The Sicilian Veil of Shame

Remembrance is a Bitter Fruit

"To forget the Holocaust is to kill twice."
—Elie Wiesel

The Sicilian Veil of Shame

Remembrance is a Bitter Fruit

Lucia Mann

Grassroots Publishing Group

Grassroots Publishing Group™
9404 Southwick Dr.
Bakersfield, CA 93312

10 9 8 7 6 5 4 3 2

Second Edition 2016
Revised Sequel to *Rented Silence*

Printed in the United States of America

ISBN: 978-0-9975677-0-0
Library of Congress Control Number: 2016940698

Cover & book design by CenterPointe Media

Dedication

I dedicate this book to the survivors of the Birkenau

extermination camp, especially my mother who,

without a doubt, made me an heiress of inner strength.

Without her Sicilian Jewish roots, which run through

my ancestral bloodline, this story would not be.

Acknowledgments

I am indebted to all who have helped and inspired me to write a book abounding with shocking, honest truth.

I am grateful to Nesta Aharoni, my publisher and friend, whose love and devotion to all my books is unfaltering; to Matthew and Joan Greenblatt of CenterPointeMedia for bringing life to the front and back covers and interior designs.

I thank my husband, Hector, with a gratitude so deep that it feels inexpressible. He has suffered good-naturedly my writer's tantrums and the many interruptions to our lives. He has also endured, without complaint, many makeshift meals. My husband's steadfast confidence in my ability to weave the fabric of my novels into a booming anti-slavery message remains my greatest inspiration.

Without the enthusiasm of these dear souls, I might have lost the courage required to research and reveal a dark past that was to me, and might still be to others, rife with pain and danger. Yet write the past I must.

Spinning in my mind for many years have been the unheard voices of those whose lives have not been vindicated and whose bravery has been dishonored.

At last they receive their due.

Table of Contents

Author's Note

I am the daughter of a Birkenau survivor. I have employed fiction to recount a true story that sheds light on the horror of the German massacre of Jews. Without pride, I confirm I am also a descendant of both the Genovese and Vecchio crime families.

The Sicilian Veil of Shame is based on the lives of some real people and events. To protect the safety of the individuals concerned, their names, professions, and descriptions have been altered, as has been mine. As the events in this story unfold, you will recognize I had a good reason for doing so.

Taking an author's license, I have embellished some details for dramatic effect.

Of course, Truth, like Beauty, oft' lies in the mind and eyes of the beholder.

A life grown in tragedy searches to find

An answer to why she was left behind,

A past so black and blue,

Not black and white.

Who will stand victorious in this fight?

A truth to be told about this life and past.

Be together here with closure at last.

Her hand is cold, her face pale,

The truth lies behind the *Sicilian Veil.*

-CMR-

Prologue

"The very first part in healing is shattering the silence."
—Anonymous

The year 1998 started well for Brianna, an emotionally grounded law student living in Vancouver, BC, Canada. But from Valentine's Day onward everything in that ill-fated year changed for the worse, turning Brianna's happy, contented life into a living nightmare that would send her across several continents searching for the truth. Eventually, Brianna ended where it all began in 1933, in Solicchiata, Sicily.

(The following is a recap of *Rented Silence*, the first book in Lucia Mann's African series.) In late-August of 1998, the British newspaper *Mail on Sunday* printed a headline that sent shockwaves around the world.

AFRICAN WOMAN IS MURDERED FOR SAVING THE
LIFE OF A CAUCASIAN BABY IN 1945.

For Brianna McTavish, a successful law student, the announcement of the murder of Anele Dingane in the Republic of South Africa would be the beginning of a series of lost, grey, and shapeless moments. Brianna's 1998 was a year of inconceivable challenges.

It all started months earlier, in mid-February of that same year. Brianna was dealing with the sudden disappearance of her mother, Lynette, who had up and left her Canadian home without a word. Concerned and worried after not hearing back from her mother, Brianna set out across treacherous mountain roads to Lynette's home. Once there, Brianna did not find her mother. Instead, she discovered what Lynette had left behind, a series of cassette tapes. Brianna listened in absolute horror as her mother narrated her chilling memoir, accounts of her unimaginable human suffering in South Africa (desertion, abduction, and abuse … in all their forms). Brianna heard many names mentioned for the first time. Among them were the following:

- Alan Hallworthy, a wealthy, cruel plantation owner who lusted for the bodies of young girls, even that of his own five-year-old daughter.
- Shiya (Brianna's mother's African name), a white newborn rescued from an intended grave. She lived five idyllic years in the bush before she was captured, tormented, and eventually freed.
- Anele Dingane, a black runaway slave who saved Shiya's life and suffered the consequences for the rest of her days.

After destroying the tapes, Brianna made up her mind to travel to South Africa hoping to find her mother. After she arrived and tracked down Lynette, both women attended the funeral of Anele Dingane, and then came face-to-face with the woman whose misfortune had started this chain of tragedies: Maria Teresa Genovese, Brianna's biological grandmother.

Brianna grew to become a bitter and lost soul. She crossed continents in an effort to unravel the truth of her mother's life. Eventually, she ended up where it all began in 1933, at her grandmother's estate in Sicily. From the moment Brianna arrived on the island, she traveled a twisted path that cut her off forever from her previous comfortable, fulfilling life in Canada.

CHAPTER ONE

August 1998, Villa Favola, Sicily

"Seek yourself before you venture into the unknown.
What you are truly looking for is rooted inside."
—Anonymous

B rianna's thousand-watt smile had vanished.

Standing on the enormous balcony of a rented villa set peacefully in a small bay thirty-five miles from Palermo airport, she wrapped her arms around her swollen abdomen and looked lost.

Brianna had hit rock bottom. A never-ending progression of unforeseen events had worn her out. She tilted her head upward and shouted to the heavens, "I need my head shrunk."

A sea breeze from the Gulf of Solanto brushed her face as she gazed at the lemon trees lining the steps that led past the swimming pool below. With tear-blurred vision, the twenty-three-year-old released a gloomy, prolonged sigh. At any other time she would have been thrilled to be wrapped in this Mediterranean summer climate, a far cry from the unpredictable Canadian weather she was accustomed to. At any other time she would have delighted in the breathtaking vistas of this seafront haven: the crystal blue waters of the Gulf, the moored seafaring vessels, and the intoxicating scents of tropical plants. At any other time her fragile nerves, now as tight as a drum skin, would have been uplifted by the magnificent sights, smells, and sounds of these sunny surroundings.

Brianna had always been a mixture of a lion and a lamb: a highly spirited soldier marching for truth combined with a thoroughly vulnerable woman. She felt like a bottle bobbing in an intangible sea—hoping to solve the puzzle of her mother's disappearance, yet again.

Brianna was in a strange land, twiddling strands of her beautiful hair, unable to speak or understand the local language. She was searching for her mother, Lynette Martinez, also known by her African name, Shiya. To Brianna, Lynette had performed more escape tricks than Houdini. Her current whereabouts were a mystery, as were those of Maria Picasso Genovese, Lynette's mother and Brianna's grandmother. Brianna's search revealed that Maria's phone number was not listed in any phone book. But then, how many Mafia people *want* to be found?

Brianna remained blithely unaware that her presence and her fanatical quest to find her mother would not be welcomed by many of the locals. A flood of tears burst through her dam of guilt and self-blame. The tall Latina spun on her heels and rushed inside her opulent accommodations.

In her bedroom, Brianna choked on the blood of emotional wounds as she wondered how she was going to pull back the layers of her messed-up life and reach a sensible center? Crossing her legs in a yoga position, she whimpered like a scared child. How had her dream of becoming a successful prosecutor—with big court trials and adrenaline-pumping investigations—come to such an abrupt end? She was reluctant to blame her unplanned pregnancy, or beat herself up over the recent breakup.

Was her fiancé, Roberto, a thorn in her side?

Most definitely.

Brianna robotically rotated the diamond ring on her fourth finger. Her lost, bitter heart compelled her to question herself. *Why didn't I fling it back at him?* Was it because there was still hope for them? She missed him, loved him, and simultaneously hated his guts. She blamed *him* for the breakup.

In their South African hotel room, before she had left for Sicily, his chauvinism had been in full display: "... *I'm the man of the house ... you'll do as I say ...*" He had ruffled her independent feathers. He had revealed his true colors: "Life has to go on, Sweet Pea. We are a couple now. When we're married, I'll take care of everything, including our finances, especially the money your *rich* mother gives us for a *big, fat* wedding and the birth of her first grandchild. If your mother wants to empty her Swiss bank account for us, our child will want for nothing."

Brianna's brows had stretched to their limit when she heard him gloating. She had thought she knew Roberto, but his cruel, money-grabbing remarks were too much for her. She regretted having ever told him about her mother's financial status.

Angry as a charging bull, Brianna had let him have it. Many heartless words were exchanged before Roberto had packed his bag and stormed out of her life.

She knew now that he wasn't going to change his stripes. *Once a zebra* always a zebra!

With her body still locked in a yoga pose and her jaw thrust forward, the stark reality of her recent breakup stabbed Brianna's heart. Would she ever be called "Sweet Pea" again? Were all of their shared goofball moments over? Could their bond, which felt like that of soul mates, be redeemed? At that moment Brianna didn't think it could. *What really goes on in a man's mind?* she thought. Her immediate answer was that Roberto had been insensitive, unemotional, and oblivious to anything a millimeter below the surface. If she had been willing to stoop to his level—with nasty opinions and attitude reversals—she could have dropped a bombshell of her own, the one-night stand she had had with her mother's lawyer and the fact that she wasn't sure whose baby she was carrying.

A week ago, during their lovers' quarrel on the dark continent of Africa, Brianna had glared at the audacity of the man she loved after she learned he had two faces. She had been tempted to hurt him back, but she had bitten her tongue and preserved her dignity—and her ironclad secret. She just couldn't bring herself to confess that she wasn't sure whose child she was carrying.

Today she was far from enchanted by her pregnancy. Adoption had crossed her mind, but the idea of a stranger raising her child was unthinkable. While all the possibilities, the "ifs," muddled her moral compass, Brianna rose from the floor, flung herself onto the bed, and buried her mascara-streaked face in a pillow. No matter how hard she tried to dispel the face of the other man, the more haunting his image became. A sneer of self-loathing crossed her full lips. "What the hell?" she howled outwardly, while her guts repeatedly screamed *Idiot, idiot, idiot! You messed up ... big time!*

Brianna felt like kicking herself. But there was nothing she could do about the oppressive guilt she was carrying. A one-night stand with a man she hardly knew was foolish. "Oh, no," she whispered, trying to rid herself of his image, which was stuck in her brain like a gramophone needle sticks in a groove.

Suddenly, his likeness was overshadowed by the appearance of another person, her beloved mother, whom Brianna had always regarded as a cross between a saint and a warrior. *Thank heavens!* Hadn't her mother gifted her with a passport to a better life? But where was she? Was she well? Was she getting the medical treatment she needed to control her brain cancer? Was she happy? Was she sad? Did she have regrets? Did she miss her only child?

Brianna's thoughts were interrupted by a shudder that originated at her toes, rolled up her body, and terminated at the top of her head. She gave herself a mental slap. *I don't want to look back.* But her tumult wasn't letting her off the hook that easily. The reflection of what had happened in the South African Edward Hotel after her spat with Roberto was vivid.

Brianna and her mother had recently gathered in South Africa to attend Anele's funeral. Lynette had been devoted to Anele, the runaway slave who had saved her life when she was left to die as a discarded infant. Anele had raised Lynette, at that time named Shiya, for five idyllic years in her village kraal.

Now in Sicily, after Anele's internment, Brianna began packing for her return flight home to Canada. She walked from her hotel room to her mother's suite to tell her she was ready to go.

Brianna knocked on her mother's door.

No response.

She waited a minute.

Still no response.

She knocked louder.

Again, no response.

When her mother failed to appear, Brianna rapped so hard on the door that her knuckles hurt. But the only reply she received was an eerie quiet. Brianna bent her head and yelled through the key slot, "Mom, hurry up. The taxi is waiting."

The silence coming from her mother's room was not golden. Instead, it prompted tear-your-hair-out frustration in the edgy girl. Brianna had a gut feeling that rose and roared: *Oh, no! Not again! This can't be happening again!* The thought was almost too much for her to swallow.

Brianna darted down the hotel's plush walkway. She hit the elevator's "down" button with such force that the tip of her index finger bent backward.

The elevator doors opened and carried Brianna to the ground level, where she dashed to the reception desk.

"Can I help you?" the cheerful hotel clerk asked.

"Give me the key to room 402," Brianna demanded. "Hurry!" she urged. "It's an emergency!"

The receptionist didn't question or hesitate. She reached for a spare key sitting in a slot behind her.

Brianna snatched the key and dashed back to the elevator, where she tapped her sandaled foot impatiently, and exhaled loudly. The ride up to her mother's room seemed to take forever. Her hand was shaking as she slipped the pass key into the slot. She barged into her mother's room and saw an empty suite. Lying on the unmade bed was a note written on hotel stationery:

Palermo Airport Hotel

"*Forgive me, Brianna. I can't go back to Canada with you. I have to finish the jigsaw puzzle that is my life. I love you, my precious daughter.*
  I'm forever yours."
~Mom

Brianna smacked her tongue in contempt. She was mad, but she was determined to not become a psychological hostage to her mother's continual "up-and-go" behavior. This disappearance was more than the heartbroken and frustrated daughter could fathom. Alone in a foreign country … again! If she tried to find her mother, would she be chasing shadows? No. Brianna believed in miracles.

Even so, Brianna surrendered to an emotional nosedive triggered by the sharp edges of her mother's inconsideration. Lynette's disappearance was a bitter pill to swallow. Anger swelled in Brianna's eyes, forming a field of red. Through compressed lips, she spat, "Goddamn you, Mother! Why do you keep doing this shit?" Her outburst was quickly followed by a silent afterthought—*Running away never solves anything*—which was swiftly followed by a scoff—*Look who's talking! Like mother, like daughter.*

Brianna tossed her head back to tune out her rising bitterness. She no longer wished to beat herself up about could be, should be, why, and wherefore. She planned to find her mother—to resolve the abandonment issues she'd felt most of her life—then leave Sicily for Canada, where she would birth her baby. Brianna, normally an optimist, thought a little help from her guardian angel would be fine right now—if she had one, that is.

Brianna admitted she had more questions than answers: Would she regret the choices she had made, stepping onto an island that was more tangled in lies and deception than she could imagine? Was she prepared for history to repeat itself? Was she equipped to face a journey that could bestow life or death?

Unknowingly, Brianna's eventual decision to forgo her former life would prove to be the worst choice. Her mission was destined to end badly. Her fate was sealed. A ubiquitous cloud of impending danger would nearly cost Brianna the lives of her unborn twins. She did not yet know that two tiny heartbeats were pulsating rapidly in her womb. If she had been aware of it, she would have lost control. In her circumstance as a single mom, one child was bad enough, two, the end of the world!

Brianna headed for her rental car. She needed to clear her head, get lost on unfamiliar roads, and distract herself from her troubles.

After driving around for what felt like ages, she parked on a cobblestone street near a row of cafes. The baby book she was reading warned her to avoid caffeine, but pregnancy advice was the furthest thing from her mind. She was going to order the biggest mug of espresso the café offered.

After downing two cups of coffee and a couple of rich pastries, Brianna felt better—for the time being. She left the fortifying cafe and began to walk, attempting to minimize the assault on her stomach.

Brianna found herself staring up at a restored medieval church,

Santa Maria della Valle. Its open cathedral doors beckoned her as warmly as they welcomed Sunday worshipers to the noon service. Dressed in solemn clothing—black pants and shirt—and boasting a dark olive complexion, brunette hair, and brown eyes, Brianna blended in with the Sicilian locals. She began to climb the ancient stone stairs, which echoed with the footsteps of bygone rulers and overzealous knights. She hesitated on the top step and clicked her tongue. *What the hell am I thinking? I don't believe in God.* She shrugged and thought, *I have to start somewhere.* She wanted to ask someone about the service, but a major drawback presented itself—her nonexistent native tongue.

Oh, what the heck. I'm here.

Briana stepped through the arched doorway and entered the ancient place of worship. She made her way to a back-row pew, sat down, and looked up. She was awestruck by what she saw: magnificent stone sculptures, blue stained-glass windows, an enormous bronze cross, and a statue of Saint Mary surrounded by hundreds of smoking candles. Mesmerized, she wondered how many people over the centuries had sat in her very seat. She let her imagination fly, conjuring up a knight in shining armor, whose sword clanked against the wooden pew. Her mind's eye entered the pageantry of Camelot and Sir Lancelot's eyes saturated with love for Lady Guinevere.

Brianna's musings vanished abruptly when she felt a harsh poke to her hip. She stared at a little boy dressed in his Sunday best fidgeting on the seat next to hers. "Hi," Brianna said softly.

He stuck out his tongue through his missing front teeth, but his impish behavior did not induce Brianna to smile. Instead, she delivered a scolding. "That's not nice." When the boy reached out to prod her waistline, Brianna grabbed his hand midair. "Stop that, you little brat! How would you like it if I poked you in the belly?"

He yanked his hand out of Brianna's grip, waggled his wavy head of hair, curled his lips into a sneer, and was about to repeat his game when ...

The weight of a prayer book came crashing down on his head. His mother ended his fun before Brianna had a chance to restrain him.

The boy's lower lip quivered as he buried his assaulted head in his mother's lap. The woman's face was flushed when she leaned in to whisper something to Brianna. Brianna guessed the lady was apologizing, so she bobbed her head in acceptance.

Brianna could no longer romanticize about ancient jousters. Instead, she imagined what her life would have been like if she had not so impulsively left every shred of her existence behind in North America. Her eyelids squeezed shut. The "saved document file" of her life so far opened to reveal some stark facts. Brianna lowered her head in shame and mouthed, "Oh, what have I done?" She began gnawing at fingernails that were already sensitive and raw. Her core values prompted her to consciously accept her wrongdoing. She, alone, was accountable for her sexual stupidity. It was idiotic for her to sleep with a guy she didn't give a fig about. What had possessed her to end up in bed with ...?

Goosebumps invaded every inch of Brianna's flesh. If her mother ever found out ... Brianna shivered. Her mom would surely give her a mouthful, maybe even a slap. Brianna's mom had a propensity for speaking her mind, be damned the consequences.

Brianna's thoughts flashed back to an earlier conversation: "You have always been a guarded soul," Lynette had told her daughter. "I found it unsettling to try to touch you deeply throughout your growing years and during your teenage rebelliousness. I responded to you in a way that was natural to me. I treated you as an adult, someone who was old enough to know better when, in fact, you were but a child searching for adult wisdom."

After that day of self-examination, Lynette had never again divulged or admitted she had failed as a mother, yet the years she had suffered guilt over the standoff she had created with her daughter continued to nibble at her. She had felt ashamed at doing nothing to correct her relationship with her daughter, but she didn't even know how to fix what was broken in her own life. Lynette was who she was. She was not going to put on a painted face for anyone. Her only child would just have to live with that.

Brianna glanced up at a statue of Jesus on the Cross. Even though she wasn't religious, she knew her baby would not receive the same jubilant welcome. She released a long sigh and chided herself. *Enough is enough. It's time to stop self-flagellating.* Brianna was smart enough to know that punishing herself wasn't going to help her overcome her challenges. She had to be strong for the innocent life growing inside her. *Forget about what has already passed … concentrate on the now … the future.*

A moment later Brianna became overwhelmed with a silent scream of frustration. All of this involuntary recall was affecting her sanity. She shrugged, trying hard to look on the bright side, to be positive, but that wasn't happening. Instead, Brianna hated herself. After becoming more and more agitated, she fled the church.

As her high heels clip-clopped on uneven cobblestones, she hot-footed her way down the street toward her car. Not far from her vehicle her stomach rebelled. Undigested pastries splattered over jagged gray stones.

"Dammit!" Brianna muttered as she tried to reclaim her equi-librium. Straightening her body to a soldier's stance, she cased her surroundings. Not a person in sight, thank heavens. But she did spot a skinny terrier heading her way. The thought of the dog chomping on her upchuck triggered Brianna's stomach to heave and gag. *I have to get out of here.* Her heart wrangled with her chest as she rushed away from the unsavory scene. After she was seated in the car, she opened her driver's window and smelled her blouse. When she was satisfied that the stench of vomit had not attached to her clothing, she took off at breakneck speed.

Back in the villa Brianna ran a bath. She dumped a whole bot-tle of lavender foam into the water. Immersed in bubbles up to her chin, she closed her eyes and strategized her next move. She didn't want to call *him* because *he* was the last person she wanted to speak with. But what choice did she have? Her phone directory search had not helped one iota. He was her mother's attorney, and, in a way, he was hers, as well. Would her mother's confidant and best friend have an answer for her? But the thought of hearing his accented Guatemalan voice set Brianna's teeth on edge. To tone down her tension, she began singing at the top of her lungs—*One Week,* a hit single by Barenaked Ladies. The villa was isolated, so she might as well, even though she would never win a talent com-petition. Brianna was tone deaf.

Thirty minutes later a squeaky-clean Brianna, invigorated by

her long soak, entered the bedroom. From her unpacked suitcase she pulled out a pair of high-waist shorts; an oversized, pink,
sleeveless top that covered her belly comfortably; and pink flip-
flops. She swept up her long hair into a ponytail. Although she
was eager to put her new plan in motion, her telephone call would
have to wait. She was famished. She checked her wristwatch: 1:30
P.M.

With her pink toenail polish blending in with the marble floor,
Brianna headed for the outdoor kitchen. She followed the smell
of unknown delights. The housekeeper assigned to the villa was
standing in front of the tandoori-style stove filling the air with lip-
smacking aromas. The short, plump, rosy-cheeked woman greeted
Brianna. *"Buon giorno,* Signórina."

"Buon giorno, Rosa," Brianna returned in her best pronuncia-
tion.

Rosa pointed to a table covered with a crisp, white, linen table-
cloth. Brianna raised her eyelids in disbelief. *Surely all of that is
not for me.*

Her chef had prepared enough brunch dishes to feed an army:
chicken breast laced with fresh basil and olive oil dressing, and
spicy sausages lying in a bed of rotini pasta. The smorgasbord of
delights was matched with a basket brimming with freshly baked
ciabatta rolls and a bottle of Riserva, a vintage red wine.

"*Mangiarsi,*" Rosa said while motioning Brianna to eat by
moving her own hand up to her mouth. Rosa then turned and left
the outdoor dining area.

Brianna poured herself a generous glass of wine from the
bamboo-sheathed bottle. She quickly downed half of it. Within

seconds, a rush of alcohol gave her a fuzzy feeling. Her inner voice urged her, *Eat before you faint.* As she dove into her food, she added, *Just as well. I'm not a health nut! I need comfort food—and as much booze as I can get.* The effect of the alcohol on her pregnancy was the furthest thing from her mind.

The meal was more than appetizing. It was scrumptious. The best she'd had in a long time. But halfway through, she felt a bear growling deep down in her stomach. She didn't need a crystal ball to understand what was going to happen next. *Serves you right!* she chastised herself. *You shouldn't have stuffed your face and drunk the wine so fast.*

With her hand clasped firmly across her mouth, Brianna bolted from the table. She barely made it to the bathroom. Straddling the porcelain bowl, she retched until she was spent. Afterward, she splashed her face with cold water and looked into the vanity mirror. She didn't like what she saw. *Yikes! I look like I've been bar hopping all night.*

Brianna reached for the cell phone in her shorts' pocket and flipped the lid. When the "no signal" flashed, she made a "what-the-heck" face. Obviously, cutting edge satellite technology hadn't yet reached these shores. The words "now or never" ran through her head as she dialed the in-house phone. The device on the other end rang a few times before a recording cut in: *"You have reached the home of Miguel Carlos Rodriquez. I'm sorry I'm not able to take your call. Please leave your number and a brief message, and I'll call you back."* Beep.

She took a deep, steady breath. "Mike, it's me, Brianna. I need you to ..."

Mike's heart raced with elation as he picked up the phone and said, "*Cariño*, where are you? I've been worried sick. I've left umpteen messages on your cell phone."

Brianna turned purple with anger. Through gritted teeth she bristled, "Don't call me darling!" Adding salt to the wound, she finished, "I'm not your darling and never will be!"

Falling back on his professional manners, Mike, her mother's lawyer, chose not to bite. His voice was calm. "What can I do for you, Brianna?"

"Has my mother contacted you?"

"Yes, she has," the cool, masculine voice replied.

"Did she tell you where she was staying? Did she leave a contact number?"

"She did. I have her address and number."

Brianna's fist punched the air with joy. The shiver travelling up and down her spine was exhilarating.

"Great! Can you give it to me, Mike?"

"Yes, of course," Mike answered. "But first I have to tell you that your Roberto has called here a few times. He wanted to know if I'd heard from you, if I knew when you are coming back. The poor guy sounded heartbroken about your breakup. You should call him."

A sudden rush of tears stung the backs of Brianna's eyes. Roberto hadn't even bothered to ask how her pregnancy was going. In a way she was thankful Mike didn't know about the baby because the last person she wanted in her pending motherhood picture was her mom's lawyer. She had not kept in contact with Mike after that fateful, one-night stand, something she gravely regretted. Even hearing his voice now on the other end of the telephone made her cringe with shame.

Prompted by a crushing hurt felt deep in her heart, Brianna gritted her teeth to prevent her rage, her distain for Roberto, from betraying her. But that didn't stop her from making a spiteful decision: Roberto was never going to see his child! She would make sure of that. Seconds later, she released a prolonged sigh, bringing her mind back on track. No, she shouldn't let her angry emotions interrupt her plans. Not now. Not ever. She took a deep breath before speaking into the telephone receiver. "If Roberto calls again, tell him I have no idea when I'm returning to Canada. If it makes him feel better, he can put my stuff into storage. I'll send him an international money order for the rental costs."

Brianna perceived a moment of uneasy silence before Mike spoke. "Brianna, what's happened to you? You sound so bitter. Not like you at all. And what are you going to do about law school? When there was no immediate reply, Mike added, "Are you going to contact the administration, or do you want me to do it?"

Brianna didn't want to continue talking with Mike about things she felt were none of his business. Thinking quickly, she replied, "Mike, I'm using a prepaid phone card and there are only a few minutes left. Please, give me the information I need."

She scribbled down the details on the villa's complimentary notepad. She was about to hang up on Mike without as much as a "goodbye" when his barely audible voice cut her short. "*Cariño*, I miss you so much," Mike purred. "My heart is full of love for you. Please come back to me as soon as ..."

Brianna hit hard. "Aha! What's the matter, Mike? Worried your *wife* might be listening in on your conversation …?" Click. The beeping sounds accompanying the hang-up rang in Brianna's ears. Still gripping the receiver in her hand, Brianna speculated gloatingly: "You're busted! Your wife was listening to your call!"

Changing her direction of thought, Brianna slapped her thigh. *How could I have been so dumb?* Spitting nails, she exclaimed, "I'm a bloody moron!"

She didn't want to recall that ill-fated meeting, but her memory triumphed, spilling out a video of her blatant flirtation: doe eyes gazing and eyelashes fluttering. Her mind replayed her stupid, superficial mistake. And add to that her tussle with an excessive amount of tequila. But all of her excuses were bullshit.

Brianna had been instantly attracted to Mike, a muscular, older man with smoldering good looks and a charismatic, charming personality. His neatly trimmed goatee and long salt-and-pepper ponytail were seductive. He could easily have adorned a page on a hunky male calendar. The more time Brianna spent with him that day, the more she had been attracted by his conquistador charm. Without weighing the consequences, she had slept with him. How she had managed to return to Roberto without a trace of "What-the-hell-have-I done?" can be attributed to shame mingled with self-disgust. She had been able to erase the "I'm-only-human" from her mind, until this moment.

Now, Brianna felt acute discomfort as even more shame piled on and overwhelmed her. She began humming Canada's national anthem, which momentarily helped to drown out the guilt. Then she lifted the telephone receiver and waited.

"*Pronto,*" the voice on the other end greeted.

"Signóra Moschetta, I need your help," Brianna said. "Where can I hire a cab driver who speaks English as well as Sicilian?"

Lusia (the owner of the villa) answered, "Signórina Brianna, mostly standard Italian is spoken here now. Do you speak any Italian?"

"No," Brianna replied.

"Then I will send a cousin of mine," Lusia offered. "He speaks many languages, including Sicilian. When do you want him?"

"I'd like him to come now, please?"

"Okay. I'll phone him right away," Lusia said. "Have a good trip, wherever you are going. And if you're not home for dinner, I'll tell Rosa to leave a prepared meal for you in the fridge."

Brianna smiled. She liked Lusia the moment she met her. The woman's warmth could melt a chocolate bar. "Thanks, Lusia."

"You're most welcome."

Brianna made her way into the master bathroom, which housed the largest claw-foot tub she had ever seen. She threw some water on her face at the sink, cleaned her teeth, brushed her hair, and put on a little makeup. She then walked into the bedroom, removed her engagement ring, and placed it in a bedside drawer. She stuffed her yellow-and-black backpack with a bottle of water, a packet of biscotti biscuits, and a change of clothing, just in case. It never crossed her mind that in her condition she might need some TUMS®. A capricious thought triggered a wily smile: Like a keen hunter I will ferret out my prey, and if I don't get lucky, then I'll eat fattening *Italian food!* But seriousness overcame her whimsy as she verbalized one of her mother's favorite sayings: "Come hell or high water, I'll find you."

Brianna continued to organize herself for her upcoming trip.

A half-hour later an outdated, red-white-green, 1937 Fiat 1100 saloon pulled into the villa's driveway. Brianna didn't know what to think. The vehicle looked as if it belonged in a museum. So did the driver. He was hunched at the shoulders, overweight, and well past his retirement years. But what triggered her to take a second look and then grin was his attire. The cabbie looked as if he had just stepped off a 1950's gangster movie. He wore thick, pinstriped serge pants; a buttoned-up black-and-white waistcoat; and a la-pelled jacket with a handkerchief in the pocket. He finished off his Roaring Twenties attire with a black fedora and black-and-white dress shoes. Brianna laughed as she wondered, *Is this glossy image fabricated for tourists, or is this man stuck in a time warp?*

Brianna was greeted by a gap-toothed smile and an extended hand. The driver's grip was firm and warm.

"Buon giorno, Signórina," he said. "My name is Giuseppe Antonio Moschetta." His withered, sun-beaten face took on a glow of pride. "I'm at your service. Where can I take you?"

Brianna smiled. His articulation was great, and his high-pitched voice was amusing. She returned the greeting. "Buon giorno, Giuseppe," she said in her best Italian. "It is nice to meet you."

The driver smiled warmly as she handed him a slip of notepaper. "Here's the address."

Brianna noted Giuseppe's bushy, slate-grey brows arch and lock above his Audrey Hepburn sunglasses. She didn't know what to think when he began to mutter incoherently. She was even more puzzled when he lifted a gold medallion from around his neck, placed it to his lips, and kissed it, as if he were warding off evil.

Brianna wished she were a mind reader.

Giuseppe removed his glasses and made eye contact with Brianna. His intense stare unnerved her. She did not react with her usual self-confidence.

"Signórina, you can tell me to mind my own business," Giuseppe said, "but why do you wish to go and see this woman? She's not a good person. This woman is quite mad!"

"So you obviously know Maria."

Without hesitation he replied, "Absolutely. I know her well."

Brianna detected a hint of derision and a change of tone in his voice. Giuseppe hadn't finished making his point. "I was born in the village of Solicchiata long before Maria was born. And I worked in the vineyards for this family. My cousin, Paolo Girrdazzello ..." His lips clenched tight. He had said enough. He didn't want to be reminded of this relative who had *destroyed* so many lives, including those of his own family.

There was no doubt in Giuseppe's mind that Maria had something do with his family's demise, but, mostly, he didn't want to cross paths with the now reigning Mafia boss. She was not to be trusted. She had lucrative liaisons with the most powerful drug cartels in the land, all of which had put Sicily back in the seat of power over American organized crime.

Everyone knew that Maria was a disturbed individual, a fatally flawed personality who occasionally slipped into madness, and that she boiled with a bursting hatred for men. In Giuseppe's opinion, her loathing prevented her from loving anyone. Maria Genovese's outward strength disguised her inner fragility. She was a bird's wing that had been mauled by a cat. No Band-Aid could hide the long-term effect of what had happened to her in the past.

Even though Giuseppe had intimated intrigue, Brianna didn't want to waste time pondering it. She was raring to go, to see her mother. She didn't give two hoots about her grandmother or care a fig about the driver's assault on her character. And she wasn't about to kowtow to the cabbie. Standing with her legs apart, hands on hips, and shoulders stiff, she made herself clear. "If you don't want to take me, I'll find another driver."

Giuseppe, his jaw set, had little choice but to respond, and quickly. He needed the money, and, according to his cousin Lusia, Brianna had plenty of it.

Giuseppe's hands extended outward in defeat as he agreed. "Okay, Signórina. I'll drive you, but only to the village," he said while avoiding her glare. "From there you can walk up the hill to the gates."

His response didn't cut any mustard with Brianna. Mind games were not on her agenda today, so she simply asked, "How far is it to Solicchiata?"

"About 194 *kilometres*," Giuseppe estimated. "I drive only on the back roads, not the highways, so it will seem much longer."

Her immediate thought was *yikes!* His vehicle prompted her next question. "Are you sure this old car can make the journey?"

Like a cat that had swallowed a canary, Giuseppe smiled, patted the hood of his old car, and said, "No *problemo*. Floria is a good girl. She goes up and down bad roads like a mountain goat."

Brianna chuckled. Her quirky driver was definitely likeable.

Giuseppe was thinking the same thing. He looked at the plump girl (he hadn't caught on yet) with the gorgeous smile and the straight, whiter-than-white teeth, and his eyes twinkled. He bowed as if he were presenting himself to a queen and said, "*Amuni,* Signórina."

Brianna smiled at his gallantry and played along. "Thank you, kind sir, but I haven't a clue what you said?"

"In Sicilian it means … *let's go.*"

Brianna responded heartily. "I'm ready when you are."

Her driver opened the rear car door, took her arm, and helped her into the vehicle. *Chivalry is not dead,* Brianna mused. This would never happen with a Canadian cab service.

Giuseppe climbed into the driver's seat and turned the ignition key twice. Floria coughed into action emitting dragon plumes of exhaust smoke. The old gal was ready to rock and roll.

Brianna, ensconced onto the car's faded, split-leather back seat, had hardly gotten comfortable before beads of perspiration began collecting on her forehead. The humidity in the vehicle was so intense, it took her breath away. She leaned forward and said, "Giuseppe, can you turn up the air conditioning. I'm melting back here."

"Sorry, Signórina," he replied in an *oops* voice. "The car doesn't have it."

Brianna rolled the window down as far as it would go. *I could have bought an air-conditioned Mercedes, instead of riding in this piece of junk.*

That was far from the truth.

The large bundle of cash her mother had left behind for her in Canada had dwindled considerably, but the law student wasn't concerned. Hadn't her mother always topped up her bank account when she needed her to? Her mother had always been a generous pushover, and, as a result, had not taught her daughter financial responsibility. Brianna was in for a nasty surprise. As the Joni Mitchell lyric goes, "You don't know what you've got 'til it's gone."

Need versus want became a more appropriate measure.

Pedal to the metal, Giuseppe sped away from the villa and headed for the outskirts of the city. Brianna gripped what was left of a door handle and clung on for dear life. Floria's shock absorbers had seen better days. Brianna's rear end, repeatedly lifted from and dropped onto the back seat, was the least of her discomforts. Her driver began serenading her. His rendition of Mario Lanza's *Santa Lucia* was more than Brianna's sensitive ears could tolerate. To put an end to the torture, she tapped Giuseppe on the shoulder and asked the first question that popped into her mind. "Why were you so reluctant to take me to Maria's place?"

Through the cracked rearview mirror, Giuseppe's squinty eyes sought hers.

"Do you understand the word *Mafia*, Signórina?"

Brianna puffed out her cheeks and countered stiffly, "Of course I do, Giuseppe! I wasn't born yesterday! We have them where I come from, also."

"Then I tell you. Solicchiata is not the place for an American tourist," Giuseppe responded informatively.

Brianna released an indignant sigh. "I'm not American, I'm Canadian. And I'm *not* a tourist," she retorted. "I'm going to visit my grandmother, who owns the estate …"

Bang … wallop. Floria jolted to a stop. Her passenger rubbed her jaw, which had collided with the back of the driver's seat. It seemed that Floria's brakes were in better condition than her bodywork and shock absorbers.

"Jesus!" Brianna shouted, gently stroking her belly. "What the hell is wrong with you, Giuseppe? You nearly broke my neck!" She was about to add "Not to mention my baby's neck" but thought it best not to.

As if a foul odor had hit his nostrils, Giuseppe's upper lip curled in disgust. His inflamed eyes sought hers. *Oops!* Brianna thought, assuming that her blasphemous outburst had upset him. Should she apologize? Nah. He'd get over it. It couldn't get any worse … or could it?

Giuseppe gripped the steering wheel and made a U-turn. "I must take you back to the Villa Favola. You'll have to find someone else to drive you."

The color of anger rose in Brianna's cheeks. She released an exasperated huff and retorted, "Are you crazy? You can't turn back now!"

Giuseppe pulled Floria farther onto to the curb, yanked up the hand brake, and swiveled his body in the driver's seat. He raised his head over the headrest and said, "For a moment you had me fooled, Signórina Brianna," he said cuttingly. "It is well known that Maria has no children!"

Brianna defaulted into courtroom mode. With a sharp attorney's tone she countered, "Wrong, Giuseppe. She definitely has one daughter, whose name is Lynette Martinez. She's my mother, and she is staying with her mother, Maria Picasso."

Giuseppe didn't flinch. He was a former police interrogator, and he followed his instinct. With his hands folded calmly on his lap, he apologized. "Forgive me, Signórina, for doubting you, but let me explain. When Maria returned home, long after the war, she claimed her legal rights to the grand estate. The announcement was in the newspaper. She declared that she was childless and that upon her death the estate was to be sold by the courts, the proceeds going to an orphanage outside Palermo."

Brianna responded truthfully. "I don't know anything about that. But I do know that she is definitely not childless. I'm living proof!" She wanted to say more, but hesitated. *Was trust an issue here?* She thought long and hard. After all, Giuseppe knew Maria better than she did. Brianna took a deep breath before saying, "Giuseppe, I don't know you from Adam, and I want you to promise never to repeat what I'm about to tell you."

He nodded.

Brianna moved to the front passenger seat and—omitting the sexual details of her mother's ghastly child abuse—filled Giuseppe in with snippets of her mother's life before coming to Sicily. During her narration, she thought her driver's astonished eyes were going to bug right out of their sockets. She wasn't surprised by his dramatic response.

Giuseppe reverently crossed himself and said, "May God protect you from all evil. It's not your fault that you have the blood of the woman who is never seen without her veil. I'll tell you this: she has a mean streak a kilometer wide when she is angered. She has had many people murdered for nothing more than looking at her the wrong way. Evil has reached into her body and plucked out her soul. And if Satan ever considers giving up his throne, it will be to Maria ..."

Giuseppe abruptly clammed up.

Wow! That's about as nasty as it gets, Brianna thought. But she wondered if, indeed, Maria carried the blood of her forefather's sins. The thought that her own blood was genetically connected to Maria's didn't enter Brianna's mind.

There was no question Giuseppe was evading.

Never judge a book by its cover ...

Giuseppe's portrayal of Maria was not flattering. Nevertheless, Brianna couldn't defend the woman's reputation without knowing the whole truth.

Her nonjudgmental stand would soon bite her in the rear, but for now she proclaimed, "I'm not going to be hypercritical. There are always two sides to a story. And to tell you the truth, I couldn't give a damn about my grandmother. It's my mother I want so desperately to see."

"Yes, indeed," he said bobbing his head. "I'll get you there as fast as I can."

Brianna returned to the rear seat, and Giuseppe shifted Floria back into gear. They were off. Floria was ready to rock and roll again, but this time she was pumped up.

Moments later Brianna's natural curiosity got the best of her. She had to ask, "Are Maria's parents still alive?"

"No. They are both dead."

"When and how did they die?"

Giuseppe unleashed a big sigh. "Following Maria's abduction, Sofia Picasso, Maria's mother, suffered many sleepless, broken-hearted nights. Eventually she went mad and committed the mortal sin of hanging herself. She died a horrible, lonely death."

Giuseppe, devoutly religious, couldn't forgive or forget Sofia's unholy actions at the time of her death. He recalled how he had wanted to spit on her grave. Only recently had he learned that a Rabbi from Italy had conducted Sofia's service. Giuseppe's Catholic principles were redeemed.

Brianna was deep in thought. Apart from the few unproven details she had gleaned from her driver, she couldn't add anything to the topic. However, that didn't prevent a big dose of empathy from seeping into her decent heart. She had always been a sucker for a sob story. "Oh, that's dreadful! Why did Sofia do such a terrible thing?"

Brianna, sitting on the edge of her seat, was all ears.

"The kidnapping of her only child ate away at her ..." He stopped mid-sentence to look at his passenger through the rear-view mirror and see if she'd caught on. When she didn't blink, he confirmed, "It was Maria, your grandmother, who was kidnapped."

Brianna's mouth opened as she had an "Oh, my God!" moment. She just couldn't wrap her mind around this horrible event, so she asked the least gut-wrenching question she could think of. "When did this happen?"

"In 1943, the night of her tenth birthday, little Maria was stolen from her bedroom for ransom, right under the noses of her parents." Seeing Brianna's shocked expression, he added, "Let me explain. You see, kidnapping, especially of children of the rich, isn't anything new here on the island, or anywhere else, I suppose. It has always been a 'way of life' for many in Sicily, and it continues that way to this day. In Maria's case, it was first thought that one of Don Alberto's many known enemies had taken her in retaliation for something or other. As it happens, though, I've been told the kidnapper was a person they least expected."

A frown creased Brianna's forehead. "Who was that?"

"Um … I don't … um … know," Giuseppe stammered.

Brianna's looked at him with an "I'm not stupid" expression, certain he was deliberately evading her question. She was good at reading faces and identifying speech patterns of people who were hiding things, but she just couldn't bring herself to grill Giuseppe over this. "Did they catch whoever took Maria?"

"No."

Brianna stated a fact. "Obviously, Maria survived to make it home."

"Yes, but she didn't come back to Sicily until 1955."

Brianna vocalized her calculation. "*Twelve years!* Where was she before that?" Brianna was too smart for her own good. It would be her undoing.

"I don't have the answer," he replied. "Maybe you can ask her yourself. What I can say is that the gentle, kind little girl I knew as a child died during her absence. It gets worse, Signórina."

Giuseppe's recitation continued. "Her father, Don Alberto, *re-fused* to pay the ransom. That's why Sofia killed herself."

Brianna was astonished. "Why on earth didn't he pay the kidnappers? He obviously wasn't short of money. And what happened to him? Why did he die?"

"The Don was shot dead the day Sofia was laid to rest in a Genovese cemetery. Some say the shooter was one of Sofia's many

Spanish brothers, all of who had always hated Don Alberto. Others say it was the kidnapper himself. Still others say it was a revenge killing for what the Don did to his cousin, Father Rupolo, and so on ..."

Brianna cut in. "I can understand the kidnapper wanting to blow the Don's brains out for not giving him money. And yes, a hate-filled brother would have wanted to kill the man who had sent his sister to an early grave. But what the heck happened with the priest?"

Giuseppe didn't weigh his answer or his language, "Uh ... the Don cut off his balls and watched him slowly bleed to death."

Brianna gulped hard. "You've got to be kidding!" she exclaimed. Her mind couldn't conceive of this horror. "Are you *serious?*" she burst out, at the same time thinking *nobody could make this stuff up!* The story was beginning to sound like the script of a horror movie, and she felt as if she were sitting in the front row. She quickly snapped back to reality and asked, "Why?"

"All I know is Don Alberto believed that his cousin, Father Rupolo, had molested the kidnapper when he was young, made him sick in the head, and that's why the boy took Maria."

Brianna was unconvinced. With a sharp mind she said, "I'm not educated as a clinical psychologist, but from a lawyer's point of view, that doesn't make sense."

The opinionated ex-cop argued, "It does to me. The boy was angry, and his heart was disturbed. The sinful violation of his body sent him over the edge. He couldn't go to the Catholic Church with his story. No one would have believed his word ... his accusation ... against a man of the cloth. He couldn't have gone to his own father. It's a shameful thing for a male to be violated by another male. He wanted to distance himself from his molester, but this is a small island. He needed money. His employer, Don Alberto, looked like the way out of his misery. Or so the foolish boy thought."

Brianna was no stranger to shocking revelations, but this was a different kettle of fish. She tucked a clammy strand of hair behind her ear and said, "Uh-huh! From what you've told me, it seems that you also know this person well."

Brianna had talked Giuseppe into revealing what he had tried to deny only minutes ago. He did, in fact, know who kidnapped her grandmother.

"I do and I don't," was the driver's vague reply.

Giuseppe fell into a deep silence giving Brianna the opportunity to digest what she had heard. But her determination to quiz him was overshadowed by a more pressing need. Her bladder felt as if it were about to burst and embarrass her big time.

"Giuseppe, can we stop somewhere," she pleaded. "I need to use the bathroom."

"For sure, Signórina Brianna," he responded. "I know just the place."

With pressing urgency, Brianna barged ahead of Giuseppe into a tiny, spotlessly clean café. She used the bathroom and, upon exiting, found her driver standing in a dining patio that was draped with colorful flower baskets. Being a gentleman, he stood until Brianna was seated.

For the second time that day, Brianna thought, *Chivalry is not dead!*

A moment later a friendly, inquisitive waitress presented herself and took their orders. After writing down their requests, she dallied at their table, yakking in torrents to Giuseppe, who translated her last comment. "She wants to know if you are my daughter."

"Tell her I'd be honored if I were your daughter," Brianna said with a wink.

Giuseppe beamed.

While they were waiting for their meal, Brianna sipped espresso from a dainty cup and studied the ruddy face of her fatherly driver. She couldn't help thinking how much she missed her own father, Lionel Martinez. That familiar emptiness triggered a feeling of contempt in her. Could she ever forgive her mother for keeping her in the dark all those years about her biological bond to her "stepfather," Lionel, who raised her? Before Lionel died, Brianna had known him as her stepfather, not as her bio dad. On a set of recorded tapes, her mother had shockingly revealed that Lionel had, indeed, been Brianna's biological father and that Brianna had been conceived years earlier, long before Lynette and Lionel found each other a second time years later. At the time of the revelation, Brianna had been mad enough to strangle her mom. She wished she would have known that her "stepfather" was, in reality, her biological father.

Brianna reflected on the explanation her mother had given her when they met up in South Africa at Anele's funeral.

"You have to move on. I did what I had to do. I pray at the end of the day that you've been helped by my decision more than you've been hurt by it."

No use in crying over spilled milk. What is done is done ... kaput ... over ... finished.

Brianna felt as though she had moved on, but she would never forget the Hispanic man who had raised her until his accidental death in her teenage years. She believed his ashes were scattered somewhere in El Salvador, but she had only her mother's word on that.

Lionel's death had left a big hole in Brianna's heart. If only she had known when he was alive that she was his child.

After learning the truth about her biological father from her mother's tapes, bitterness crept into Brianna's heart. She had rebelled against her "beloved" mother, calling her ... well ... a disgusting word no decent woman should utter.

Brianna's reflections were interrupted by the arrival of her meal. She didn't waste a moment diving in to the prosciutto sandwich piled with cheese, local mushrooms, and mildly hot red peppers. She drank a couple of espresso refills, each one as thick as tar. It all hit the spot.

Brianna's fondness for her driver grew deeper when Giuseppe insisted on buying her meal. He would not take no for an answer. In return, without his knowledge, she left a generous tip.

With her hunger assuaged, a caffeinated Brianna was ready to rumble in Giuseppe's rust bucket for the next leg of the journey.

Settled on the back seat, Brianna dug in her backpack and removed a small book, a tourist guide, she had purchased at the Palermo airport. It opened with these words: "The political state and unrest of Sicilian society in 1860 influenced the etymology of the words 'Mafia' and 'Omerta' (a code of honor embodying absolute silence when questioned by law enforcement). In 1876 Romualdo Bonfadini, an Italian magistrate, stated that 'Cosa Nostra' (Our Thing) was not a secret society but a 'way of life,' an 'attitude of mind ...'"

Giuseppe glanced at Brianna. Her head was bent low. He interrupted her by asking, "What are you reading, Signórina?"

"Oh, it's a book about how the Mafia started."

His laughter was warm and rippling. "You don't need to read a book, Signórina. I can tell you the real story that my grandfather Salvatore told me as a boy."

Brianna closed the book. "Sure," she said. "Why not hear it from the horse's mouth?"

Giuseppe happily obliged her. "You see, the Mafia was actually formed thousands of years ago. Sicily, after the Byzantine rule, was invaded by Arabs. Many captured islanders were shipped to North Africa as slaves. The people who were left behind, my ancestors, revolted and tried to kill off the invaders with homemade clubs, which were no match against the invaders' steel swords. Those who were not slaughtered fled to the mountains. The Arabs were relentless in pursuit, calling out '*Mafina*,' which means 'Refugees, you can't hide from us.' Taking cover by day and killing by night, these brave fighters were nicknamed by the island compatriots 'the Mafia warriors.'"

Brianna's three loud sneezes brought Giuseppe's storytelling to a halt. "Sorry about that," she apologized. In the back her mind, she hoped her sneezing wasn't the beginning of a viral cold. She had heard a restaurant worker *ahchoo* behind the partition that divided the café's seating area from the kitchen.

Giuseppe continued where he had left off. "I have another story, a more credible one, about the beginning of the word 'Mafia.' Would you like to hear it?"

Brianna bobbed her head.

Giuseppe cleared his throat and continued on, as articulate as a history teacher. "After another invasion, this time by the Normans, the islanders had had enough of slave masters. From a concealed cave in the Nebrodi Mountains, Genio Genovese ordered his band of fighters to kill the invading soldiers while they slept. The next day, in retaliation, the French Captain burned down villages, killing men, women, and children. The marauding Frenchmen didn't stop at traditional murder, though. They raped every woman and girl before they killed them. When one mother found the mutilated body of her eight-year-old daughter lying on the church steps, she cried, '*Mia ... fia, mia ... fia,*' which means 'my daughter ... my daughter.'"

Brianna's hand was clamped tightly over her mouth.

Giuseppe's horrid tale continued. "Later that night, the girl's father and a band of local men surrounded the French camp, shouting 'French *bastardos*. You'll all die by the hand of the Mafia before the sun rises.'"

His words became a blur when, with little warning, a sour feeling rose in the pit of Brianna's stomach. She didn't have to guess what was coming next. "*Giuseppe, stop the car!*" she implored.

When Floria started to idle, Brianna flung the door open and sprinted to a grassy area. A projectile of undigested food, which felt like gallons of coffee and a bunch of bile, hit the embankment. Standing by her side, Giuseppe gently patted her shoulder. Brianna was flushed red with embarrassment. The driver had his own reason for her throwing up. "Foreigners are not used to our strong coffee. I have a bottle of soda water in the car. It always helps me when I drink too much caffeine."

"I'm fine. Thank you. I have a bottle of spring water in my bag," Brianna said.

Giuseppe was developing a fondness for his passenger. "If there is anything I can do for you, don't hesitate to ask."

Brianna smiled warmly. "I think we should get going before it gets dark."

Brianna climbed back into the car, grabbed a handful of Kleenex, and lowered her head from view as she wiped off any vestiges of vomit. But she couldn't do anything about the taste of bile that lingered on her tongue, teeth, and the roof of her mouth. She would have given anything for an oral rinse, a peppermint candy, or a stick of gum.

With gears grinding, Giuseppe drove slower this time, giving Brianna the opportunity to enjoy the scenery. Despite Sicily's turbulent history, it was an idyllic, friendly island.

It was going to get even better.

Brianna was awed by the serene surroundings Floria was driving through. Beneath a clear blue sky, late afternoon light carpeted the landscape with a kaleidoscopic of hues: straw-colored fields, orange and yellow citrus groves, and earth-brown nut orchards. Sheep dotted the hillside, their heads bent as they grazed happily. A shepherd boy sat on a rock watching over them. These idyllic sights brought on a rush of words. "Wow," Brianna said. "It looks so peaceful. I could live here forever quite happily."

Giuseppe smiled but was not as accommodating in his own mind. *No. You wouldn't want to live here,* he reflected disapprovingly. *It is not the tranquil village I grew up in. Don Alberto's vendetta ended that.*

The village of Solicchiata lay ahead nestled in the shadows of Mount Etna. It was sunk as deeply in the valley as it was in poverty. Giuseppe carefully navigated the hairpin turns leading him down the steep, one-lane road that was the only access in and out of the village. The street was especially treacherous for vehicles with bald tires. Brianna was too preoccupied with the scenery to acknowledge the bumpy discomfort of the ride.

Brianna delighted at the display of holy shrines, dilapidated stone dwellings—some now no bigger than shoeboxes—swirls of smoke belching out of outdoor fireplaces, and women parked on wooden chairs preparing food. As the car snaked its way toward her destination, men, women, and children stopped what they were doing to stare at the colorful car, driver, and passenger. Brianna greeted the gawking folks with a regal wave of her hand. Giuseppe was enjoying the "celebrity" status and said, "They must be wondering why a Messina-plated taxi is driving among them."

"I guess so," was Brianna's response.

The bright, warm sunlight filtering through the car window was overshadowed by Brianna's nervousness and excitement. Her flesh tingled as she anticipated seeing her mother. But what kind of reception would she receive—cold or warm? She casually asked Giuseppe, "Which house does my grandmother live in?"

Giuseppe clicked his tongue at her lack of knowledge. "Maria doesn't live in these poor houses, but she does own every last one of them. She lives in a grand place up the hill." He pointed. "It's over there … a short drive."

Brianna leaned forward and poked her head out the window. The red, late afternoon sun was disappearing over the western mountains, and dark clouds were moving eastward. Overcast skies obscured the sun's fading rays. Straight ahead, all she could see was dense forest.

Giuseppe pierced through her absorption. "See that cottage over there?" he gestured. "That is where I was raised. And the one next to it was the home of my Uncle Cesare, Aunt Raphaela, and cousin Paolo. They are all gone now."

"Gone where?"

"They were *chased* …" He emphasized. "Were run out of their home and have never returned to the island, not that I know of."

"Who chased them from here and why?"

"Why" was becoming Brianna's word of the day.

Giuseppe swallowed several times before answering. "It's a long, sad story."

Brianna's knew her chatty, informative companion was going to walk her into the past, whether she wanted to go or not. Could it be any worse than what he had already divulged about Sicilian honor? Brianna decided to let him continue uninterrupted, even though she was distracted by passing images of village dwellings. These rundown shacks looked no different from the slum houses she had seen in the black townships of South Africa. Plastic wrap replaced missing glass panes; and structural decay, rotting wood, and poor roof coverings were visible. However, Brianna could not dwell on these hardships any longer. Instead, she stepped back into the past with her narrator. Throughout Giuseppe's story, Brianna's brows raised and lowered as frequently as a bride's underwear.

CHAPTER TWO

January 4, 1943, The Village of Solicchiata, Castiglione de Sicilia

"My soul, like a ship in a black storm is driven, I know not whither..."
–John Webster

A light dusting of snow sprinkled the red-tile roof of the tiny limestone cottage at the edge of the Genovese vineyards. The winter storm on the horizon was about to blacken the spirits inside this modest home.

The back door was violently thrust open, nearly ripped off its hinges—and not by the wind. In a cloud of flour dust, thirty-year-old Raphaela Girrdazzello hit the floor, along with a lump of bread dough she had been holding. Her rotund body was a tight fit under the butcher's table. Paralyzed with panic, she held her breath. With an Italian-designed hat hiding his face, a tall man, his body powerful from hard work, approached the butcher's table. He bent his six-foot frame down to make eye contact with the terrified, hunkering woman below. With her brown eyes wide as the Alcantara River and her double chins quivering, Raphaela let out a sigh of relief and a reprimand. "You scared me! Whatever possessed you to almost break down our door, and why are you home so early?"

Cesare grabbed his wife under her armpits and yanked her to her feet. Raphaela looked straight into her husband's blazing, demonic eyes. She didn't know what to make of the spectacle. So she hurriedly made the sign of the cross with her powdery hand. Had Lucifer gained a new disciple? She clicked her tongue. What a stupid question. Wasn't her husband employed by the Devil himself: Don Alberto Genovese? Raphaela latched hard onto his hand, dug her fingernails deep into his skin and said, "Husband, what's happened to make you take on the look of the *diaula*?"

When Cesare pulled away from her tight grasp, blood instantly rushed back to his numbed hand. His weather-beaten face was contorted as he towered over his petite wife. He didn't have the luxury of time. He ordered, "Pack some food. Make sure you bundle enough for a couple of days. Put on your winter coat, shawl, and sturdy walking shoes. We are leaving the island. Hurry, we have to go *now!*"

Raphaela's chubby face scrunched with incredulity. "I don't understand!" she cried.

"You will do as I say!" He ordered his wife. With a condescending wag of his finger, he continued bullying her. "Do *not* question my authority!"

After a long, uncomfortable silence, Raphaela gathered the courage. "In God's name, please tell me why we have to leave the island so quickly. I thought we had no secrets between us."

Cesare's narrowed eyes intimidated her. "Do you want me to take a whip to you, woman?"

Caught off guard by his rough language, Raphaela's saliva curled into a dry, tight ball in her mouth. This wasn't the gentle soul she had married. She didn't recognize this beast. He had never threatened her before. Like a traditional Sicilian wife, she had devoted all of herself to her husband—did what she had been told without question. But this time was different. Instead of seeing her loving husband, she saw a monster. A gut reaction to his words prompted her to pursue the truth. She could no longer stifle her anger, and she was tired of struggling for the right words. "You're acting like a *stunata!*" she spat. "What's happened to make you behave like the village idiot?"

Cesare immediately counterpunched. "I'm not a madman. I'm a desperate man." He released an irritated, raspy sigh. "You have no idea how much trouble we are in."

Raphaela's forehead took on the appearance of well-traveled tram tracks. She cleared her throat and demanded, "Talk to me."

Cesare turned his head away from her intense stare. He couldn't bring himself to tell her the truth. Not at this moment. She would become hysterical in disbelief, and that would delay their departure. Even he was having a hard time taking in what had happened earlier that day at the estate house. Suddenly, his brain snapped and his frayed nerves exploded. He snatched the nearest object and shattered the silence.

Countless Shards of glass from a nearby lamp formed ranks on the floor like gladiators.

Raphaela dropped to her knees and clasped her chapped hands in prayer. "Hail Mary, full of Grace …"

His wife's petrified expression melted Cesare's fury. He quickly drew her into his arms and held her shaking body. He whispered in her ear, "Darling, please forgive me. I've loved you since you were twelve, on the day we met in church. Please don't question the purity of my love. You know I would never hurt you, but I beg you, do as I ask without question or we will both die." He spun on his heels and made for the back door announcing over his shoulder, "I'll be back in a moment."

The hair on Raphaela's neck stood straight up. She was numb with unanswered questions. She didn't know what to think. But obey she must. A torrent of mingled emotions raced through her mind as she robotically reached for her black sweater, thick winter coat, and shawl. From a small table she picked up a string of rosary beads and a hand-drawn art piece of the Virgin Mary, crafted in pastel colors and gold leaf. She placed the items in her coat pocket. Her mind raced back to reality. She asked herself how her afternoon off from kitchen duties could end so badly. She wondered: *What in the world is going on?* She was being ordered to leave her homeland without explanation.

The aroma filtering through the back window made her head turn. Outside the back door sat two smoked pork hocks—in a large metal pot above an open wood fire—that she had "liberated" from her employer's cold-room. Raphaela knew she had broken the Holy Commandments and the civil law. If she were caught, she would pay the ultimate price. Guilt nudged her. Raphaela hoped God would grant her absolution in these bad times.

Like most other villagers, Raphaela and Cesare were poor, but they counted themselves more fortunate than most. Both were employed by the Genovese family. Raphaela was the head cook, and her husband was Don Alberto's butler, bodyguard, and gofer. But neither had seen wages in almost three months. In wartime Italy, basic foods were under strict rationing and, therefore, practically nonexistent. Many starving families had resorted to smuggling—a big risk—only to end up behind bars. In addition, great masses of German troops stationed on the island drew heavily upon everyone's scarce resources. Except for those of the wealthy landowners, who, on the whole, controlled the black market prices. They didn't have to hand over their crops to the government storehouses, and they practically owned the government and the *carabinieri* (national police), who set up roadblocks and paid informers to catch farmers and starving villagers. In Raphaela's reckoning, her rich but tight-fisted employers wouldn't miss the hocks from their larder, which to this day was bursting with delicacies no villager could ever afford, at any time.

A couple of hours earlier, with the stolen delights hidden under her thick coat, Raphaela had rushed home (a brisk thirty-minute walk) to prepare a special meal, a birthday surprise for her thirty-nine-year-old husband. She had planned to spring a second surprise on Cesare after he had a full belly. She was pregnant, definitely. Women know these things. She was twelve weeks along with their second child. After her first missed cycle, she had waited out the following two months to make sure. Now she wondered how he would react to the news of the theft and the baby. As a devout Catholic, would he admonish her about the theft? Would he be overjoyed about having another child? Probably not, but there was nothing he could do about it now! It was God's will.

For many years Raphaela had longed for another child. Cesare had argued against it. "Darling, we can barely feed ourselves or send our son to school, and often we don't get paid for our labor. No, no, no. You will just have to wait until our fortunes change."

Raphaela recalled her reply. "That will never be, Cesare! We are unfortunate, uneducated country peasants who are penniless."

"Then I'll get a second job to make more money, if it will make you happy."

"And I'll find extra work, too," she had added cheerfully.

With a face as long as the skirt she was wearing, the crestfallen Raphaela—devoted wife, mother, and homemaker—dampened the fire. She carefully removed the hocks from the hot pan and wrapped them in a dish towel. As she stretched her arm under the kitchen table toward her market basket, her troublesome thoughts thickened into something akin to sticky, dripping hog fat. How had this day of celebration turned into a mysterious, chilling mystery? How could she tell Cesare her happy news? Where would she birth their baby? Would her unborn child survive their journey to God-knows-where? The gravity of something forgotten suddenly hit her like a meteor.

Like a wild windstorm, she flew outside and saw her husband approaching her. She ran toward him and grabbed his wrist. In a voice that betrayed her fear, she stammered, "Wh-at about Pa-olo, our son? I can't lea-ve without him."

Never in a million years could Raphaela have anticipated her husband's response.

Cesare's ebony eyes blazed like red-hot coals. "*Madone de*

mia!" he swore vulgarly. "I have no son. And if I did, I would kill him with my own hands. We went without so we could provide him with private education. I even forgave him when he let us down and was expelled. Even Father Rupolo warned me he was a troublemaker."

Raphaela folded her arms in defiance and argued protectively. "He's not a bad son." Justifying her statement, she added, "Paolo was bullied, nearly beaten to death. That's why he quit school."

Cesare glared at his wife with a look that could have frozen an Inuit. "If you know what's good for you, Raphaela, you will never speak his name again. The *shekoo* (donkey) is as good as dead."

Raphaela's lips, clenched tightly, locked in her scream.

Ten years earlier, on a foggy January morning in 1933, Don Alberto Vincenzo Genovese paced in his living room. Although he worried about why it was taking so long, the twenty-nine-year-old was feeling lucky today, but not blessed. To distract himself from his eagerness, the expectant father looked out a balcony window festooned with flower boxes that were sprinkled with a smattering of light snow. Gone were the delightful fragrances of snapdragons, annual wildflowers, and *sparacelli*—the wild asparagus that grew in these planters. He visualized what lay beyond the high stone walls that barricaded his magnificently restored, eighteenth-century estate house: acres and acres of grapevines that produced traditional wine—a lucrative business that had been passed on from father to son for the past two centuries. Today he could name his heir.

Alberto stroked his thin, neatly trimmed, black mustache and thought: *Should I be worried?* How many hours has she been in labor? It was far too long for his liking. As time crawled by, Alberto clasped his hands until his knuckles paled. Would it do any good to ask God to intervene, hurry the birthing of his son into the world? The prospective father shook his head. No. He'd be wasting his breath. He could never be favored by the higher powers. He had blood on his hands. He had broken all the commandments, been excommunicated from the holy church; he had been damned and marked for the rest of his natural life.

The Don exhaled loudly through his nose, almost a horse snort, as he shrugged off his gloomy thoughts. All he wanted to do now was barge into the bedroom and find out what was happening. But he knew better. If he tried that, the elderly village midwife, Concetta—who had birthed him and most of the other babies in the community—would have his guts for garters. Men weren't allowed in the birthing room. Period! That was the custom. He would just have to wait this out. If all went well, Sofia, his third wife, would give him the son he longed for. But a cautionary inner voice wasn't as supportive. *Are you sure of that? Have you ruled out your past failures? Have you forgotten your legacy, the Genovese curse?*

For too many years to count, non-angelic forces had penetrated the living arteries of the Genovese bloodline. Would the introduction of Sofia's royal Spanish blood help repel the ill fate?

No. Fates are predestined.

Less than three years ago, Alberto's first wife, a mere slip of a girl, had died shortly after the birth of their stillborn daughter. His second wife, not much older than the first, had passed away from unknown causes in the third month of her pregnancy. Ever since these tragedies, Alberto often questioned the awful legacy left to him. This was one of those times. Hadn't his grandfather, Don Calogero Stefano Vincenzo Genovese, sired twelve daughters before he got lucky? At age seventy-five, the devout Catholic broke his marriage vows while his wife, Violetta, was away visiting her family in Palermo.

In her absence, Calogero ordered his trusted butler to go into the village and bring him a ripe young girl who'd be willing to sleep with him for a healthy sum. The servant served his master well, as did Rosia DeBenedetto. But as fate would have it, or rather the curse would have it, the dirty old Calogero died from a massive heart attack the day after he had bedded the thirteen-year-old.

When his grieving widow caught wind of the village talk—her husband's infidelity and Rosia's ensuing pregnancy—the scorned Violetta threatened the girl, her parents, and immediate family members with death. Deeply shamed by their only daughter's un-wed condition, and fearing for their lives, the head of the DeBene-detto family simply handed his daughter, Rosia, over to Violetta. They had dodged the bullet, but Rosia was not so lucky. She would have welcomed death if she'd have known her fate.

Violetta had the panic-stricken girl carted off to a remote Car-melite nunnery where she birthed a baby boy in secrecy.

After the birth, some gossiped that Rosia was never allowed out of her cloistered confines and that she eventually became a nun. Others rumored she was shipped off the island to God knows where. Still others presumed the heartbroken girl had been mur-dered. Only Violetta knew the facts, and she was not going to tell.

The truth was buried somewhere in the hearsay.

Hell hath no fury like a woman scorned!

As none of her daughters were legally entitled to inherit, Violetta schemed and won in her fight against the male-heir tradition. Her fortune in gold (valuable for bribes) granted the matriarch all the power she needed. Rosia's baby was baptized in the Catholic Church and documented as Calogero's legitimate child and valid heir to the Genovese estate. Had Violetta's evil intentions and the Genovese family's spilling of innocent blood for centuries been the cause for the family's bad luck? So it seemed.

The day the ten-day-old infant boy was delivered to the estate house, Violetta wanted nothing to do with him. The child's sparkling hazel eyes were ugly reminders of his biological mother. Violetta did, however, bequeath him her husband's middle name. He became Stefano Vincenzo.

Unaware of his humble beginnings, Stefano Junior adored his governess, a woman brought in from Palermo, who devoted every minute of her life to the outgoing child. But the vivacious boy wasn't fond of his so-called mother, Violetta, who seldom spoke to him. Regardless, he was a happy, bright boy who excelled at his private schooling. At age fifteen he took over the Genovese vineyards like a pro. A year later, Violetta arranged his marriage to one of her many nieces. The union was a disaster; their differences were as dramatic as night and day. They hated each other. However, nine months later, a son, Alberto Vincenzo Genovese I was born as the new heir to the Genovese fortune and vast farmlands.

Would the Genovese curse be broken at last?

Can hope be worse than despair?

As Don Alberto waited for the birth of his child, his heart missed a beat when he heard a knock on his study door. He said with urgency, "Come in." A disappointed scowl crossed his mouth when he saw who it was.

Cesare, age twenty-nine, was not only the Don's childhood playmate, he was also the family butler. Dressed in a classic tailcoat, white starched shirt, and black tie and pants, Cesare announced, "Your guests have arrived, Don Alberto. They are waiting in the main dining room."

"Have you put out the champagne and my finest wine and cigars?"

"I have, Don Alberto," Cesare replied respectfully.

"Good," Alberto said. "Then we will toast the good health and prosperity of my son, Alberto Stefano, Jr., when he enters our lives. On this note, how is your son doing?"

The question brought a bright smile to Cesare's dark, handsome face. "Paolo will be five-years-old next week, and already he's helping me plant our garden. He's such a good boy."

"I'm pleased to hear that."

Alberto lit a cigar. A billowing smoke ring coiled its way to Cesare's defenseless nose. He held his breath to prevent the cough that was threatening to escape his assaulted lungs. No one in his family smoked. They couldn't afford this luxury.

The Don added, "Paolo will be able to play with my son, just like we played, Cesare. How old were you when you came to work in the fields for my father?"

"I was five, sir." Cesare mused with a hint of disdain. *We are the same age! Wasn't that worth remembering?*

"We had some great times, didn't we?" Alberto laughed. "I'll never forget the time we got caught looking at that dirty magazine. Do you remember?"

With a half-smile creasing his lips, Cesare answered, "I do," but inwardly he wasn't pleased. He recalled how he had been thrashed by Don Stefano and how Alberto got nothing more than a "that's-my-boy" look. On many occasions Cesare had taken a beating for the wrongdoings of his playmate.

Even though Alberto was *farsi rispettare* (highly respected), there was no mistaking the merciless blood he carried. The mixed-blooded Don Stefano, Jr., Alberto's father, had indeed inherited the merciless Genovese genes. There wasn't a trace of Rosia's gentle nature in him. Stefano was a sociopath, a cold-blooded killer with a stone-cold heart. Growing up around Alberto, Stefano's son, Cesare knew firsthand of the legendary power and ruthlessness of a Mafia family. However, Alberto, the new Don, was more feared than his father because he was highly educated. Schooling meant power.

Alberto had attended university and received a degree in Business Economics. People who had wealth and education were always regarded with fear on the island. Over half of the interior Sicilian population was illiterate, including Cesare. More than anything else, he didn't want his son to end up like him, in a lowly position slaving for others for the rest of his life. This proud father had plans for his son, Paolo.

He took a second job working late hours in the vineyards, especially at harvest time, to put money aside for his son's education.

Now, in spite of the inward fear he had of Don Alberto, Cesare worshipped his boss and looked admiringly at him as a man who made men and women tremble in his presence. Alberto was the highest ranking *copa* of the region and was also feared among his flock of black sheep. And he was the best dressed man, at all times. Today Alberto was wearing a crisp white, long-sleeved shirt that accentuated his perfect pearly white teeth, his best feature. At five-foot-eight, Alberto was slightly paunchy and, to say the least, unattractive. He'd not inherited his handsome father's genes, or the fine porcelain features of his mother, Claudia, Violetta's first cousin.

Alberto's hideousness only added to his menace. Apart from his good teeth and thick, black hair, his dark olive face was as oval as a melon. He had prominent cheekbones and a bulbous nose, almost phallic looking. His eye color was that of unpolished ebony. The smell of money had lured in his many female admirers, but Sofia was the one who had netted him.

Cesare hadn't taken to the Spanish socialite as he had to Alberto's other wives. He felt that Sofia had bewitched his childhood friend when she met him at the funeral of Don Stefano two years earlier in 1931.

The late *Padrino* (Godfather), Stefano, Jr., was an old-style *copa* to a band of men who faithfully enforced his idea of justice. (The term "Mafia Boss" would not be used on the island of Sicily until World War II.) For many years before Sofia was born, Stefano had done business with her aristocratic, Jewish family, whose ancestry could be traced back to the fifteenth century. It was rumored that Stefano had crossed Sofia's family and they had put a hit out on him. An assassin's bullet had, indeed, marked his end. Stefano's killer was never found. That's how it was in the Mafia world. One day you ruled the land, and the next day you lay buried in it.

While carrying out his butler duties at Stefano's wake, Cesare had observed the twenty-year-old Sofia, who defined Spanish beauty. Attired in expensive, couture funeral garb, the tall blond with stunning green eyes put her seductive powers in play. Pulling Alberto aside at every available opportunity, the recently widowed Sofia linked her arm around his waist, touched his cheek, and whispered sweet nothings in his ear. There was no doubt in Cesare's mind that the Spanish widow was up to no good. Did she suspect Alberto was responsible for the car bomb that killed her parents shortly after Don Stefano's death?

Only the march of time would reveal the answer.

One hot summer afternoon, not long after Stefano's funeral, Sofia turned up on the estate bearing lavish gifts. She brought a purebred Arabian stallion, a Bugatti sports car, and several oil paintings—abstract Spanish artwork—that Cesare and the rest of the household staff thought was ghastly. However, the distasteful art was nothing compared to what happened next. In less than a month, with Alberto's father and former wives hardly cold in their graves, Alberto and Sofia secretly married in Palermo. Much to the chagrin of the Catholic Church and Alberto's relatives and friends, a local magistrate legalized the union. No one was to know that the Spanish widow had emphatically refused a church wedding. She had done it once, and was not about to do it again.

Kept in the dark until the last minute, Cesare was more than shocked. This wasn't the Alberto he had known. The now reigning Don had not missed a Sunday Mass in the Genovese chapel since he was a little boy. He kept a thumb-worn Bible on his nightstand and a picture of the Virgin Mary above his bed. From the day of the wedding on, Alberto's faith in God pretty much failed to exist. The Supreme Being was ousted to make room for the love of a woman.

Smitten from the day he met the funny, beautiful, and smart Sofia, Alberto was willing to give up everything for the sultry seductress. He was madly in love with her. He chose not to hear cautionary words from the village priest, Father Bettino, or from his faithful friend and servant, Cesare.

The day after the couple returned from their honeymoon in Tuscany, tongues wagged in disbelief throughout Solicchiata, and especially among the household staff congregated in the thirty-foot, L-shaped Genovese kitchen. "Their unblessed marriage and any children they may have will be in mortal danger," declared one bystander.

"Their souls and their offspring will be damned for all eternity," said another.

"Don Alberto's ancestors must be turning in their graves."

A cleaning woman bewailed, "Sofia could have converted to our faith." The woman rubbed her temple as if thinking what to say next. "She could have had a blessed Christian marriage." The house cleaner didn't know that Sofia had been *forced* at a young age to convert from Judaism to Catholicism in order to marry her first husband. Her power hungry father had stopped at nothing to ensure a stream of wealth flowing into his pockets.

The maid wasn't finished giving her pennyworth of ill feelings. "How is Don Alberto going to explain this to his cousin, Father Rupolo?"

"That's one priest who will probably never set foot here again," added another servant.

"She's a Jewish witch!" someone else bitched.

The scandalous kitchen chatter was riper than the odor of the room's hanging cloves of garlic, until Raphaela put her foot down. She said angrily, "I don't wish to hear another bad word about Mistress Sofia." "She's been good to us ever since she moved in here …" A loud, contemptuous snigger cut the cook short. When Raphaela looked in the direction of the sound, she put her hands on her hips and challenged, "If you have something to say, *Normanne*, spit it out."

The twelve-year-old kitchen helper gripped tightly the mop handle she was holding. She hated being referred to as the product of bygone Norman conquerors, just because she wasn't a typical Sicilian with dark skin, hair, and eyes. Yes, she was different. Her eyes were bright blue, her hair red, and her face pale. Large freckles mapped her natural pallor. Even though she was genetically different, it didn't give others the right to taunt her. Just for once, she'd liked to be called by her real name—Teresa Maria.

But that wasn't going to happen.

The fiery little redhead glared at Raphaela. Teresa was ready to battle. "It's all right for you to say she's good, but I haven't been paid since she took over," she claimed. "I need money to feed my mother and father. They haven't had work in ages. My heart hurts for them to go so hungry."

Raphaela let out an indifferent sigh. "We all have families to feed, and if it wasn't for the leftover food she allows us, we would all starve. Just be grateful that you have a job. There are loads of girls in the village who would love to clean floors just to eat a piece of leftover ham. Now go about your business and let me go about mine."

Teresa's body language spoke volumes. "My mama said that if I don't get paid, I'm to leave this cursed, evil place and find work elsewhere."

Raphaela shook her head. She wasn't going to get into a futile argument with a child. "Then go. No one is stopping you. But I assure you, there's no work to be found. Not in these parts. And if you head for the city, you may find yourself in a worse position. I've heard some awful tales about landowners beating their servants. Don Alberto has never laid a hand on any of us."

Teresa rolled her eyes and said, "But that's going to change, Raphaela. He's going to get mad if their unblessed baby dies or worse ..." She gulped air. "What if it turns out to be a girl?" she said. "Maybe he will get rid of her and choose me for his wife. He likes me you know. He always looks at my breasts."

Raphaela nearly dropped the soup pot as she began to laugh. "Dream on, silly girl! You are the last female he'd ever look at." But she silently agreed that Teresa had hit the nail on the head regarding the gender of the child. The cook was painfully aware of what happened in this house when his last child died. He made life unbearable for the servants, shouting at them for no reason.

But he had never hit any of them. Not like his father, Don Stefano, had done. Raphaela knew that if something were to go wrong this time ... she crossed herself for protection. She knew that a birthing problem now would affect not only the family members in the Genovese estate house, but those who worked for them, as well.

From that day on the sword of Damocles hung over all their heads.

At a quarter after one that afternoon, a newborn's wailing could be heard throughout the house. The kitchen servants clapped in unison.

"A strong pair of healthy lungs," Raphaela commented. "This male child is going to make it."

"This girl child is going to make it!" Concetta announced as she entered the staff's work space.

Many mouths flew open.

Raphaela's face paled in shock. "Dear God in Heaven! Not again."

Teresa seized the moment with the talons of a predator. "See? I was right," she gloated. "He's cursed for breaking from the Catholic Church. God punishes those who do wrong by Him ..."

Teresa's words were cut short. "Do I get to finish the sentence?" she grumbled.

Concetta thrust a bloodied sheet into Teresa's hands and ordered, "Get this washed. It will keep you from ..."

Concetta was startled by Cesare's presence.

With his hands clasped behind his back, Cesare walked over to his wife, Raphaela, and understood by the look on her face that she knew. He pulled her aside and whispered in her ear, "Don Alberto is not a happy man. He won't even look at his daughter. He's getting drunk to drown his sorrows."

"Oh, this is so sad," Raphaela responded. "He'll get over it when she gets pregnant again."

"Something tells me that is not going to happen," Cesare said. "Enough of this loose talk or we'll both be fired. Don Alberto wants you to make fresh espresso, and I'll take him some of your delightful pastries. Maybe the sweetness will soften his bitter heart?"

"I doubt it," Raphaela replied. "As long as I have known him, his heart has been sour as vinegar."

In another room, alone with his thoughts, Alberto slumped in a gargantuan armchair, his arms folded and his feet tapping as if they were playing drum pedals. At the same time he fiercely ran his fingers through his wavy black hair. He was disappointed, but all was not lost. She'd be pregnant again in no time. He would get busy as soon as she was fit. Seated nearby, Alberto's Mafiosi comrades commiserated, one by one.

"She's young. Don't worry. It will definitely be a boy next time."

"Maybe ten boys before she's too old to bear anymore."

"You better get busy right away making a son!"

"My wife gave me a daughter first."

"Enough!" Don Alberto snapped, slamming his hand on the table. His fiery eyes and gritted teeth were enough to dismiss his guests. To their retreating backs he said, "I wish to be alone. Cesare will see you out."

The quiet gave him room to vent. He thrust his hands into the pockets of his tailored trousers and stomped across the room like an uncontrolled child in the throes of a temper tantrum.

Upstairs, giving away to utter exhaustion, Sofia closed her eyes and wept.

CHAPTER THREE
Ten Years Earlier, Sofia del la Llerna Picasso Genovese

"Magna est veritas et pravalebit—For great is truth and shall prevail."
—Thomas Brooks

Sofia, age twenty one, was hurting. Her thin aristocratic face was pale, and her eyes were puffy and swollen from crying. It was supposed to be a day of celebration. She ran her fingers through her newborn's wispy black hair and said tenderly, "My heart is breaking. But don't worry, little one. I love you and want you, even if your father doesn't." The baby's eyelids opened. Her almond-shaped eyes, the color of emeralds, focused on Sofia. Pride mixed with sadness saturated the new mother's heart.

Sofia stared into the innocent eyes of her child and silently pledged the promises made by almost all mothers. She even promised things she was unsure she could keep, such as to protect her daughter from everything bad, even if that meant protecting her from her own father. "Yes, my beautiful daughter, Maria Teresa. I am your mama. You are my firstborn. Soon you'll have a fine brother to protect you."

The married couple's bedroom was enveloped by the still of

night, perfect for a healing sleep, but Alberto was a no-show. Sofia, alone in the bed, didn't feel she had let her husband down, but she did feel intensely his rejection of their child. It hurt beyond words. She harkened back to the long journey—the up and downs—of having his baby. She recalled announcing the pregnancy. Alberto had jumped up and down on a chaise lounge, just like Tom Cruise had done on *The Oprah Winfrey Show*. But it was what he did for her during her pregnancy that prompted her to smile. He had lovingly rubbed her swollen limbs, laid his head on her distended belly, stroked her head when a headache hit, ran warm baths, and placed fresh fruit and flowers on her meal trays. He had showered her with hugs and kisses, but he had abruptly halted lovemaking. Everything had changed.

Being generously endowed, Alberto had secretly blamed his manhood for what had happened to his previous wives and their unborn children. His face had never been more solemn and serious. "I don't want to hurt my son before he's even born," he had told her.

Of course, Sofia had laughed. But no amount of sexual temptation, not even strutting around in sexy lingerie—a red bustier, black stockings, and garters she had ordered from Paris—had changed his mind.

An hour after the delivery, Sofia held the still unwashed Maria at her breast. Despite her love for her child, Sofia's mood was darker than the stormy night sky. Having a baby, especially the first, is challenging, both physically and mentally. But it wasn't postpartum depression—the baby blues—that turned her heart as black as carbon. As the baby sucked, Sofia ran her fingers over the embroidered initials—A & S—on the top bed sheet and asked herself why the man she'd fallen in love with and married would not even look at his beautiful daughter. She knew all about his previous failures to produce a son, but that wasn't going to happen to her. She would give him a son. She was sure of that.

Males dominated Sofia's gene pool. She was the last child (and the only girl) born to Count and Countess de la Llerna Picasso. Sofia had eleven brothers. She had led a sheltered life of privilege, money being no object. She grew from a lanky teenager into a mesmerizing beauty who attracted men of all ages—but none that her father or brothers approved of. At age sixteen, she announced that she wanted to attend university to study architecture. Having had the best private education possible, she longed to continue on to an exciting career.

"Out of the question," came her old-school father's reply. He made it clear that a woman's place is in the home. "Universities are for men, not foolish-headed girls!" he had said. "No. And I forbid you to mention this stupid notion again. You will marry as soon as I find a suitable match."

Sofia begged her mother to intervene, but to no avail. Unbeknown to Sofia, the wheels of an arranged marriage were already turning. When her mother hinted at this, Sofia had vowed that she would make life a living hell for whomever her parents had chosen.

Hell made an entrance when Fernando Ortega, a distant cousin of the King of Spain, was invited to escort Sofia to a ball held at her parent's home. He was dressed in matador gear: white knee socks; tight, black pants reaching to his knees; and a white dress shirt and red jacket. As in bull worship, Fernando removed his Spanish-styled hat and bowed before her. His outfit and physical features enticed more than an animal rage in Sofia. She gagged. The weasel was at least three inches shorter than she ... and balding. His scrubbed-clean face showed a multitude of pimple eruptions, and his crooked teeth were tobacco brown. It was more than Sofia could take. She turned tail and ran.

With the hem of her sequined, cream, tulle ball gown trailing behind her; her gold, high heels clattering over marble tiling; and her crystal filigree earrings swinging, she fled upstairs, slammed the door, and locked herself in her bedroom. No amount of persuasion could bring her out.

Two months later, in the Burgos Cathedral, a sullen seventeen-year-old Sofia had said "I do" to the relative of the King of Spain. She walked down the rose-petal aisle in a gorgeous, white wedding dress with a dropped waist, tasseled belt, and close-fitting head-dress. It would have been the perfect attire for a happy, romantic bride, but not for the crestfallen Sofia. Her face was as long as the ropes of pearls hanging around her neck. This day was to be the start of an unconsummated marriage because, thank God, Fernando preferred men. Rather than endure this loveless farce, a part of the bride's mind wished her new husband would step on a roadside bomb. But there was no way she could get out of her marriage, as divorce was out of the question. Catholics didn't divorce, for any reason. And now she was one of them. That day she vowed never to let go of her true faith, her Jewish upbringing.

Sofia didn't have to suffer the humiliation of her husband's sexual preference much longer. He contracted syphilis, went mad, and died in a hospital exactly one year after they were married. Sofia swore never to marry again, but her controlling father had other plans. "You will remarry any person we choose or you will be sent to a Catholic convent!" A disdainful, defiant look crossed Sofia's chiseled features. She angrily protested. "Become a nun! Never ! You can't make me enter a convent! I am a born Jew, or have you forgotten?"

"Have you forgotten that you denied your true faith?" her father questioned.

"Your memory is feeble, Father," Sofia blasted. "It's because of you that I converted! It was your pathetic wish or, should I say, crazy idea for me to marry Catholic royalty ..."

"Sofia!" her mother shouted, cutting off her daughter's angry tirade. "Show your father respect, immediately. He wants only what is best for you. And there aren't too many noble Jewish families left in these parts."

Sofia wrung her hands. It was a pointless argument. What was done was done. She rushed from the room when her father raised a balled fist and approached her. It wouldn't have been the first time he had laid a hand on her. She fled outdoors into the maze on her father's estate. She wanted to be lost forever in a labyrinth of walking paths, but she was not alone.

Her brother Noah was exercising the family's mastiff in the grounds' spectacular network of gardens. Noah, the sibling closest in age to Sofia, hugged his sister and gave her the perfect way out. "Dear Sister, don't despair. All is not lost. The new *latifondista* (landowner) of the Genovese farmlands will spare you the fate of wearing a penguin suit at the convent!"

Her heart had nearly jumped out of her chest when she heard the confession that followed. "Don Stefano, Jr., the old bastard who double-crossed father, we took him out. You can pretend to be our representative at his funeral the day after tomorrow."

If Sofia was shocked, she didn't show it.

CHAPTER FOUR

January 1933, Maria Teresa Picasso Genovese's Entrance into the World

"What shall be the maiden's life?"
—Scott

It felt like a lifetime later, but Noah's slippery plan had worked. She was Don Alberto's wife and the mother of his first child. As soon as she was able to get out of the delivery bed, she went in search of her husband. The first person she saw was Cesare. "Where is Don Alberto?" she asked.

"He left this morning on business, Mistress Sofia," replied Cesare.

Sofia made eye contact with the servant. Something wasn't right! Her sixth sense perceived that Alberto's loyal servant was lying, protecting his master. With Cesare a few paces behind her, she searched the two-story house. In the last of the twelve bedrooms, Sofia got the shock of her life. Her heart sank when she opened the door. There, lying naked on the four-poster bed, was Teresa's older sister, Natalia. The startled teenager grabbed the bed linen to cover her bareness, and closed her eyes tight. Her thin body trembled. She was terrified. What would Sofia do to her? Would she get out of this home alive? Should she make a run for it? Natalia pulled the bed cover over her head. "God give me strength!" the outraged Sofia cried hysterically, looking away from the scene. She turned to face Cesare standing in the doorway with a sheepish look on his face. "Where's the *bastinado*?" she demanded.

The butler lowered his eyes and head and bit the inside of his cheek before replying. "He's gone to Palermo, Mistress Sofia."

She thrust out her arms and boomed at Cesare. "When your boss gets back, tell him I'm going to shoot his brains out." And if she wanted to hit him, she wouldn't miss. Sofia was a sharpshooter. She had learned this skill at the age of nine. Sofia had never missed a hunt.

With his tongue glued to the roof of his mouth, Cesare watched speechlessly as Sofia approached the bed. She hugged the trembling girl and softly said, "I'm not mad at you, child. It's not your fault that you were seduced by my despicable husband, but I think for both our sakes you should get dressed, find Teresa, and go home, the pair of you. I can't have you or your sister working here again. Do I make myself clear?"

The wide-eyed girl nodded.

Cesare couldn't help but admire his wronged mistress for not taking revenge on her servant for the inappropriate behavior of her husband. Cesare had never cared for Sofia, until now.

The mistress of the house whirled around and, with her gypsy-styled skirt flapping, returned to her bedroom. This time she didn't shed a tear. Instead of feeling sad, she felt demoralized. The rejection of their first child was unthinkable, and the sexual abuse of a servant was devastating. She wished she had never met her husband! But she had no one to blame but herself. She was trapped in her own making. She was her own worst enemy.

Weeks passed since Maria Teresa Picasso Genovese was born, and, remarkably, the family's coexistence was not fraught with discord, as the staff had predicted. The strong-willed Sofia, like a sirocco breeze belching out hot fumes, carried on after what would prove to be one of her husband's many indiscretions.

Let sleeping dogs lie.

However, Sofia couldn't wrap her mind around her husband's ongoing rejection of baby Maria. It went against every maternal fiber in her body. Sofia didn't give a rat's arse if her husband never paid any attention to her ever again, but she would have given anything for Maria to have a loving, nurturing father. Sofia would wait a long time for her wish to come true.

One afternoon Sofia opened her carbon-encrusted heart to the old midwife, Concetta. "My heart is breaking," Sofia sniffed to the only person she felt she could trust in the house. "Isn't Maria the most beautiful baby? Why won't my husband even look at her?"

The ancient woman sucked in a deep breath, and compassionately placed her hand on top of Sofia's. "Signóra Sofia, the makings of men's minds are a mystery to all women. I think he's just a little upset and will soon be by your side," she said glibly. Concetta actually knew Alberto better than Sofia did. She had birthed the Don, watched him grow into a strong-willed young man. His immature stance on the newborn was nothing new to the midwife. Would he change? She didn't think so. She believed if Sofia produced a son, then, and only then, would the spoiled Don have a change of heart.

Would the Genovese blight then be over?

Not while clocks keep chiming.

Sofia had fertility issues. Unable to get pregnant for five years and desperate to produce an heir, she took every fertility herb known to mankind.

Don Alberto went into a deep, dark depression and blamed the family curse for his inability to bear a son. It wasn't until a bubbly, angelic, five-year-old Maria—wearing a frilly, pink summer dress—ran into his study, climbed onto his lap, gave him a big mushy kiss, and said, "I love you, Papa. Why don't you love me back?" that the Don began to thaw.

Tears stung his eyes as his conscience began to plague him with feelings of guilt and anger at himself for his outrageous behavior. Oh, the priceless years he had lost. He looked deep into his daughter's beautiful eyes for the first time. They took his breath away, as had Sofia's eyes all those years ago. For the first time since she'd been born, he embraced Maria tightly, showered her with kisses, and admitted, "How could I have been so blind? Forgive me, little one. I'll never reject you again."

From that day on, Don Alberto became a good father, the kind who played and wrestled on the floor. Father and daughter were inseparable.

The Don was devoted to his remarkable, bright, willful daughter, whose intelligence impelled her to read at an early age. Maria excelled at her schoolwork. She had a private tutor from the age of four. She could read Latin, her favorite subject, and did extremely well in arithmetic, history, and geography. When asked by her parents what she wanted to do when she grew up, her rely was, "I'm going to become a doctor so I can heal the vineyard workers who can't afford hospital fees."

In the days that followed her husband's change of heart, Sofia couldn't have been happier. She enjoyed watching the father and daughter develop a strong bond, even though her relationship with Alberto (especially in the bedroom) had soured somewhat. Later, following a full-term stillborn birth, she was deeply saddened to learn that another pregnancy could end her life. Imagining not being around to watch Maria grow was all it took to prevent another conception.

Sofia had her tubes tied.

CHAPTER FIVE

Five Years Later, a Birthday to Forget

"Many a happy dream can darken into your worst nightmare."
—Anonymous

Anew year, 1943, had just begun, and Maria was blossoming. She stood above average height for her age, looked much older than her ten years, and was stunningly beautiful. Naturally, and thankfully, her genes expressed primarily her mother's side. Much to the Don's displeasure, Maria was ogled by men on the streets; even some of his business partners slipped up and gazed at her far too long.

Men would not play a part in Maria's life, though. Not yet anyway. Her father had plans for his only child. As he had no male heir, she was to inherit everything he owned legitimately—and not so legitimately. Only time would tell if she developed the street smarts to operate the heroin trafficking and protection rackets he had run since his father death.

Today was Maria's tenth birthday.

Don Alberto bought her a palomino pony. The birthday girl was tickled pink, and she named her new charge Alfonso. Alberto was proud of Maria as she learned to ride like a pro. When they rode through the estate together, she could easily keep up a gallop alongside his spirited stallion, Diablo. And she always insisted that Cesare's fifteen-year-old son, Paolo, the stable boy, join them. Maria and Paolo had become inseparable. She told her father they'd be best friends for life, just like he was with Cesare. What she didn't tell her father was that she had a crush on the tall, good-looking boy, who was not yet old enough to shave. To her, he was a heartthrob. If she knew that her little-girl crush would have dire consequences, she would have hit him with a manure shovel and made sure he never woke up.

But for now, it was time for birthday celebrations.

That evening, in a bedlam of celebratory spirit, the mansion was jam-packed with party guests. Maria was Cinderella on her way to a ball. The ten-year-old sidled down the staircase dressed finely and fashionably in a lilac-and-white, ankle-length dress, and ballet shoes to match. Her long hair, styled in curls, hung down her back. Around her neck hung a diamond encrusted emerald and-pearl-necklace that had been passed down in the Picasso family from generation to generation. It was reputed to be more than 200 years old. A local band played popular wartime boogie tunes, and then a famous classical guitarist from Palermo, hired especially for the occasion, strummed the birthday song. Everyone sang. After this joyous moment, Maria blew out the candles on her chocolate cake and beamed with happiness. She hugged her mother and father and then skipped between the tables where she hugged all 100 guests.

At the stroke of midnight the exhausted birthday girl said her goodnights and headed upstairs to bed. Sofia accompanied her delighted daughter to her room, removed the hundreds of gifts resting on her custom, four-poster bed, and said, "My darling daughter, sleep tight, and Mama will see you in the morning."

Sometime later it happened. Maria didn't hear the sash-window being pried open; nor did she see a snow-covered figure gingerly climbing through it. Suddenly, a damp hand was clamped over her mouth. Jolted from a deep sleep, Maria's eyes grew as wide as saucers. She wanted to scream, but couldn't. It was too dark to make out the identity of the shadowy figure looming over her. His foul, garlic breath assaulted her nostrils. "Don't make a sound, Maria," the intruder growled. "If you want to see your mama and papa again, you'll do as I say," he threatened while slowly releasing his grip.

There was no mistaking *that* voice. It was imprinted on her heart. Rubbing sleep from her eyes, Maria bolted upright. "What are you doing in my bedroom?" she admonished fierily. "My father will kill you if he catches you here."

CHAPTER SIX

The Next Morning

"Some people sell their souls, and live with
a good conscience on the proceeds."
—Anonymous

Sometime around eight o'clock in the morning, Sofia, still in her nightgown, headed for Maria's bedroom. She opened the door to greet her daughter with a loving "Good morning, darling." But her eyebrows arched with surprise. Maria's bed was in a shambles. Tousled bedding, looking as if it had been wrestled off the mattress, had been thrown on the floor. This was not at all like her meticulously tidy child, who insisted on making her own bed each morning. Without a second thought, Sofia assumed her daughter was already dressed and in the bathroom. She was about to head in that direction when her eyes noticed the flimsy net drapes wafting. Strange, she thought. Maria was not only a neat freak, but she was also a stickler for closing her bedroom window at all times.

As Sofia pulled the sash-window down, something caught her eye. She took a second look. Why was an oak ladder propped against the wall? No external repairs or painting were planned. Sofia quickly reopened the window, stuck her head out, and frowned.

In the snow she saw two sets of slushy footprints leading away from the house. Her brain was numb with confusion. Then her heart began to pump with fear of the unknown. She didn't notice the puddles of water inside the bedroom, on the floor below the window ledge. She turned tail and rushed down the hallway toward the bathroom on the same floor. It was empty. "Maria! Come out," Sofia shouted, as if her daughter was hiding somewhere.

Sofia's low-heeled slippers clattered on the marble floor. Downstairs, she rushed into the kitchen. "Raphaela, have you seen Maria? Has she had her breakfast?"

"Come to think of it, no, Signóra Sofia," Raphaela responded. She studied her mistress's worried face. "Is something the matter, Signóra?"

The cook received no answer.

Sofia rushed toward the dining room.

With his elbows resting on the table, Alberto was reading the newspaper while munching on scrambled eggs and porcini mushrooms. "Where have you been?" he grouched. "Your breakfast is getting cold."

"Alberto, have you seen Maria? She's not in her bedroom or bathroom."

The Don didn't look at all worried when he replied. "She's probably at the stables with Alfonso. I swear those two are joined at the hip! She enjoys the stable work as much as the riding. She's probably still mucking out the stall." A huge smile erupted on his face. "She'd marry that darn pony if I would let her."

Sofia stared her husband down. "Alberto, it's no laughing matter. Maria is missing."

"Don't be so dramatic, woman. She's a ten-year-old with a mind of her own. She'll turn up when she's hungry."

"Humph. That seems unlikely," Sofia argued. "She never leaves the house without eating cook's special Maria breakfast."

This was certainly true, Alberto thought. Maria loved *fichi d'India* (prickly pears) soaked in honey.

Sofia scratched her head and then remembered. "Did you order outside repairs to the house?"

"No. Why do you ask?"

"I found Maria's window wide open. You know she hates that. And there's a ladder against her bedroom window."

"What?" Alberto said, looking perplexed. Then his wife's words hit home. He flung down his knife and fork, and pushed the dining chair back so hard it crashed to the floor. All that could be heard were his heavy footsteps bounding their way up the stairs. Sofia was hot on his heels.

He saw the melted snow puddles and the dribble of blood on his daughter's pillow case. Nearly bowling Sofia off her feet, he pushed past his wife, flew downstairs to the annex (the staff's dining area), and bellowed at the top of his lungs, "Cesare! Go to the stables. Get Paolo to saddle two horses, and bring them around to the courtyard. Hurry, we have little time."

Naturally, the butler asked, "What's happened, Don Alberto?"

"Some *bastardo* has kidnapped my daughter."

Cesare couldn't believe his ears. It was every parent's worst nightmare. How could this have happened? One minute the child was safely tucked into bed, and the next, gone. And Maria enjoyed a good life—no broken home or lonely childhood—a protected life ... until now. It could easily have been one of the many estate employees, Cesare reasoned. The culprit was probably not a passerby. The estate was too well guarded to let some stranger waltz in. It had to be someone who wanted revenge for some wrong Alberto had done. Retaliation was the way of life on the island; feuds between ruling crime heads were not uncommon.

Cesare couldn't have been more wrong. His mistaken assumption was about to hit him square in the jaw.

Alberto headed for the gun cabinet in his study, removed two shotguns, and, feeling as crushed as harvested grapes, swore revenge. "When I catch whoever has her, I'll blow his fucking head off."

At the stables Cesare was surprised to find the outside doors still bolted shut. He undid the heavy latch and entered. There was no sign of his son, Paolo. And by the looks of things, the horses had not yet been served their early morning feed. Nor had their stalls been mucked out.

Cesare was perplexed. His son was an early riser, and he took his duties seriously. Cesare scratched his chin. Where could he be? But the butler didn't have time to ponder this question. He quickly saddled the Don's black stallion and a mare for himself, gave them each a handful of oats, and walked them to the courtyard where Alberto was waiting.

Above them, Sofia's loud, lamenting wails could be heard from Maria's bedroom. Without a glance in her direction, the two armed men rode through the estate tracking the footprints, one an imprint of adult's footwear and the second the barefoot impressions of a child. As they neared the vineyard boundary along the tracks, Alberto spotted his field workers hard at work. "Have any of you seen my daughter?"

"No, *Latifondista*."

They rode on.

At the border of Alberto's property, the footprints vanished. But the estate owner spotted deep impressions made by the hooves of a mule or donkey drawing a cart through the snow on a disused dirt road. The Don scratched his chin. His servant immediately offered his advice: return to the estate house and get more help. Call everyone. Check seaports, roads, and homes and all owners of mule-drawn carts. Cesare wanted to reassure his boss by embracing him, but the pulsing veins popping out of his master's neck were a sure sign of a beating if he dared approach what was left of Alberto's sanity. Cesare felt wooden from the neck down.

The men galloped back to the house in frightening silence.

Waiting for them in the doorway was a hysterical Sofia, who had chunks of hair missing from the crown of her head. When she spotted her husband, she screamed like a stuck pig. "Alberto, Alberto, come quick! Raphaela found this in the henhouse."

What she clutched in her hand would send Alberto over the edge. On Maria's lined school paper, a note read: *"Listen carefully! Leave 50 million lira in gold in a bag under the rock marked with an 'X' on the Garibaldi road before sunset today or you will never see your daughter alive again. One of your 'slaves' must make the drop. Don't get smart. You are being watched. If I see police, I will kill her. After I have the money, a note will be left under the same rock telling you where you can find her. Choose your next steps wisely."*

Bang!

The shotgun blast left a gaping hole in the ceiling. Sofia hit the floor screaming. Cesare stood like a statue, every nerve-ending rooted to the floor. Alberto fired a second shot. Covered in a rain of plaster dust and with venom oozing out of every pore, the Don would make a decision that would destroy not only Maria's life but his, Sofia's, and all those who lived on the Genovese lands. He shrieked, "*Merda!* I'm not going to pay one coin to the *bastardo* who has my daughter."

Cesare placed a hand over his forehead and closed his eyes. He had been in the family long enough to know that a true-blooded Genovese would fight to the death to get a loved one back. Refusing to pay the ransom for Maria was unfathomable. But then Alberto had always been the odd one. Like his father and grandfather, he had no moral fiber. Even the most intelligent men can be wrong sometimes, Cesare reckoned.

Sofia couldn't believe her ears. She turned red with rage. "*Aricchi Du Porcu!*" ("You are like the hairs on a pig's ear!"), she shrilled at her husband. "How can you say that? You are one of the richest men in Sicily! It's a paltry sum for the return of our child." She wrung her hands. "For God's sake, Alberto, she's your daughter … your only child and the heir to your estate! I'll pay the money myself."

"You'll do no such thing," Alberto thundered. "My father taught me never to bow down to bullies who think they can rob you. He also taught me that we have a barrel of apples, and that a bad apple might be in this barrel. This apple has to be removed, and if it isn't, it will ruin the rest of the apples. That's how it goes in my world!"

Sofia didn't know how to answer that, but she did have the smoking gun.

She dug in her skirt pocket and placed a silver ring in the palm of her hand for all to see. "I found this in Maria's room," she announced. Then she curled her lips into a contemptuous sneer. "It belongs to your bad apple!"

Alberto stared hard at the plain band. There was no doubt who owned it. He turned and grabbed Cesare's wrist in a vice-like grip. "I gave him this ring last December on his fifteenth birthday," the Don raged. "You and your *bastardo* son are fucking dead!"

The atmosphere in the room plunged down to the murkiness of a tomb.

With his face pale in disbelief and in fear of his life, Cesare argued, "Don Alberto, Paolo would never do such a thing … kidnap Maria! He loves her like a sister. There must be a big mistake. Maybe he gave it to Maria. Maybe she found it and was going to …"

Cesare's mouth shut when he saw Alberto's balled fists. The Don wasn't buying his servant's declaration of his son's innocence. "You better find him and prove me wrong, or your head and everyone who has Girrdazzello blood will be executed," Alberto said without a flinch of uncertainty.

With a stubborn jaw set, Cesare left the front door wide open and ran as fast as his legs could carry him down the hill through the landscaped gardens and toward his limestone cottage. While the servant fled Alberto's wrath, the Don's head was buried in his hands. For the first time since he could remember, he wept. Sofia went to her husband and wrapped her arms around him. Their soul-wrenching sobs permeated the canvas of baby Maria's painted portrait hanging above the fireplace.

CHAPTER SEVEN

The Aftermath of Abduction

"Sometimes we have to fight our way out of the dark
because the light doesn't come looking."
—Anonymous

In her urine-soiled nightgown, Maria was lying in the back of a cart under snow-covered bales of hay. Her muffled sobs were barely audible. Blindfolded, gagged, and hog-tied, she questioned why he had trussed her up like a chicken. She thought he was her best friend. He'd been the love of her life! She had dreamt of marrying him when she was older. Where was he taking her and why? Bouncing from side to side, she was frightened. Blazing tears of fear rolled down her dirt-encrusted face. When she heard someone coughing nearby, she realized she wasn't alone. But she couldn't cry out because of the gag in her mouth. She wondered who was driving the cart.

A slim, red-haired woman dressed in peasant clothing and a black wool scarf whipped the white-faced donkey. The twenty-two-year-old *Normanne* yelled, "This is not the time to get stubborn, Shekoo." Fraught with trepidation, Teresa wanted to get off this back road. It wasn't safe. Too many smugglers used this route.

Even though her cart looked uninviting to thieves, she couldn't risk being stopped.

Another thought made Teresa's lips part in a cold smile. She believed vengeance to be the only true justice. Hadn't she and Paolo been nothing more than year-round slaves—morning, noon, and night—for the Genovese family? If she and Paolo encountered no hiccups, she would have the last laugh at the people who had made her life so miserable. She was proud that she had planted the seed of their plan in Paolo's mind. So here she was, helping kidnap the daughter of a despicable man, the one who had bribed her older sister, Natalia, to have sex with him. Natalia had confided to Teresa, "I hated every minute that ugly man's wine-belly was on top of me, but mama is sick and the money he gave me would buy medicine." That image made Teresa madder still. She whipped the donkey harder. "Get a move on, you stupid Shekoo!"

Teresa drove the cart behind deserted, Byzantine, monastery ruins, and reined in the donkey under nearby dense shrubbery. She jumped down and rushed to the back of the cart. "We're here, darling. You can come out now. I made it without anyone seeing us."

Paolo, his eyes bloodshot from an allergic reaction, brushed the straw off his clothing and out of his tousled, unevenly cut hair, which looked as if it had been styled with a sharp rock. Muttering under his breath, he reached under a bale and dragged Maria out by her feet. He threw the shivering child over his shoulder, clamped an arm around her midriff, and rushed through the ruins toward a subterranean basement, a place he had hidden as a child.

Rodents scurried into dirt holes as Paolo made his way blindly through the bowels of the ancient building. He sucked in his breath. The stench of animal feces and urine, along with other obnoxious odors, overpowered the depths of the ancient relic.

On that same day, another awful scene was playing out in another place.

The sun was setting fast behind Monti Nebrodi (Italian Continental Apennines), silhouetting the mules and their riders. Cesare was used to long riding sessions, but it had been awhile since Raphaela had ridden a horse, let alone a mule. Cesare couldn't afford to slow the creatures down. They'd not traveled far enough in the daylight hours, and darkness would soon be upon them. He knew that the odds of making their escape from the island were minimal. As well as Mafia informers, roadblocks were enforced by the German occupiers and the *carabinieri*. Cesare feared the tipster island police the most. They couldn't go to a higher bidder than Don Alberto! No one, not the protected rich nor the vulnerable poor, was safe from his sociopathic rage.

Cesare had been witness to some of Alberto's brutal punishments. He couldn't bear to think about them, but the reflections of the Don's cruelty won. He remembered when a local farmer who supplied the Genovese family with fresh pork had dared to raise his price. Only his teeth and a piece of his jaw bone were found in the man's pig sty. Poker faced, the Don had said to the man's grieving widow, "If you want my advice, dear lady, destroy those vile, flesh-eating creatures before they eat you, too. Out of respect for your husband, I'll never eat another piece of ham."

Cesare recalled rushing from the scene, exploding privately with laughter at the Don's joke. His mirth had dissipated when someone who worked on the Don's books also dared to ask for more money. Cesare knew exactly where that young man's body was buried. Cesare had done his master's bidding without question. When asked by authorities about the missing man's whereabouts, Alberto had shrugged and said, "Don't know him. Name doesn't ring a bell."

The runaway butler recalled yet another murderous incident, one he didn't wish to recall now, but one that his mind insisted on playing. A widow, whose son worked in the Genovese vineyards, had asked for his wages in advance. Alberto had lunged at her and strangled her with his bare hands. Cesare had cried and blessed the woman's soul as her ashes were scattered in the wind. Now, all who bore the Girrdazzello name were on the Don's hit list. Cesare couldn't bear thinking about his circumstances anymore, so he concentrated on the task at hand. Would he succeed?

With no moon or stars to guide him, and without sufficient time to plan a favorable escape route, Cesare decided to head for the Port of Messina, an ancient city that stood on the Eponymous Strait, a gateway into Italy. They had to cross a mountain range, which was the least of his concerns. He knew the trails well. As a boy, his adventurous spirit had often led him into the mountains.

Cesare turned his head backward when they reached the beginning of a tumble of limestone hills that ended where the sea began. He wanted to make sure Raphaela was keeping up in the slushy snow. He had given her the more docile mule, an old mare that seemed to have a mind of its own; it lagged far behind because it was constantly trying to reach the grass growing under the ledge. His heart was heavy as he looked at the silhouette of his shawl-draped wife, her head hanging low. She looked so forlorn. He waited for her to catch up. Noticing the grimace on her face and the whiplash marks on her skin, caused by contact with tree branches, he asked, "Are you sick?" That was a foolish question. She was sick at heart. She had been wrenched from her life without any explanation. He hadn't told her everything. He had said, "Just go … now!" She hadn't even had time to grab all her belongings. She was able to take only the most basic necessities.

The relentless stress of running away and of her secret pregnancy was gripping Raphaela's body and mind. Why was life with Cesare so exhausting? She craved the life of a normal married couple, one filled with love, tenderness, and children, and, of course, boring domestic chores. What she needed now was to put her feet up—to rest, relax—because her legs and back were aching after straddling the mule for what felt like hours.

"Are you okay back there?" Cesare shouted.

"No. I'm not okay. I'm sore," she yelled back. "And I have to pee."

"Can you manage for a little while longer?"

Cesare knew these mountains as well as children know their ABCs, so he coaxed her: "I just want to get off this path and make it to the forest canopy up ahead." He knew there was a cave not too far away where they could rest up for the night.

Raphaela sighed. She had been anxiously holding her bladder. Since she was used to relieving herself often, the pressure to urinate felt unbearable. "No. I can't wait," she protested.

Cesare let out a sigh of discontent, walked over to his wife, and helped her off her mule. He took her arm, led her to a bushy patch, and turned his back on his wife's private moment.

Raphaela bunched her skirt up around her hips, pulled down her underwear, and squatted. Not wishing the urine to get on her shoes, she positioned her feet as wide apart as they would go. When she looked down at the urine flow, she noticed it was dark. There was no mistaking the discoloration—amniotic fluid mixed with blood. She heard whistling in her ears as her blood pressure rose. Her heart beat rapidly as a pain hit her like a boxer's blow to the gut.

Raphaela didn't cry out. She knew the cramping was a labor pain. A woman instinctively knows these things. Her body was expelling her precious child, the one thing she wanted more than anything in the world. She silently cursed Cesare. *Damn you, husband.* However, anger was fruitless. Nature was taking its course. The consistent, pulsating contractions were undeniable. With her face contorted in pain and tears rolling down her cheeks, she lowered herself onto the damp soil and spread her legs wide.

Cesare's back was to her when he impatiently called out, "What's taking you so long?"

She didn't answer. Instead she rubbed her small, swollen belly, letting the natural rhythms control her body. She pushed and pushed, letting out a loud animalistic growl, "Noooo …!"

Cesare rushed to her side. "What is it? What's the matter? Are you hurt?" His eyes grew wide and his hand clamped over his mouth when he saw blood pooling around his wife's privates. Stupidly, he asked again if she was all right. She screamed at his idiocy, "Do I look like I'm fine! I'm losing our baby."

Cesare, immobilized like a stunned mullet, gawked at his wife. Then he blurted out another foolish question, "Are you sure?"

Raphaela shook her head … *Men!* "I was going to tell you back at the cottage, but you didn't give me a chance. I wanted it to be a wonderful birthday present."

Cesare remained silent. Nothing he could say now, foolish or otherwise, could ever untangle this sad situation. His heart was as heavy as a cement block as he gazed at his sorrowful wife. Had he been so engrossed in his work at the estate house that he had not noticed she had gained weight and been unusually moody?

Raphaela looked into her husband's eyes. She couldn't see his anguish because a cold emptiness had seeped through her. But she did allow him to hold her hand.

Three hours later the spontaneous abortion ended. Lying grotesquely between Raphaela's legs was a recognizable three-inch fetus covered in a thick blood clot. It was surrounded in a reddish-brown membrane and immersed in a mixture of earth and blood. Raphaela's body was spent, and she felt isolated in her grief. Eventually her tears were reduced to a steady trickle, and she began to breathe normally. But she didn't want to breathe. She wanted to die, too, with her baby.

If she had been able to garner the strength and courage, she'd have heaved herself off this mountaintop. She felt the wet mountain air brush against her grief-stricken face, but the coolness didn't dampen her fire. She glared at Cesare, who was standing over her in silence, his mouth agape.

"You've killed our baby!" she shrieked.

Cesare groaned audibly. He could not dispute her accusation, so he remained silent.

Grief overcame her rage. "I have nothing left anymore. I don't want to live. Please let me die. I just want to be with my baby."

Cesare's face turned as pale as hers. He wrung his hands and looked up at the heavens. But no words of prayer escaped his lips because Raphaela's scream shattered him—mind, body, and soul—while it rendered still the surrounding beech forest and sent a falcon screeching into the sky.

At daybreak the sun rose on a new day.

With a long, drawn face, a glum Cesare dug a tiny grave. He wrapped the tiny mite in his wife's shawl, buried it, and placed a small, granite rock on top. At the same time, Raphaela wasn't mourning the loss of her baby's life. Instead, she was mourning the loss of her own spirit and hopes. A happy picture popped into her head. He had been such a good baby, her firstborn. When Paolo was accepted into one of the finest of Roman Catholic schools— Duomo in Palermo—her love for him filled her with joy. She would work twenty-four hours a day, if need be, to help pay his tuition. Father Rupolo (Alberto's cousin) had remarked that his protégé would go far in the world. He had the intelligence to become whatever he wanted to become. And he had the makings of a great priest. But that once-in-a-lifetime educational gift ended in nothing short of a failure.

If Raphaela and Cesare had known that *child grooming* at the hand of the priest was part of the curriculum, they would have thought twice about their only son's education. Shortly after Paolo had turned eleven, when he was on one of his school breaks,

Raphaela noted a drastic change in his well-mannered, vibrant personality. He became moody and argumentative, and threw daily temper tantrums. He no longer wanted to go fishing, horseback riding, or attend festivals, let alone church. Nothing could be done to appease her son's festering temperament. Not even Cesare's scolding. "You had better behave yourself! Father Rupolo told me about you beating up a classmate and stealing from others. I didn't raise you to become a common thief and bully. Your mother and I work our fingers to the bone so you can go to school. If I hear one more word from Father Rupolo about your disrespectful behavior, I'll take my belt to you."

At age twelve, after repeatedly running away, Paolo was expelled. It broke Raphaela's heart. Cesare, on the other hand, was livid. His hard earned money had gone to waste.

As time went by, Cesare forgave his son and managed to procure a job for him at the Genovese stables. The scrawny little boy grew into a handsome young man, taller than his father. His long, black hair and chestnut eyes complemented his deep tan, and his muscles rippled through his shirt. The girls in the village fought over who would date him first. But Maria was their competition. The two of them were always seen riding across the fields together. Paolo was happier than he had ever been. He wasn't thrown out of his home, as had happened to so many kids who were left to fend for themselves among the town's human garbage: pickpockets, prostitutes, dope fiends, and beggars.

More time passed.

One day Paolo was washing the horse muck off his hands when he saw her for the first time. Her red hair glowed like coals in the hot sun. Wearing the skimpiest of dresses, leaving nothing to the imagination, the much older Teresa pranced up to him like a deer. "Hi, handsome," she cooed." I'm Teresa. I've not seen you before."

The teenager blushed. It was love at first sight. "I'm the but-ler's son," he stammered. "My mother, Raphaela, is the house-keeper and head cook here."

Teresa smiled at him. "I was going to sneak up to the kitchen window, but I'm sure you can help me."

Paolo's eyes lit up like a Christmas tree. "Anything." he said. "What do you want?"

"Could you please ask your mother for some food ... anything she can spare ... vegetable peelings and a little olive oil. My family is starving."

Paolo's legs couldn't have carried him faster to his mother's workplace.

After that first encounter with the older girl of his dreams, the smitten boy not only stole food from the mansion, but also stole money from his mother's savings jar.

Seven years his senior, Teresa had no qualms about the thievery or of seducing the teenager. He was hers, bought and sold. Her young stud's testosterone levels were at their maximum levels, and Teresa was more than an ego boost to his budding manhood. It was his first real taste of sex.

Paolo and Teresa began an affair. Every night, after Paolo's chores were done, the lovers met secretly in the old chapel on the Genovese estate. Naturally, Paolo wanted to marry Teresa; he even offered his silver ring, a birthday gift, to seal the deal. But she laughed at the silly, romantic boy and told him it would be impossible. Her parents would never agree, nor would his. But Teresa did plant the first of many bad seeds in his head. "If we had lots of money … and I know a way to get it … we could go to Italy, get married, and have a great life together without anyone saying, 'She's too old for you! She's not a decent Catholic girl. Her sister's a prostitute!'" The last part of her sentence flew by Paola. "How do we get this kind of money?" he asked innocently. "There's a war going on."

"Darling, trust me."

"Oh, I do," purred the lovesick boy.

"Great. Then I will tell you my plan …"

CHAPTER EIGHT

That Same Day, Somewhere in the Nebrodi Mountain Range

"You can never plan the future by the past."
—Edmund Burke

The cool mountain wind bore silent witness to Cesare's inner pain as life and death played heartless games on them out on the Nebrodi.

Cesare undid the clasp of his chain and laid the religious medallion under the rock laid to protect the fetus's grave from predators. Like most traditional Sicilians, Cesare was superstitious and believed that vengeance is the only true justice. Blood or no blood, he hoped Don Alberto had found Paolo and administered righteousness before all of his relatives. Cesare's Girrdazzello bloodline—and there were not many members of it—would be executed to get to the truth. Would Raphaela's family also suffer from Don Alberto's wrath? Probably, Cesare reckoned. No one would be safe.

The grieving father glanced at his wife, who was standing sullenly by his side. Although she was in a fragile state of mind, he felt the time had come to tell her what was going on. It was the only way he was going to redeem himself and the unblessed soul of their dead baby. He took her arm, led her to a rock, told her to sit, and said, "We need to talk."

During the horrible disclosure, disbelief crossed Raphaela's already sorrowful face. It was just too much for her grieving heart to bear. But the heart never lies, she told herself, and Cesare had never before lied to her. She wrung her chapped hands. "I'll pray for his soul, but he is still my son. I can never hate him, only what he has done. Mother Mary and all the Saints forgive him."

Cesare nodded, but not wholeheartedly. It would take more than a miracle for him to forgive what Paolo had reduced them to—fugitives in fear of their lives. With their arms wrapped around each other, the grieving couple held each other in a tight embrace. A low-lying blanket of mist obscured the entrance to the large granite crag. Cesare was thankful for the camouflage, but he noticed Raphaela shivering. "Are you cold, dearest?"

"I am a little," she replied.

"I'll go and gather some wood."

Cesare lit a small fire. The spiraling smoke fumes were obscured by mist. He turned to his wife and said, "Try to eat something and get some rest."

But neither of them could eat the food that Raphaela had packed. Nor did sleep come easily—not because of mourning, but because of toads. The giant amphibians made their presence noisily known; they were not happy about sharing their domain. However, Cesare wasn't the least bit bothered by his warty companions. He knew it was the other animals that lived on the mountain he had to worry about: wild cats, foxes, weasels, and snakes.

While her husband pondered the unknown, Raphaela, a survivor, pulled herself out of the past and began to focus on the present. She stood up and threw her blood-soaked undergarments into the fire, wondering if they had enough money to replace the necessary clothing. She was afraid to ask.

Cesare looked at his wife and at the burning material, but he remained silent. No words could put out the flames of hell he believed he was destined for.

The next morning, as the first rays of sunlight warmed their cold bodies, the silent couple mounted their mules. Holding Raphael's bridle, Cesare led her toward the summit along a cold, granite-studded trail.

A million questions invaded Raphaela's mind: Where were they going? Where would they stay? How would they feed themselves if they had no money? Would she ever be able to put flowers (jasmine was her favorite) on the tiny grave? Would she ever bear another child or see her dear son, Paolo, again. Something startled her, but she dared not look.

Never before seen in this wintery month, a tiny butterfly with bull's-eye markings landed on her hand. Raphaela's heart beat with positivity. She believed the butterfly was a sign sent from heaven. She pulled her rosary from her pocket and began praying, "Hail Mary, full of grace ..."

CHAPTER NINE

August 1998, Brianna's Extreme Highs and Lows

"Everyone craves for truth, but only a few like the taste of it."
—Tusher Chauhan

Floria zigzagged up a steep hill on a winding mountain road worse than any logging road Brianna had ever driven on in Canada. Giuseppe drove alongside the high stone walls toward Maria's home, which was still completely hidden from view. "This is the start of the Genovese private grounds," he informed his passenger. "And ..."

Giuseppe's talk about the surroundings began to blur. A disconnected Brianna leaned forward. "Giuseppe, what happened to Maria after her father refused to pay the ransom?"

"That I don't know, Signórina Brianna," he replied truthfully. "What I can tell you is that the child Maria I had known and loved returned home with hate in her heart for all men. That's why her place is guarded by women and why only females work at the mansion and in the fields.

"Not even a priest is allowed on her estate. Dealings with other regional bosses are conducted by telephone or, on rare occasion, at a meeting in the old chapel at the bottom of the Genovese vineyard."

Brianna frowned. "How do you know all this?"

"My wife, Lena ... she has since passed away ..."

"I'm sorry to hear that."

"Thank you, Signórina. But as I was saying, times were very bad for our family, not only during the war, but well after. So when Maria returned home, my wife went to the house to ask for work. Maria sent her packing when she found out who she was." Giuseppe took a breath. "Yes, I suppose she was a painful reminder. You see, my youngest daughter, Teresa, was Lena's spitting image."

"Was? Does that mean she is also dead?"

"Yes," Giuseppe answered in a despondent tone. He didn`t tell his passenger that he was the only survivor of his once large family.

"Oh, how sad," Brianna commiserated. "If you don't mind me asking, how did Teresa die?"

Brianna saw Giuseppe's grimace in the mirror. If he didn't reply, that was okay by her. She didn't wish to drag him back to something he obviously didn't want to talk about. But he more than surprised her.

"Signórina, my beautiful, spirited daughter, Teresa, was shot by a German in Rome during the war." A sigh escaped his lips, ending his disclosure. "We have come to the entrance." He brought Floria to a halt and pointed to his right.

Brianna opened the car door and stared. She had never seen anything like it. A massive padlocked gate loomed above her. It looked as though it had come straight from the set of a horror movie.

The gate and the walls connected to it were covered in weeds and thick brambles replete with thorny, arm-length porcupine barbs stretching out like fingers jutting out of an angry heart. But it was the name *GENOVESE* written above the gate in large wrought iron letters that caused Brianna to frown. Why would a Mafia family have their name prominently displayed on their gate? Wasn't that stupid? Advertising where you live? But that thought was soon washed away, replaced by an exciting tingle on her skin. *Mom, I'm here,* she mouthed.

Giuseppe's eyes were glued to his feet. He wasn't so thrilled. His skin was creeping with shivers, and the hair on his head stood up. He wanted to be gone, and he said so. "I'm happy for you, Signó-rina. You will see your mother, but now we part company. The sun is behind the mountains, and I have a long drive home."

Brianna was disgruntled. "You can't leave me here!" she pro-tested. "What if they are not in?"

"Oh, Maria never goes out."

"Ah, come on, Giuseppe," Brianna manipulated. "We had a deal, that you would wait here until I told you otherwise. If you want more money, I'd be happy to make it worth your while."

Giuseppe, his arms limp at his sides, discharged a defeated sigh. "Very well, Signórina. If you are not back here in, say, one hour, then I'll leave."

Brianna pulled out her purse and removed some money. Her driver's old eyes glistened when he was handed the large wad.

"See. I mean well," Brianna said. "We can sort out any differ-ence in the fare when you take me back to the villa. Okay?"

Giuseppe stuffed the U.S. currency into his pants' pocket and said, "I'll park over there." He pointed to a concealed spot. "Go and ring the bell."

Brianna's heart was beating a thousand miles a minute. Her mother was behind this fortress gate. But before she could see her, she had to get inside.

Perfumed purple flowers sheathed with weapons of their own entwined themselves around the rustic, copper-encrusted bell. As Brianna's fingers sought to reach the device, she struggled to maneuver through the prickles. "Damn!" she cried, plucking a spike from her bleeding finger. Finally, she carefully pulled the bell's cord. Lurch, the gangly Addams family manservant, popped into her mind. Grinning, she mouthed his famous greeting, "You rang?" The sound of frenzied barking quickly cooled her wit, and did nothing to calm the butterflies jabbing her insides with spiked boots.

It sounded as if the hills were alive with packs of wild dogs. Peering through a wide gap in the fence, Brianna saw no signs of life. With shaking hands, she rang the bell again. Then, suddenly, from out of nowhere, a beast was in her face. Her heart pounded as she reflexively jumped back.

The black horse—snorting stinky, hot breath—was bigger than any other Brianna had ever seen. She looked up at the rider, seemingly in her late thirties, who glared at her as if she were a homeless dog. The woman was stunning, with long, black, windswept hair; intense, round ebony eyes; and a deeply suntanned complexion. But Brianna's reflection on the woman's beauty was interrupted when the guard unbuttoned her jacket and revealed a pistol tucked into her waistband.

Brianna clasped her hand over her mouth in shock.

The keeper of the gate yelled something at her. Brianna quickly responded. "I don't speak ..." Another kind of bell rang in her head. "Hang on a minute. She turned and called, "Giuseppe!" at the top of her lungs. "Come here. I need you to translate for me."

Brianna, shifting her weight from one leg to the other, waited.

Giuseppe was nowhere in sight.

"Some helpful translator," Brianna grouched through gritted teeth. *Ah well,* she thought. *Here goes. "No parla Siciliana. Mia chiama ..."*

A deafening sneeze followed by a globular projectile of horse snot cut short Brianna's attempt to introduce herself. "Thanks a friggin' lot!" Brianna sniped, wiping the disgusting slime off of her clothing. When she looked into the rider's face again, it was creased with course laughter. Brianna wasn't laughing, though. She was in attack mode. "Do you speak English?" she demanded haughtily.

"What you want, *Americana*?" was the heavily accented women's response.

"My name is Brianna. I'd like to see Maria Picasso Genovese. You see, my mother is ..."

The horsewoman cut in, "There is no one here by that name."

"Are you kidding me?" Brianna was tired, hungry, and not in the mood for mind games. Like a strong tailwind, she blew, "Bullshit. Her name is above the friggin' gate!"

The woman leaned forward in the saddle. "Go home, *Americana*," she ordered.

Brianna, her Latin blood boiling, flared. "I'm not going anywhere ..." She wanted to add "bitch" but had second thoughts. "You can flash your gun as often as you like. It doesn't scare me. I've come to see my mother. If you don't open the gate, I'll climb the goddamn wall."

"You're out of your head! The dogs will eat you alive. Donna Maria doesn't see anyone without an appointment."

This is absurd, Brianna fumed inwardly. She removed her designer sunglasses, made intense eye contact with the woman, and went full throttle. "I'm her goddamn granddaughter! I don't need a fucking appointment!"

Francesca Zanatta dismounted and came closer. *Yes. This girl is a spitting image of that face in the portrait that is hanging in the living room.*

An eternal silence took up residence between them.

From the corner of her eye, Francesca spotted Giuseppe fiddling with his trouser zipper. "Who is that man?" she queried.

Brianna turned her head to the side then back to the horsewoman. "Oh, that's my driver."

Giuseppe adjusted his trouser belt and glanced in their direction. Then, muttering under his breath, he shot out of sight. Brianna didn't know whether to laugh or not.

The gatekeeper didn't pay Giuseppe's shenanigans much attention. She was unable to get the similarity between Sofia de la Llerena, Maria's mother, and this foreigner out of her mind. "Wait here," she said gesturing to Brianna with her hands. "Don't do anything stupid. I'll be back."

Francesca didn't give Brianna time to respond.

A cloud of dust and the sound of galloping hooves penetrated the muggy air as the guard sped out of sight.

Brianna leaned against the gate. Her head was throbbing. She had to calm the emotional storm threatening her queasy stomach. But it was too late.

She retched what was left of her midday meal.

Brianna felt a hand caressing her neck, but she was past embarrassment. "You need to see a doctor," a concerned Giuseppe said. "He lives not far from here."

"I don't need a doctor," Brianna countered. "I know what's wrong with me."

Giuseppe didn't press Brianna further. Instead he informed her, "Signórina, I have to get something to drink. I'll give you the phone number. Call me there." He made a beeline for Floria when he heard a horse's galloping hooves moving in their direction.

With the reins of a second horse gripped in her hand, Francesca led both horses to the gate. She dismounted, opened the lock with an ancient-looking brass key, waved Brianna through, and began frisking her. Brianna shoved back hard. "What the hell are you doing?"

"I'm checking for weapons."

Brianna, now hopping mad, could have socked her.

When the indignity was over, she snapped angrily, "Happy now?"

Francesca cupped her hands along the side of the black horse. Brianna stared at the waiting hands and protested, "Hell no! I'm not getting on that monster! I don't have to tell you, I'm pregnant."

"Women around here ride until they are ready to drop. Can you ride a horse?"

"No."

"Then I suppose you'll just have to follow on foot. It's quite a way."

Almost pushed beyond her limits, a grimacing Brianna traipsed behind the three butts, Francesca's and the two horses', up a steep, cobbled driveway lined with dwarf palms and enormous cacti. The sound of Francesca talking to herself nonstop drifted on a gentle breeze. She sounded like a diesel truck sputtering after its motor has been turned off.

Part way up the hill Brianna took a deep breath, filling her lungs with the countryside's exotic perfumes: jasmine, honeysuckle, and bougainvillea. She became so engrossed in the spectacular landscaped gardens that she didn't see an offset cobblestone. She tripped and fell into something dark and squishy. She made a face and yelled "Eww!" as she struggled to hold back the gag reflex. She froze in her tracks and shouted to her escort, "Wait!" Francesca spun in her saddle and asked, "What's the matter?"

Adding insult to injury, Brianna uncomfortably disclosed, "I fell in a pile of dog shit!"

Francesca's straight face dissolved into giggles. Her chortling fueled Brianna's anger. "It's not funny! Where can I wash this off?" she asked, holding up her mucky hands. She wiped what she could on the grass.

Francesca winked and nodded her head toward the mansion. "Follow me."

Brianna's "washroom" had a hypnotic effect.

Set in marble, the larger-than-life stone lion fountain spurted gallons of water from its mouth. Francesca's face crinkled in mirth as Brianna sprinted toward it and washed off the offensive mess in the cold water. Then, smiling broadly, Brianna followed the cackling Francesca on their last leg of the journey. A few yards up the path, Brianna's mouth involuntarily opened and shut. She couldn't help wondering if she had traveled back into medieval times. In front of her, nestled in an enchanting forest of olive trees adorning the highest hill in the vicinity, was a mythical-looking, gray-stone building. It was impressive. The arched windows, reaching upward and finishing in majestic points, were heavily barred. Fearsome gargoyles caught Brianna's further attention. They were set on the buttresses of this restored, two-story mansion built in the beginning of the eighteenth century. To Brianna the place looked like a medieval stronghold with a panoramic view of the surrounding hills.

An even more welcome sight was briefly visible on the other side of the front door. Her heart leapt. Inhaling deeply, she fought to control her nerves. Behind the six-panel, glass front door, she was sure she caught a glimpse of her mother walking by. Brianna couldn't wait a moment longer. She was on cloud nine.

Riding a roller coaster of happiness, Brianna ran through a cobbled courtyard bejeweled with exotic plants in enormous clay pots, toward the entrance to the house. The enormous bronze door-knocker looked as if it belonged on a Norman cathedral. Brianna didn't bother to knock. She opened the door and stepped into the entry hall. Long accustomed to removing her footwear, a Canadian habit, she paddled barefoot over the inlaid marble in the airy, open foyer. She was not surprised by the opulence: a passageway filled with a smorgasbord of lavish, period furniture and walls filled with large, framed masterpieces. The impressive art-work looked like museum quality.

Brianna's eyes came to rest on a particular painting, a com-missioned portrait in a heavy gilt frame. The artist had captured the dark, wild beauty of a young girl: windswept black hair, spell-binding green eyes, and a Mona Lisa smile. Next to this piece was a painting in stark contrast. It was an older girl holding a broken heart in her hands. There were tears of blood streaking down her face. What Brianna didn't know was that this artist had captured how Maria felt when she had returned home all those years ago. Brianna's focus on the painting was broken when an out-of-breath Francesca sneaked up behind her and said, "Come this way."

Brianna followed her escort, who ushered her into a stately reception room. Even without the glow of a crackling log fire, the enormous white-marble, open-hearth fireplace was magnificent, as was the furniture. The tapestry drapes could have belonged in a palace, and a vintage crystal chandelier hung from an ornate cof-fered ceiling. It bathed the room in splendor. But Brianna thought the celestial figures on the ceiling, angels in various poses, looked out of place in this Mafia residence. White roses and lilies arranged in a stunning crystal vase caught Brianna's eye. It was sitting on a Roman-styled table and was bathed in pearlescent light. The bou-quet's aroma intoxicated her and helped to sooth her jittery nerves.

The door opened.

Brianna faced a tall, heavily veiled woman dressed in fu-neral garb. Black matronly shoes completed her somber ensem-ble. Standing behind the first woman was a silver-haired, female mammoth of indeterminate age. She was taller than a tree and had bushy black hair that a bird would be happy to nest in. Her moustache and other facial hair were untouched. The word "Sasquatch" came to Brianna's mind. She wanted to laugh at her own silliness, but, instead, quickly refocused her attention on the veiled woman. She didn't know how to address Maria, or even if her grandmother understood English.

Brianna extended her hand. "Hi. I'm Brianna, Lynette's daughter," she blurted awkwardly. "We met briefly at Anele's funeral in South Africa. I've come to see my mother. Where is she?"

Maria's handshake was stone cold, just like the silent, deadly moment they were sharing. Brianna felt like road kill waiting to be devoured.

A stony quiet permeated the room like cold storage before Maria began to speak. Exuding calmness, she said, "My daughter is resting." Gone was the *ees* speech of her youth. "You can see her in a moment, but first we should talk." She patted the back of a plush, white, leather sofa. "Please, sit down."

Although slightly accented, Maria's fine English astounded Brianna. How had she learned to speak the language with such perfection? The last thing Brianna wanted to do was talk to the woman she wanted to knock out. Shiya's traumatic taped revelations of Maria's actions when her daughter was born, and the scene at Anele's funeral, were still fresh in her mind. But Brianna did as she was told and sat down.

Maria, reeking of vanilla bean perfume, joined Brianna on the sofa. "I must say, this has come as a surprise. We weren't expecting you. But I'm happy to meet my granddaughter in different circumstances."

Brianna was taken aback by Maria's soft and comforting tone. This person was nothing like the character she had imagined her to be on the day of Anele's funeral: a wicked-faced witch with razor teeth and a searing voice that put the fear of God into everyone. This Maria appeared totally opposite, seemingly sweet and harmless. Had Giuseppe exaggerated his depiction of an evil monster? One thinks of evil as dark and sinister, but Maria was gracious, the perfect hostess. Or so Brianna thought.

For the moment Brianna couldn't read her grandmother's expression, but the law student was intuitive and studied the woman's body language. An inner sense warned Brianna not to be easily fooled. She would eventually learn there was a lot more to her biological grandmother than meets the eye. It wouldn't be long before Maria showed her true colors, which she kept hidden behind her security blanket of intricate, black lace.

Having lacked a real childhood but functioning well day to day, sixty-five-year-old Maria's attitude could often be childlike. For her, throwing a tantrum wasn't anything unusual. She could stomp her feet and turn beet red. Behind her warm, intelligent, and sophisticated personality lurked a torn, embittered woman. Maria was an angry soul who raged with hatred that grew out of the darkest period of her life, a time that ripped away her innocence and compassion. Until now she had only divulged that period of her life to Shiya and one other person. Even though Maria returned to the traditional life she had lost—one filled with long lunches and late afternoon strolls—she never perused the street markets or attended religious festivals or church. Maria seldom left her gated fortress.

As Maria patted her granddaughter's clasped hands, Brianna noted a silver ring on her wedding finger. Was she married? Where was her husband? *Duh! She's wearing funeral garb,* Brianna's inner voice scoffed.

Maria began bombarding her with questions. "When did you arrive? Did you come straight from the airport? How did you get here?"

In short sentences, Brianna filled her in.

"You had a long drive then," Maria responded when Brianna ended. "You must be thirsty. Would you like something to drink?"

"Sure. I'd love a glass of ice cold water." She really wanted a *stiff* drink to calm her jittery nerves. But her conscience reminded her of the risk of drinking hard alcohol—fetal alcohol syndrome in babies. A *shame-on-you* shudder tingled down her spine.

Maria turned to her faithful watchdog. "Battistina, go and get a jug of iced spring water for this young lady and a jug of lemonade, in case she prefers that."

The servant bobbed her massive head and left.

Brianna scoffed internally. *Young lady! I'm your granddaughter and I have a name! And you are about to become a great-grandma!*

Maria folded her hands on her lap and said, "Your mother has told me so much about you. How proud she is of you. I believe you intend to become a lawyer. After the baby is born, that is."

Apprehensively, Brianna twiddled her hair. She was itching to see her mother and did not want to get caught up in small talk with a woman whose eyes and face she could not see. "Well, I'm not sure about those plans right now," she replied.

Quickly changing the subject, she said, "You have a beautiful home, from what I've seen so far."

"Well, thank you," Maria said. "I'll have to show you around before you leave."

Brianna heard the door creak open again. Expecting the yeti's reappearance, Brianna didn't turn her head. If she had, she'd have seen Shiya dressed in a bathrobe, her face pasty, and her "electrocuted" blond hair growing in tufts after having been shaved off in the South African hospital.

"Hello, Love," Lynette said. "I must say, I'm shocked to see you here."

As if a flea had bitten her, Brianna jumped from her seat and, nearly knocking the fragile woman off her feet, bear hugged her mother. "Mom, it's so good to see you." At that moment Brianna felt as if a thousand pounds of weight had been lifted off her chest. Shiya didn't feel the same, nor did she share the joy. With a long face she grouched, "For crying out loud! How did you find me?"

"I called Mike."

Shiya shrugged her bony shoulders. "So much for attorney-client privilege," she huffed. "I've a good mind to fire him." She looked deep into her daughter's teary eyes and melted. "How long can you stay?"

"For as long as you want me to."

Shiya raised her eyebrows. "I don't like the sound of that. Explain?"

Brianna knew her mother would balk so she responded quickly. "What would you have done in my shoes, Mom? Wouldn't you go looking for the person you loved beyond all else?"

Shiya's response wasn't what Brianna wanted to hear. "You

get on the next plane, go home to whatever-his-name-is, have your baby, and finish your studies, which I paid an arm and a leg for. Then I'll come and see you and my grandchild," Shiya ended heartlessly. It didn't surprise Brianna. Her mother had never been an actual maternal figure in her life.

Brianna became angry when the no-nonsense Maria decided to have her say in the matter. "You only get a once-in-a-lifetime chance at a good education. Believe me, I know. I wanted to be a doctor but never got the chance. So you'd be foolish not to see your studies through. Your mother is doing fine here and getting the best medical attention. So there is no need for you to worry about her."

Brianna let loose a long sigh. Two against one wasn't fair. Brianna suddenly developed an allergy to the truth. "If it's okay with you, I'd like to spend a couple of weeks here."

Shiya examined her daughter's face, searching for a trace of deception. One step ahead of her, Brianna's blank expression was unreadable.

"It's a deal," Shiya said. "You're a smart girl. You'll catch up in no time."

Smarter than you think, Mother, was her internal response. Another thought nudged Brianna. "Where's the phone, Mom?" "I need to let Giuseppe, my driver, know that I'm not returning this evening."

In the privacy of Maria's study, two rooms down from the reception area, Brianna spoke to Giuseppe at the arranged telephone number and informed him that she planned to remain at the estate house and that she would personally call Lusia in the morning to cancel her stay there. She finished with, "Giuseppe, I'd like you to ask Lusia to pack my stuff. Can you bring my suitcases here? I'll pay you for the return trip."

At around eight that evening, after a superb, three-course rural meal—tortellini soup followed by pasta primavera and lemon sherbet—mother and daughter spent hours chatting in the bedroom on the second floor. Shiya explained that when she arrived, Maria had arranged a visit with a top cancer doctor. The bullet entry wound had long healed, but she did have some brain swelling. Her headaches had escalated to a point worse than she'd experienced before the shooting. Surgery was necessary to relieve the pressure and examine the growth of the cancerous tumor. Shiya knew she was living on borrowed time. Had the day come to reveal the last, shocking secret to her daughter? How would Brianna handle it? Would she fall apart? Would she ooze hatred into her mother's soul, leaving it to rot in purgatory?

Brianna interrupted Shiya's thoughts. "Are you sure *these* doctors over here know what they are doing?"

Shiya laughed. "Sicily isn't a backward country, Brianna. Palermo Hospital has the best neurosurgeons in the world. So don't worry. I'm in the best of hands."

Brianna wasn't so easily convinced. "I'll go with you to the hospital then," offered Brianna. "When do you have to go?"

"Dr. Giovanni Caldrese is coming to see me tomorrow morning."

Brianna stared at her mother. "A guy!" she exclaimed.

It was Shiya's turn to stare. "Did I hear you right?"

"My taxi driver told me that Maria didn't allow men into her home! And that everyone who works for her here is female. So far I haven't seen any men."

Shiya closed her eyes for a moment and sighed. It was a small world. She wasn't going to disclose the fact that Dr. Caldrese was a "closet" gay, hence his acceptance into Maria's abode. So she simply answered, "My mother is not what you think. She had her reasons for abandoning me, but that's all in the past. I have forgiven her. We have moved on. When one gets to know her, she is a loving, kind soul."

At this moment in time, Brianna couldn't argue with that; however, she would deliver her own verdict when the time came. But there was one thing that had bugged her since her arrival. "Mom, why does Maria wear that veil?"

Shiya rubbed her forehead. She didn't want to get into this, not now, and said so. "Oh, it's a long, sad story. It will have to wait. I have to take my medicine and get some sleep before the thumpers start. Please, ring the bell for me." She pointed to the dangling cord near the door. "I need Battistina to ..."

Brianna opened her mouth. "Go ahead," Shiya said.

"You don't need that sumo wrestler!" Brianna pouted. "That woman would give me nightmares if she had to tuck me into bed! I can help you."

"Brianna," Shiya said in a raised voice. "I never raised you to be nasty to others. Yes, Battistina is different, but she's been good to me." She took a deep breath before continuing. "She's been kind and helpful to me when I have been too sick to do the simplest things, like get in and out of the bath. Now ring the bell. Then go see your grandmother to find out which room you'll be sleeping in. You have ten magnificent rooms to choose from. Before you go, can you do me a favor?"

"Sure. I'll do anything for you," Brianna said obligingly in a playful voice.

"What do you want, Miss Shiya?"

"Madam Shiya would like ..." Lynette gestured. "Go in the top drawer over there and get my tweezers out of my toilet bag. I want you to pluck this blasted hair out of my chin. The darn thing feels like barbed wire."

Brianna, giggling like a toddler, carried out her mother's bidding. "There. All gone," Brianna announced, still holding the tweezers that sandwiched the offensive grey hair. "Do you want me to pluck your eyebrows? They look a bit bushy."

Shiya shook her head, "No. That's enough torture for one day."

Brianna chortled.

"Oh, you can laugh all you want," Shiya said, "but old age will one day catch up to you, and you'll remember this moment."

Brianna grabbed her mother's hand and kissed it. "Mom, I'll treasure the day I had to extract the barbed wire from your old face."

"Get out of here!" Shiya said playfully. "I'll see you in the morning." In an instant a serious look wiped away the fun. "Yes, we need to talk. There is something I need to discuss with you regarding your father."

Brianna weighed her mother's statement. "Mom, we went over this a million times when we were in South Africa. Look, the past is the past. I've forgiven you, so let's move on."

Shiya lowered her head as certain thoughts raised their ugly heads. She was torn. Should she tell her daughter or take the awful secret to the grave? How would her only child react? Would she hate her? And would there ever be a right moment? Brianna erased Shiya's musings by kissing her mother on the forehead. "Night, Mom."

"Goodnight, my precious daughter," Shiya returned playfully, adding, "Don't let the bedbugs bite."

The precious mother-daughter time ended too soon. Brianna didn't want to leave her mom. She wanted to sleep with her, cuddle with the woman she loved so much. She'd promised her mother that she would not bring up anything that she'd heard on the cassette tapes, which still haunted her dreams—abandonment as a newborn, kidnapping at age five, rape and abuse for years.

"See you in the morning, Mom," Brianna said kissing her mother again, this time on the cheek. "I love you."

"I love you too," Shiya purred. "Now go and get some sleep."

A contented smile crossed Brianna's lips. There was a God in heaven. All was right in the world. She closed the door behind her and began walking down the hallway. Battistina, whose peculiar gait looked as if she had broken ankles, popped out of a dark corner carrying a black bag. *Did she understand English?* Brianna wondered. "Hi. Where can I find Maria?"

"Donna Maria *ees* gone to bed," she replied brokenly.

The *ees* had a new owner.

Brianna glanced at the wall clock above the servant's head. It was nearing ten. Old people go to bed early, she thought. So she simply asked, "Where's my bedroom?"

Battistina pointed. "Mistress Sofia's room *ees* end of hallway.

Ees last room. The sleeping clothes *ees* on the bed."

Brianna politely thanked the yeti and headed in that direction. Brianna entered a massive bedroom fit for a queen. The four-poster, Spanish-styled, intricately carved bed was a *pièce de résistance*. Surrounding the large bed and bed stool were dressers, wardrobes, and Roman occasional side tables. The bed linen, sheets piped with red and gold lace, matched the tailored drapes. She noted there was no TV, which she was used to having back home. So far she had not spotted one TV in the house. Did Maria even get TV reception? One thing Brianna did notice and was glad of: The home was free of cigarette smoke.

Brianna puttered around the room taking in the majestic décor. She was mesmerized by a large oil painting. It was a family portrait, Brianna guessed, of Don Alberto, Sofia, and baby Maria. Brianna couldn't help but stare in disbelief. *Wow! I do look like her! Like Sofia.* But in the back of her mind she thought, *I hope she didn't kill herself in this room.* (She had, in fact, hung herself from the heavy brass chandelier that lit the room.) Too tired to contemplate the thought further, Brianna locked the door. Why, she had no idea.

Brianna undressed. But no way was she putting on the floral granny nightie that was set out for her. How she was going to clean her teeth was another matter. At least she had a clean set of clothing and underwear in her backpack. As soon as her head hit the pillow, she was sound asleep, only to wake up to a loud *thumping* noise. She assumed it was the old plumbing. Since she didn't believe in ghosts, Brianna drifted back to her dream world, only to awaken with heartburn. She made a mental note to ask the doctor what she could take to relieve it.

Fingers of bright sunlight streamed through Brianna's window, flirting with the drapes, caressing the bed, and sending a morning message to Brianna: *Wakey, wakey, sleepyhead. Time to rise.* Her eyes opened slowly. Yawning, she lifted her watch off the side table and got a rude awakening. She couldn't believe her eyes. It was nearly lunchtime. Why had no one woken her? Had her body been so exhausted that time had jumped forward? She dashed to the master bathroom. This volatile upchuck was the worst so far. Clutching her raw throat she stared at the flushed face reflected in the vanity mirror. This was not the live-life-to-the-fullest girl she used to be. She decided to come clean. Her mother was bound to find out sooner or later.

Brianna was wearing white, elasticized jeans, a powder blue T-shirt, and matching flip-flops when she passed Battistina in the hallway heading in the opposite direction. "Good morning," Brianna chirped happily.

The servant, her eyes cast to the floor, went about her business wordlessly.

Ah, it's your loss, you unfriendly mammoth, Brianna thought as she opened the door to her mother's room. The lights were on and the bed was unmade. But there was no Mom.

Brianna smiled as she sniffed the air. Her mother's favorite perfume gripped the room like a blast of air freshener. Brianna closed the bedroom door and hurried downstairs. Through a bay window she spotted a veiled Maria dressed in a long, black dress leaning against the wrought iron balustrades on the balcony. She was doubled over as if experiencing stomach pain. Brianna crept up on her. "I overslept," she said matter of factly. "Where's my mom?"

With her hands tightly clasped, Maria swallowed hard. She didn't want to be the bearer of bad news, but there was no way out. "Sit down, Brianna," she said, pointing to a stone bench. "There is something I have to tell you."

Every cell in Brianna's body quivered with cold. She remained standing.

"Your mother woke me in the middle of the night. Her speech was slurred, and she said her head felt like it was about to explode. I knew that she was living on borrowed time with the brain cancer which, incidentally, was inherited from my side of the family, so I had her rushed to the hospital."

Brianna's dark eyes flashed in anger. "Damn you!" she fired. "What's the hospital phone number? I need to call right now!"

Maria's reply was barely audible. "It was your mother's wish not to wake you. I had to honor it."

A lump constricted Brianna's throat before her words spilled out. "Have you heard from the hospital? What do the doctors say? Is she okay?"

When Maria didn't respond right away, Brianna felt a shiver like no other. She tried to shake off a bombardment of panic signals as she latched on to Maria's cold hand. Fighting back tears, the distraught girl pleaded, "Do you know something I don't? For God's sake, please tell me?"

Maria caressed Brianna's shoulder in a tender manner. "Sweet child, she died on the way to the hospital from a massive brain hemorrhage. I didn't know your mother as well as you did, but I'm told she had a remarkable attitude, was a fighter to the last moment. She's with the angels now, looking down at you from heaven."

Brianna's face turned ashen. Shock. Denial. Disbelief. She couldn't scream. She couldn't breathe. She couldn't cry. Then, in a split second, reality slammed into her like a tornado. *No! It's not happening!* She became weak in her knees, as if her body was melting. Her legs turned to jelly and gave way.

When Brianna opened her eyes, she was back in bed; a stranger with slate-colored eyes was at her side. Sitting in a chair by the wall, Maria was rocking with her sentinel, Battistina, at her side.

"Hello," a softly-spoken man greeted Brianna. "I'm Doctor Caldrese. How are you feeling?"

"Weird," she replied. "My head feels spongy."

"That's because I've given you a mild tranquilizer shot," the doctor stated. "Your heart rate was out of control and your blood pressure was way too high. It isn't good for you or your baby."

In her drug-induced disorientation, the doctor's words didn't register; nor did the fact that he had the same surname of her ex-boyfriend. Roberto's ancestors had come from Sicily, not Italy as Brianna had assumed.

The doctor, wearing a pink shirt, matching tie, and dark trousers reeked of aftershave. Giovanni stroked her hand, trying to spare her from feelings of dismay. "Shortly before your mother died peacefully in my arms on the way to the hospital," he said softly, "she asked me to tell you that she has loved you from the moment you were born. And knowing that she'd be missing so many special events—the birth of her first grandchild, your graduation from law school, your wedding one day, and maybe more grandchildren—truly saddened her. But she did stress that your grandmother will be here for you. Won't you, Donna Maria?" he said, turning his head toward her. Even though Maria had hardly had the chance to get to know her own daughter, she was gripped by despair and nodded in agreement. She approached the bed and shushed Brianna. "We'll get through this together. Just the two of us, I promise. And as long as I have breath in my body, I will take care of you and your child." She placed a hand over her heart. "A vow I made to your mother before she left this house."

Brianna felt as if her heart was hemorrhaging with anger. Anyone in their right mind would have choked Maria for not having the decency to wake her in such an emergency. Now she felt herself clinging to the person she wanted to strangle. She wanted so desperately to belong to someone. With her head resting against her grandmother's chest, Brianna wept. Her wracking sobs tore Maria's heart. She reached into her skirt pocket, removed a handkerchief, and tenderly wiped Brianna's eyes and her own tear-streaked face. It was the first time Maria had let tears flow so freely since her return.

The sound of the sorrow flowing from both women echoed pitifully throughout the open room. For Brianna, the feeling that all was right with the world would never return. And now she was certain there was no God in the heavens.

Everything had changed.

CHAPTER TEN

Shiya's Open Casket

"The maid is not dead, but sleepeth."
—St. Matthew

The day had come. Brianna dreaded it more than anything else. With her face free of color, drained of blood, she was led into the reception room by Battistina, whose powerful arm rested on her shoulder. This space was traditionally decorated with white roses tied with satin ribbons of the same color. On a linen-covered plinth sat the solid bronze, gold-plated casket. It was lined with velvet and surrounded by hundreds of glowing candles of various shapes and sizes. All of the mirrors were covered, and the heavy brocade drapes were drawn.

Every unsteady step she took toward the open coffin was an effort for Brianna. It felt like the first day of school, not knowing what to expect. Until now, it hadn't really sunk in that her mother was never coming home. But it was final.

Brianna glanced at Maria, who was standing at the head of the coffin. Brianna heard loud sniffing coming from underneath her grandmother's veil. Brianna wondered if her grandmother's grief was real. Was she truly mourning the daughter she could never get back? Had Shiya carried away a piece of her heart, as well? No. It couldn't be. Maria had not known her daughter throughout her life, like Brianna had known her mother. Was her grandmother's reaction guilt? Or was it a mother's genuine love and deep sorrow for the loss of her child? Brianna couldn't answer on behalf of a woman she hardly knew.

Maria was in deep thought. *This isn't fair. My heart is breaking. Mothers shouldn't outlive their children.* Yet here she was saying goodbye to her only child. Although she'd been baptized a Catholic at the Don's insistence and with Sofia's disapproval, Maria had not stepped through the doors of any House of God since childhood. She had no love for religion or priests. But she was now having a change of heart. She wanted to give her daughter a blessed send-off even though she had no idea what religion Lynette belonged to, if any. Maria hadn't bothered to consult Brianna.

Yesterday Father Bettino was more than shocked to receive Maria's telephone call. He hadn't set foot in this house since her father's time. The plump Father, wearing a black *cope* (poncho-like garment) and a pinkish-red skullcap, looked as old as the hills and as if his days were numbered. He took hold of Brianna's trembling hand and spoke softly. "Come, child. Let us pray for the soul of your departed mother. Look into the coffin at the vessel that carried her *bedda* ('beautiful' in Sicilian) soul."

Brianna took baby steps toward the open casket. She didn't know what to expect. She had never seen a dead person. She stared at her mother's peaceful face. It looked as if she would wake at any moment from a nap. The priest was right; her mother was as beautiful in death as she was in life. But Lynette's eyelids were closed, hiding her most stunning asset—her spellbinding green eyes. Brianna's lips quivered. *I'm never again going to see those sparkling eyes.* Expressionless, a heartbroken Brianna continued to stare at her mother's features. Tears flowed freely down her cheeks and fell liberally onto her mother's lifeless body.

A delicate mother-of-pearl rosary was looped around Shiya hands, and white roses blanketed her body. But it was what she was wearing that caught Brianna's eye—her mother's sending-off outfit. She was clothed in her grandmother Sofia's exquisite, pure silk wedding dress, the one she wore at her first marriage ceremony. And around her neck, dazzling in the candlelight, was a 200-year-old Picasso heirloom: a diamond, emerald, and pearl encrusted set. Under the traditional black, Spanish veil that crowned Shiya's head was a shoulder-length blond wig. It was styled exactly as she had worn it before her head surgery in the Durban hospital. Brianna marveled at the mortician's expertise: perfect makeup and false eyelashes that gave the embalmed Lynette the look of a film star. Brianna was touched by the effort Maria had expended for her mother's send-off. She wanted to hug her grandmother and thank her, tell her that she was all she had left in the world. But the sincerity of the thought stuck in her throat.

Forgiveness has a price.

Brianna leaned over and, choking back another rush of heart-felt tears, kissed her mother's cold forehead. "Mom, I'm going to miss you," she whispered. At that moment, the finality of death struck Brianna like a sledgehammer. She felt anger, and a melt-down in the pit of her stomach. "Why me, God?" she screamed. "Why did you take my mother? I didn't get the chance to spend time with her. During my whole life, she did nothing but disappear! Damn you, Mother! Damn you!"

With her hands perched on her massive hips, seventy-year-old Battistina, standing somberly at the back of the room, couldn't hold her tongue any longer. She launched an attack. "You no say bad words to the dead," the deeply religious woman protested to Brianna. "Let me tell you, your mother, she *ees* a good woman. I know this. She does not deserve your evil damnation! I don't like you!"

Brianna wasn't sure if Battistina's balled fist was meant for her.

In a flash Maria appeared before the two women. She slapped her servant in the face. "That's enough!" she barked. "Leave now, you bumbling buffoon!"

Battistina, her chin drooping to her chest, quietly left the room.

Brianna was speechless. She blamed Maria's and Battistina's atrocious behavior on grief. Although she hadn't thought much about it, Brianna had witnessed Maria's controlling ways, but nothing this ferocious, nothing that hinted at this brutal side of her. Brianna couldn't help but feel a tad sorry for the yeti. Actually, she wanted to blast Maria for being so heartless, especially at a sensitive time like this.

Now wasn't the time for such behavior, though.

If Father Bettino was shocked by the goings-on, he didn't show it. He merely stepped forward to salvage the moment. Although his words referred to Maria and the absent Battistina, he spoke directly to Brianna. "It's all right to be angry, child. It's all part of the grieving process. But remember, your dearly departed mother is free of pain, resurrected in the Lord's arms. He understands that her body still belongs to someone who loves it."

No words from him or anyone else could console Brianna or mend her shattered heart. Death was too hard to grasp. The finality was suffocating. She couldn't imagine life without her mother. Struggling with dark thoughts, her will to die suddenly overcame her will to live. Not even the child she was carrying, an extension of Shiya's genes, made a difference at this mournful time.

Brianna laid her head on her mother's chest. "Your body has stopped working, but I know you can hear me. How am I supposed to go on without you?" A flood of tears fell onto her mother's makeup, causing the heavy foundation to trickle. What Brianna did next astonished Maria and the priest and triggered them to prepare to act.

Brianna roughly lifted Shiya by the neck, and then she lost it. "You can't leave me, Mom," she screamed. "Please come back. I hate you. I hate you. I hate you," she repeated before Father Bettino had a chance to intervene.

The Father gripped Brianna's shoulders firmly and forced her to back away from the casket, allowing Shiya's affronted head to fall back onto the silk cushion. He led Brianna to a seat at the back of the room. Brianna's body dropped into the chair like a cement block.

Maria sighed heavily. Her heart went out to the girl, but consoling her granddaughter would have to wait. "Brianna, I've given permission for my gates to be opened for the villagers to come and pay their respects to my daughter. Do you wish to be present?"

"No. I'd rather not," Brianna replied. Rising from the chair, she announced, "I'm going to speak to my mother alone, in her room."

No one stopped her.

No one uttered a word.

Brianna headed down the upstairs hallway toward the room that her mother had occupied. There, she vigorously slammed the door shut and pulled the drapes. In the darkness, she buried her head in the comfort of her mother's pillow. She wanted to believe that her mother's soul, her essence, was still in this room. Brianna spoke to the air. "Mom, if you are listening, please help me deal with this. My heart is broken and I don't know what to do. One minute you were here and the next you were gone. It's so friggin' cruel. I suppose like Naboto, Anele's father, you have all seeing knowledge now, so you know about the baby and the stupid mistake I made. I wanted to tell you, but I thought you would hate me."

As she pounded the pillow, the lyrics *"You don't know what you've got till it's gone"* came to mind. Brianna whispered, "Mom, give me a sign. Show me you are here with me." But the only sound she heard was her own voice echoing against the walls. Seconds later Brianna felt like doing handsprings when she heard a cavernous thump. "Mom, is that you?" All ears, she waited to hear the sound again. But after a brief moment, Brianna's earthly logic snapped her back into reality. She made a disgusted face. *Yeah right! What's the matter with me? Since when do I believe in ghosts?* She thought of what her no-nonsense mother would have said: "The best way to deal with grief is to go through it and then get on with your life, not mope over a shadow that is gone."

That night, alone in her mother's bedroom, Brianna buried her face in her mother's robe and was comforted by the smell. She wrote her mom a letter: *Mom, you were the greatest. I know your life was short, but I am lucky to have known you. It was an honor and a privilege. You were funny, smart, and the bravest person I have ever known. I will miss your hugs, laughter, smiles, and, most of all your love, which will live in my heart forever. Love is immortal. Your loving daughter, Brianna.*

CHAPTER ELEVEN

Funeral for a Forsaken Daughter of Africa

"We owe respect to the living: to the dead we owe only truth."
—Voltaire

On the morning of Lynette's private burial, the first September rain fell from an overcast sky. The well-manicured, prominently fenced Genovese graveyard was surrounded by natural wilderness. It was a tranquil setting, and Shiya would join the many Genovese generations buried before her in the family plot. Maria wanted her daughter to rest next to Sofia, her grandmother, in the above-ground, white-marble mausoleum, a shrine erected by Maria to honor not only her mother but also the daughter she hardly got a chance to know.

Father Bettino, holding an umbrella over his prayer book with one hand and sprinkling holy water over the grave with the other, began. "Eternal rest grant unto her, O Lord, and let the perpetual light shine upon her. May she rest in peace. Amen."

Shiya's casket, head facing east, was lowered. At the same time, Brianna released a balloon with a letter attached that she'd written to her mother. As Brianna watched the balloon soar heavenward, a powerful moment of separation and recognition that she was now an orphan pummeled her. The balloon crystallized the reality. It was true. Brianna's wailing tore through Maria's heart.

Weakness triggered by emotion brought Brianna to her knees.

Battistina rushed to her side, lifted her as if she weighed nothing more than a dandelion seed, and cradled her like a baby.

"Take her back to the house," Maria ordered. "I'll be along in a minute." Maria dismissed her servants and the priest. She wanted to be alone with her loved ones. Kneeling on the grass beside her father's gravestone, she spoke to the dead. "Papa, I love you. Hug your granddaughter, Lynette." She turned her head towards Sofia's tomb. Her mother's burial in consecrated ground had caused an uproar in the Catholic Church. But Don Alberto had threatened to withdraw his enormous handouts if his wishes for a blessed burial were not honored. The Church was adamantly against him. If they bent the rules for Alberto, they would have to continue sanctioning suicide burials. It was out of the question.

The Don sought the help of Rabbi Joshua in Rome. And in true Jewish tradition, Sofia Picasso Genovese underwent *tahara* (ritual washing) and was buried with dignity and respect. Would her daughter, Maria, who didn't have a shred of dignity or respect, receive the same honor when her time came?

Do pigs fly?

In the isolation of the cemetery, Maria stood in front of Sofia's magnificent resting place with her arms hanging limply at her sides. The elaborate mausoleum was adorned with a marble statue of an angel, whose wings were lowered. Maria stepped forward and touched the outer tomb wall. Her voice was low when she said, "Mama, take care of my daughter, your only granddaughter. She has your beautiful face and eyes."

After talking to the dead for what felt like hours, Maria made her way back to the estate house. She was in no mood for merriment or socializing and was glad she hadn't agreed to the typical Catholic wake gathering consisting of eating, drinking, wailing, and consoling. The money that she would have spent was given to Father Bettino to do with as he wished. But Maria was sure part of the funds would simply slide down his throat. The black robe he wore at the funeral had smelled as if it had been laundered in wine. At the time, Maria had bitten her tongue, but a whimsical thought had crossed her mind. *It's a good thing we are not Muslims.* She couldn't have handled the lamentation at a Muslin ceremony: constant funeral prayers, tearing of clothes, stamping of feet, and pulling of hair, all accompanied by loud wailing ... for months!

Contradicting Giuseppe's interpretation of her as an ogre, Maria was a guardian angel to most in the village. Unwed mothers received the best medical attention. The elderly were provided with walking canes, wheelchairs, and other necessities. And large baskets of food were distributed at Christmas.

Back in her home, lounging in her favorite chair in the study, Maria cradled her head in her hands. She needed some solitude to rethink her intentions: retiring and handing over the legitimate wine business as well as the billion-dollar drug empire to Brianna. Could the girl handle the stress, conduct meetings with other bossy regional crime lords (held secretly once a month in a build-ing that once housed migrant grape harvesters)? And should she unburden herself to Brianna, unlock the unmentionable and stain her granddaughter's heart, mind, and soul? Should she reveal the sordid secrets concealed within the estate walls? Should she betray her daughter by telling Brianna about her mother's last dark se-cret? Maria shrugged. Would trust be an issue? Would Brianna ac-cept without question the golden Mafia rule: Don't ask. Don't tell?

Maria released a long, tired sigh. She dared not hope for too much. What the aspiring lawyer would make of this lifestyle was a worrisome question. But the fact remained that Brianna was her only blood relative, until the birth of the baby. Traditionally, the business passed down to blood relations only. Maria raised her hand, lifted her veil, and touched her face. Yes, these scars were beyond tired. It was time to exorcise the ghosts, literally. She owed it to Sofia and Shiya. They were her angels in this life and the next. She didn't want the sands of time to run out on her as they had for the two of them. For Brianna's sake and for Maria's great-grand-child, the time had come. Maria's hand reached for the bell. Mo-ments later Battistina entered, a black bag clutched in her hand.

After her body absorbed the heroin, Maria vanished into a sea of black. She felt no pain. She began to mellow. Once more she had escaped her daily mental torment. Her trusty servant, Bat-tistina, carried her to bed. But this time, Maria's drug-induced es-cape from reality was not going to give her peace. She felt herself drifting toward a Mass of pitch-black smoke. As she neared it, the putrid stench of decay filled her nostrils, while grotesque crea-tures, genitals exposed and gurgling green vomit, reached for her.

Behind these creatures from hell was a very tall black man. He was hunched and wearing only chicken feet in his earlobes. The African witch doctor wagged his finger. "Undo the wickedness of your ways, daughter of the night, for evil has reached into your soul and plucked out your spirit. If you don't heed this warning, you'll be joining me and my friends soon."

The echoes of Maria's screams danced evilly in her head.

CHAPTER TWELVE

A Fine October Morning, 1998

"And forget because we must and not because we will."
—Matthew Arnold

It was the beginning of fall, the time for olive harvesting. Chestnuts were in full swing. The nights were cooler and the days comfortably warm.

At 6:30 A.M. on this fine October morning, Brianna woke up, got out of bed, and reached for her capris. When she pulled up the zipper, it snapped off in her palm. "Shit!" she grumbled. She had packed on pounds, not only from the baby, but also from excessive eating. Rich Italian food had found itself a willing partner. Even the plaid shirt she chose was a tight fit over her blossoming breasts. She made a mental note to ask Maria where she could shop for more maternity wear. But then she shrugged, reasoning she only had about a month to go. That thought gave rise to a tinge of sadness. Her mother's death remained an open wound.

But Brianna had pulled herself together, even though there wasn't a day she didn't crave her mother's embrace. She had more or less accepted the hand that had been dealt her. Wishing her empty heart to heal, she had turned to her grandmother. Until now Maria had been loving and supportive. In return, Brianna felt she needed to offer security and protection to her grandmother, but she wasn't sure from what. Further, she wanted to speak her grandmother's language. After all, she was in Maria's land.

In the days after her mother's funeral, Brianna began practicing words on the servants. Some of them laughed. Others shrugged. Still others sniggered. A few helped her with the difficult pronunciations. But the old cook, Raphaela, never spoke and always avoided eye contact. Even so, she prepared the yummiest food Brianna had ever tasted.

Now in her eighties, Raphaela managed the kitchen single-handedly. Did she have a choice?

After a quick change into something more comfortable, Brianna was ready. Her sweatpants had never let her down. The pregnant lass headed for the kitchen to see what breakfast delights Raphaela was offering today. As Brianna entered the airy kitchen, she tilted her head and sniffed the air. "That smells good, Raphaela," she remarked as best she could in the cook's language. "What's on the menu today?"

Raphaela stared at her, dropped the whisk she was holding in a bowl, lurched forward, grabbed Brianna firmly by the elbows, and marched her to a corner of the kitchen. "You are not like her," she whispered. "You are a nice, kind girl. Please help me. He is hungry and she ..." The sounds of Raphaela's false teeth snapping shut and her starched apron swishing echoed across the roomy kitchen. Cook dashed back to her mixing bowl.

Seldom did Maria enter the kitchen at this time. She was not an early riser. However, the willowy, veiled shadow that was Maria suddenly loomed over her cook. "Breakfast is late, Raphaela," Maria admonished scathingly in English. Her choice of language prompted surprised looks from both Cook and Brianna.

Maria raised the flat of her hand high and stiffened her fingers as she scolded, "If you know what's good for you, you won't let it happen again."

Cook didn't need a translation. It wouldn't be the first time Maria had reprimanded her verbally and physically. Like most of the servants, she had occasionally been slapped hard when Maria lost her temper.

"It is ready, Donna Maria," Raphaela responded in a shaky voice. "I'll serve you and the Signórina right now."

Maria walked away from the kitchen without any polite pleasantries. No "Good morning, Brianna. How are you? Did you sleep well?" Brianna stared in astonishment at her grandmother's retreating back. "Rotten bitch" came to her mind. Maria's abrasiveness toward the amazing cook was uncalled for. Brianna knew she was staying in a house filled with weirdos; nevertheless, she knew her place. But that didn't stop her from feeling sorry for Raphaela.

In the dining room Brianna lowered herself into a high-back chair next to Maria, who still had not acknowledged her presence. Brianna followed Maria's example and decided not to offer pleasantries, but there was something she had to get off her chest. She was beginning to wonder if her grandmother showered and slept in that darn veil. Who was the real Maria Picasso, the one behind the veil?

Brianna waited until Raphaela served them laced scrambled egg with garlic and left the room. Then she lost her grip on manners and came straight out with it. "Why do you always wear that ridiculous veil?"

Underneath her mask, Maria's face contorted into that of a sad puppy. *Oh, it was only a matter of time;* she thought. Maria raised a hand to her head and removed the veil. The bright lighting from the enormous crystal chandelier illuminated her ghastly secret.

Brianna was stunned. It was unimaginable. The sight was grotesque. Pop-eyed, she quickly turned her head from Maria in revulsion. Again, without weighing her words, she blurted, "Holy crap! That's awful!"

Maria lowered her head as Brianna looked back at her disfigurement: the clumped, raised scar tissue, similar to leprosy nodules, snaking down her cheek to her neck. But it was the two different eye colors, green and blue, that most caught Brianna's attention. When she saw a tear roll down Maria's good cheek, she jumped up from the table, wrapped her arms tightly around her grandmother, and stumbled out an apology. "Oh ... I'm so sorry ... I didn't mean to be so rude. Can you tell me about it?"

For the first time in eons, Maria was ready to let down her guard and remove the emotional smoke screen that was her reason for wearing her veil. She was aware that her skin was irreparable, but now she felt ready to let go of the tragedies in her life for once and for all. Or was she?

After what seemed an eternity of pitiful sobs, Maria stared at the silver band on her finger. Why had she kept it? Why on earth was she wearing it? Why hadn't she tossed it in the sewer?

A child's unadulterated love can never be forgotten.

Maria turned to her granddaughter and declared, "I was allowed to live, Brianna, but at an awful price, as was your mother. We are victims of unspeakable crimes. In the recorded tapes she left you, and to me in person, your mother spoke of the hell she'd lived through. Her suffering was no different from mine. Now I will tell you how my privileged, happy childhood ended. How I became disfigured." Maria gritted her teeth in annoyance at the sound of a loud knock on the dining room door. She halted her words midstream.

"I'm sorry to disturb your meal, Donna Maria," Francesca said. "The gate's bell is ringing. Do you want me to see who it is?"

Maria released a long, disgruntled sigh. "If it's that's darn priest, Bettino, asking for more money, tell him to get lost. If he wants wine, give him a couple of bottles. But not my good stuff." She knew the priest's taste for the Devil's brew often overpowered his faith.

The Donna re-fastened her veil over her iron-gray hair, which she had wrapped in a bun at the nape of her neck. "Well, my dear, it looks as though our chat will have to wait."

As Maria rose from the table, Brianna pushed all seriousness aside and decided to become a goofball. She bowed to her grandmother and said in a silly voice, "Yes, m' Lady. Your wish is my command." At the same time, Brianna could not help wondering what Maria had to reveal that could be worse than what was in her mother's shocking tapes.

Under her veil, Maria composed herself, hid the earlier sadness, and smiled underneath her security mask. It felt good to have a young spirited person in her life. Most of her servants, except Francesca, were geriatrics.

Maria thrust out her arms and said, "Give *Nonna* a big hug."

Without a second thought Brianna warmly hugged her grandmother.

Alone at the table, Brianna didn't taste a mouthful of the food. Her appetite had vanished. But she wasn't going to let the food go to waste. She wrapped the breakfast remains in a napkin and headed for the dog kennel behind the mansion. Battistina had told her that Maria's favorite Doberman bitch had given birth to twelve healthy pups. As she entered the large wood kennel, the dogs started to bark. Brianna hushed them by saying, "Why are you making such a racket? It's only me." She didn't see the person riding behind Francesca in the courtyard. If she had, she would have freaked out.

With perspiration dribbling down every inch of his bare skin, the ponytailed man was shown into the reception room. "Miguel Rodriquez, Donna Maria," Francesca announced.

Mike strode across the room, hand outstretched. "Good morning, Donna Maria," he greeted respectfully.

Maria limply shook his hand. In these parts, a visitor was expected to kiss her hand in respect. Through her lace, she sized up the man standing before her. He was as Shiya had described: very handsome, could melt a woman's heart. But Maria knew better. He was, as far as she could tell, a snake in the grass. "What brings you to Sicily, Mr. Rodriquez?" she asked in an ungracious voice.

He was, in turn, assessing Maria. He pulled out a handkerchief and dabbed his brow before saying, "I've come to see Lynette Martinez (he had never called her Shiya) and her daughter on official business. I'm their attorney."

"I'm afraid you can see neither," the cool voice replied. "You have made a wasted journey. Francesca will see you out."

As loud as the colorful shirt he was wearing, Mike fired back in exasperation. "I've come a long way and have every right to see my clients."

Maria wasn't in the frame of mind for a *tête-à-tête*. Socializing with strangers was not her forte. And his demanding attitude ruffled her feathers. "You have no rights in my house, Signóre, but I can tell you this: Your long trip here has been in vain. Lynette is dead. She died a month ago, and my granddaughter is under my charge. She'll no longer need your legal advice."

It took a couple of seconds for the bad tidings to register in Mike's brain. He placed his hands on his cheeks. Cupping his face he muttered, "Oh, no. When and how did she die?"

"I shot her."

"What!"

The look of horror on Mike's face brought a whiplash of words from Maria. "You idiot!" she declared. "She died of a brain hemorrhage. As her lawyer, I'm sure you were aware of her cancer?"

Mike nodded, holding his temper in check. He wasn't happy about Maria's lack of consideration in not letting him know that Lynette had passed. "You could have let me know. I left my number with whoever answered the phone a while back."

Maria's dislike for all men was one thing, but this man was much too cocky for her liking. She vented her gallbladder on him. "Why should I have?" she persisted. "You're not a relative."

"I am … was," he emphasized, "her lifelong friend."

"That's not what she told me," Maria said with more sarcasm than the situation warranted.

Mike glared back at her. He wasn't going to accept defeat. But diplomacy was needed regardless of the fact that he wanted to strangle this pretentious woman. He clasped both her hands and gently squeezed them. "Donna Maria Picasso, at least let me see Brianna. There is something she needs to know about her father, now that her mother is gone."

In a rare moment of spontaneity, Maria mellowed. The sincerity in his voice, his pleading eyes, and soft hand gesture tugged at her heartstrings. She, too, was carrying the dreadful secret Shiya had hidden from her daughter. Better he should tell her. She turned to her watchdog, Battistina, who had slipped in quietly after Francesca had ushered Mike into the room.

"Battistina, find Brianna and bring her here," Maria ordered.

The yeti answered from behind Maria's shoulder, "Yes, Donna Maria."

The bulky woman was gone in a flash.

Maria waved to an overstuffed easy chair. "Do take a seat," she offered in a syrupy sweet voice. "Brianna can't be far."

As Mike wearily flopped down in the comfortable chair, Maria turned to her gatekeeper, who was standing by the doorway. "Francesca, go to the kitchen and tell Raphaela to prepare lemonade ... or would you prefer wine?"

"Lemonade will be fine, thank you," Mike replied.

Outside, in the dogs' pen, Brianna was sitting on the ground with one of Lady's puppies snuggled on her lap. Battistina rushed into the barn and ordered, "You come right now. Someone's here to see you."

Brianna squinted. With a "who-the-hell-could-it-be" expression, she queried, "Do you know who it is?"

"I don't know," Battistina answered. "But you better come now. Donna Maria is insistent."

Brianna gently placed the sleeping pup back onto the warmth of Lady's stomach and followed the Sasquatch into the reception room.

When she entered, Brianna was astounded.

Mike's smiling greeting, "*Hola*," was followed by his eyes fixating on Brianna's bulging tummy. Could it be his? Would she even tell him if it was? The thought made him shudder with apprehension mixed with excitement. He just had to know, so he fished. "Congratulations. You are going to be a mother. Does Roberto know?"

Brianna broke out in a cold sweat. She could only speculate as to what was going through his head.

"It's no concern of yours! Why are you here?"

Mike approached her, clasped her arms above the elbows, pulled her close, and hugged her. Brianna was shocked into speechlessness.

However, the revulsion in her body sent a clear message. Wiggling out of his tight embrace she hissed, "Don't you dare touch me ever again!"

If Mike was shocked at the telltale edge to her embittered voice, he didn't show it.

Standing a distance away from each other as if they were two gunfighters in a Western showdown, Mike said, "I'm so sorry to hear about your mother's death."

Brianna lowered her head. "It is tragic and I was devastated, but my grandmother has helped fill the big hole Mom left in my heart."

"That's nice," Mike said, trying not to look at the veiled woman he was sure was stripping him to the bone. "I'd like to have a word with you in private. It's very important."

Before Brianna could answer, an effusive Maria objected. "If you have anything to say to my granddaughter, it will be in my presence. Do I make myself clear?" Her motive? She wanted to see if Mike would give Lynette's secret away.

To Brianna, Maria was formidable, definitely in control of the awkward situation. And thank the heavens—because she, herself, was not.

Annoyance crossed Mike's handsome face. Although he was eager to talk with Brianna, he wasn't going to say anything in front of Maria. It was none of her business. Mike decided that Lynette's awful secret would have to wait. Besides, there was the other person in Lynette's and Brianna's life to take into consideration. He didn't know that Lynette was deceased. How would he take the news? Mike had no idea. But he knew one thing for sure: Brianna would be more than shocked when she found out. She would be livid.

Mike sighed heavily before sitting down again. He never wanted to keep this dreadful secret, but like a priest taking confession, he had no choice but to remain silent. He opened his briefcase, pulled out some paperwork, and, looking up at Brianna, informed her, "I've brought the university refund, your canceled tuition fees, and some other stuff that requires your signature." He searched deep into her eyes. "I must say, I'm disappointed about this cancellation. You told me on the phone that you intended to return to Canada, but it seems that is not the case. Will you finish your studies here?"

"I haven't decided yet."

With a "whatever" look, Mike handed Brianna a document. "This is the Lease Termination Agreement for the apartment you shared with Roberto. He has terminated his side of the agreement, but the landlord wants your signature before he can release the commitment."

Brianna wasn't surprised, but she had to ask, "Has Roberto moved out?"

"Yes," Mike replied. "I believe he's in the process of buying a house not far from the hospital. Everything that belongs to you is in the basement of my home. What do you want me to do with your things, seeing as you are not planning to return?"

Brianna closed her eyes for a moment. Did she want to keep any of the memories associated with her past unsuccessful relationship? No, not really. But there was one important thing she did want, not related to Roberto. "Mike, could you do me a favor, and I'll pay for the shipping. There should be a large blue tote containing photograph albums, framed pictures, and mementos I've collected over the years. It's all I have left of my mom." She felt tears threatening to fall, so she quickly added, "And I'd like my law books and my jewelry box. I put my mom's Rolex and gems in there. You can give everything else to a thrift store, unless Roberto wants any of the furniture that belongs to me. I paid a lot of money for the leather sectional. Maybe he can use it in his new place."

"I'll call him when I get back, and, of course, I will arrange for the items you want to be shipped here. But now that your mother's dead, I'm her legal spokesperson. Brianna, what I have to tell you is not easy. As executor of your mother's estate, I need your mother's death certificate in order to file her Last Will and Testament in the County Clerk's office. She had no debts or liabilities and ..." He paused and made wary eye contact with Brianna. "And if you wish to contest ...."

"Why would I want to contest my mother's will?" she interrupted. "I'm her sole heir. I have a copy. Mike, what's going on?"

"Oh, Brianna it pains me to say this." He took a deep breath, not knowing how to break the shocking truth delicately. "She left her wealth and personal belongings to a South African orphanage and to children's homes in Central America."

Go figure! Brianna's inner voice screamed. Brianna was aware that the reading of a will had been immortalized in movies, but no film could capture this reality. Was the change legally binding? She swallowed hard before she spoke. "Mike, I'm not a vulture coming out of the woodwork after someone dies, but this is mind-boggling. When did she change her mind?"

Mike felt an uncomfortable feeling creep into his heart. He detested this part of his job. "After Anele's funeral," he stated factually. "Naturally, I asked her why the sudden change and why she had chosen not to inform you of her amended document. Your mother's response was, 'Don't worry about Brianna. She is a big girl and will understand.'"

Brianna turned to Maria. "Did you know about this?"

"Yes."

"You never said anything."

"It's not my place to dispute your mother's wishes, and neither is it yours. This matter is closed." Then with purring assurance, Maria finished, "You don't need your mother's money. I have plenty. I'll support you."

"That's not the point," Brianna huffed. "I'm upset because she didn't have the decency to tell me."

"Whoa! You're sounding like a spoiled brat," Maria snapped. She came closer to the lawyer and his client and directed the next mouthful to Mike. "If there's nothing more to discuss, then this meeting is over."

Mike couldn't have agreed more. But there was one more item to deal with. He stuck his hand in his trousers' pocket, pulled out a white envelope, and handed it to the stoic-looking Brianna. "Roberto asked me to give you this."

Brianna's rigid posture said it all. She robotically stuffed the correspondence into her capris' pocket and glared at Mike. At the same time, Maria loudly cleared her throat. Mike got the message.

While Mike was putting the signed paperwork into his briefcase and preparing to leave, his thoughts penetrated the depths of his heart. Why had he made this journey? Deep down he already knew the answer. It had nothing to do with Lynette's change of heart or with the professional matters he had been assigned. It was Brianna he had longed to see. But now he, too, had a change of heart. She was no longer the vivacious young woman who had captured his heart. She was as cold as a polar iceberg and as bitter as a lime, not the woman he had fallen in love with. Not the woman he had prepared to divorce his wife for. In a way he was thankful he had made this trip. It had opened his eyes.

Without a second glance at the young woman he had been smitten with, he made his way to the door. "Well, I think that's all," he said in a professional tone. "I've a long drive back to Palermo. But I do intend to return in a couple of months to finalize certain matters."

Brianna didn't like that idea.

"Bye, Mike," Brianna said awkwardly. "Thanks for coming. Sorry it wasn't under better circumstances."

There was no *arrivederci* from Maria. As the ruler of her domain, she was cutthroat. She had wanted to grab his collar and throw him out. Shiya's confession about him seducing her in a weak, lonely moment had left a bitter taste about him in Maria's mouth. She did not know that Brianna's vulnerability had also made her susceptible. If Maria would have known, she would have pulled out the small-caliber handgun hidden in her deep shirt pocket and dropped him where he stood.

Out of what felt like obligation, Mike stepped forward, cupped Brianna's chin, turned her face toward his, and kissed her passionately. Mortified, Brianna shoved him away. She didn't have to look in Maria's direction. She knew her grandmother's eyes were glaring under her Milanese lace. Brianna could only imagine what was going through Maria's mind.

Brianna knew it was in her best interest to come clean, to confess to Maria that he could be the father of her baby. But first she'd go to her room and read Roberto's letter. She missed him. He had been her anchor until so many things in her life had changed. She missed being romanced: the dozen roses on Valentine's Day, the champagne, and the candlelight dinners. Mostly, though, she yearned for him to lay his head on her burgeoning belly and say, "That's my baby inside." She wouldn't be the first woman to hoodwink a man. She was the master of her own destiny.

Brianna sat cross-legged on the bed and began reading:

Dear Sweet Pea,

I hope my letter finds you well. Have you found your mother? I know now how important she is to you. Blood is thicker than water!

But there isn't a day that goes by that I don't think of you. I miss and love you. But I've come to terms with the fact that you are not coming home. You see, I had a long conversation with Mike. He told me you canceled law school. What a shame. You would have made the best lawyer ever. But it's your decision to quit, and I know you have good reasons.

I've changed jobs. I'm now working at the children's hospital. It's keeping me busy. I moved out of our apartment, bought a townhouse, and sold the Nissan. I couldn't bear coming home without finding you there; nor could I drive a car that still reeked of your perfume.

Oh, by the way, I've been seeing a great girl. She is a nurse. I know she will never take your place, but she has healed my broken heart. You'd like her.

Take care, Sweet Pea. I'm here for you if you ever need a friend.
Love,
Roberto

Dry eyed, Brianna crumbled the letter into a ball and flung it on the floor. "Bastard" came to mind. He hadn't even asked after the baby! The first part of his letter had hurt, but the bit about finding a replacement for her so soon really stung. She wanted to phone him. Tell him he was a dickhead and that he'd never see his child as long as she had breath in her body. But in her heart she couldn't do that because she wasn't sure. One thing she was sure of, though, was that she would be a good mother. She clasped and unclasped her hands. Not that long ago she couldn't imagine life without Roberto or her mother. But soon she would have another love in her life. Whether it was a little girl or a little boy didn't matter. The child would replace her lost loves.

Brianna stroked her swelling belly and began singing Madonna's *Ray of Light* to her baby. She wrote down two names: Shiya and Alberto, Jr. How was she going to support herself and her baby? In hindsight she wished she had not been so liberal with the money her mother had left her in Canada. The amount had dwindled drastically. And even though Maria had offered financial support, Brianna was proudly independent. The refund from the university would just have to tide her over.

What she couldn't have known is that Shiya had thought long and hard over the decision to change her will. She wanted her daughter to understand that what she and Maria had gone through would shape her new beginning as well as her baby's future.

CHAPTER THIRTEEN

Maria's Buried Wounds

"The heinous memories are burned into my soul like ink unto my skin."
—Austen

The morning after Mike made his unexpected appearance, Brianna faced Maria across the dining table.

Maria shifted her weight on her chair and looked into her granddaughter's dark, enchanting eyes. She sighed. She didn't want her past to be a burden on such young shoulders, but Brianna had left her little choice. The day before, the mother-to-be had confided in Maria, "I feel so much stronger since I read Roberto's letter. It feels like I'm shedding old skin and growing an emotionally tougher one."

Maria had become her oxygen, had kept her going. But today, for some unknown reason, Brianna felt a rush of insecurity penetrating her pores. Something awful was about to take place. She felt it. She sat rigid, as if she were bracing for a winter's storm of unknown intensity.

"Hurricane Maria," a category five, was heading Brianna's way.

Maria stroked the scars on her face. "You wanted to know how I received this terrible scarring. How I came to be so repulsive to the human eye. And how I got this ..." She rolled up her sleeve to expose a tattoo on the underside of her forearm. It was simple and bleak. It almost looked like a barcode. Brianna leaned closer to get a better look. The marks were numbers. She fixed her gaze on the indelible design.

Brianna was only twenty-three, and what she knew about the Holocaust was limited, but there was no mistaking the mark of a concentration camp victim. But as far as she knew, Maria wasn't Jewish! Secrets always intrigued Brianna. She was all ears. Before the day was out, she'd wish she hadn't been so eager.

"To truly understand, Brianna, you'll have to step back in time with me and walk in my shoes. But first, you must swear the code of silence ... Omerta. Do you understand the meaning?"

"Of course," Brianna assured without batting an eyelid. She'd watched many Cosa Nostra movies. A flashback to one particular scene made her shiver. "Are you going to cut my hand and burn a religious effigy in it?"

Maria gave her the scornful eye. "*Omerta* is not the lurid prose of movies. What I'm asking you to do is to vow ... never to reveal any Mafia secrets ... you hear or see in my home ... never become a *traditura di lu cori* ... traitor to the heart ... not even under threat of torture or death. You must have total obedience to me. Never betray me or the Mafia faction. No questions asked. Avoid any and all contact with authorities. Refuse to give evidence to the police. If you accept this, I will confide in you."

Although troublesome alarms sounded in Brianna's head, she robotically nodded and agreed. "I accept, Nonna."

Maria ran her tongue over her dry lips. She had tried hard to forget, and she had, in a way, moved on—until now. Could she handle resurrecting the ugliness all over again? She wasn't sure.

"Brianna, I'm going to take you back to my childhood, how it was taken from me, and how I returned to Sicily a changed woman." She took a long, deep breath. "How my life ended when I was kidnapped the night of my tenth birthday."

CHAPTER FOURTEEN

January 1943, a Sicilian Monastery's Dark Secrets

"Thou cam'st on earth to make the earth my hell."
—Shakespeare, Richard III

Underground, in the monastery's network of catacombs, little Maria was terrified. What was happening? Why were Paolo and Teresa so cruel to her? She couldn't call out; the tightness of the gag ensured that. Blindfolded, she didn't know whether it was day or night. She was hungry, thirsty, and in desperate need of the bathroom. The birthday feast the night before was about to present itself and embarrass her. So she began chewing on the gag her kidnappers had formed from her nightie. Finally, the material gave way. "Help me! Help me!" she yelled. Apart from the reverberating echo of her voice, she heard nothing. She went into survival mode. She had to free herself, but how? The strapping that was binding her arms and legs was unbearably tight.

Maria sat upright, drew up her knees, and lowered her head. She began biting the knot that fastened her leg bonds. After what seemed like eons, she freed herself of the lower restraints. Being double jointed, she was able to contort her supple body. Slipping her arms under her buttocks, she brought them to the front and undid the knot binding her arms with her teeth. Only one restraint was left. She flung the blindfold onto the dirt floor. However, she might as well have kept the blindfold because she couldn't see a thing in the pitch black. Taking one step at a time, with her arms spread wide, Maria began to shuffle through the darkness. She froze in place when she heard a rustling noise. "Is anyone there?" she called out.

Not a sound. Gingerly, she moved on, tripping several times over unknown obstacles. She heard the rustling sound again. This time there was no mistaking the gnawing of rodents. Fear propelled her legs. Cut and bruised, she crawled up a stairway toward a faint ray of light only to be halted by a boot pressing her head to the dirt. Paolo was livid. His prize had broken free. "You little shit!" he screamed. "You're not going anywhere until I get my money."

A dark, puzzled look crossed her light features.

Teresa asked, "How on God's green earth did she free herself?"

"Obviously, you didn't do a good job," Paolo scoffed.

Maria, restrained once again and back in the underground holding cell, pleaded for her life. "Please let me go. Take me home. My mama and papa are going to be worried sick."

Teresa laughed. "That's exactly what we want them to be. That's why they'll pay up."

Maria didn't know how to respond to that. She was young, but not stupid. The pair had taken her for money, but could they risk freeing her afterward? She knew who her kidnappers were. Maria shuddered at the thought. Her light chatterbox ways descended into a heavy silence.

Teresa was illiterate but she could tell the time. She pulled the fob watch from her skirt pocket and smiled. She had stolen the piece from the Don's study before she'd been fired. He didn't even know it was missing. "Only one hour to go," she informed Paolo. "I'll get changed now and make sure my sister is waiting for me at the crossroad as planned."

After Teresa changed, Paolo smiled admiringly. Teresa could have passed for a man in his pants, shirt, and cap. He hugged and kissed her. "Be careful, darling. Hurry back. I can't wait to start our life together, even if it's on the run," he laughed. Wearing only his underpants, socks, and boots, he began humming a romantic tune to Teresa.

It sickened Maria. If she'd had a gun, she would have shot him dead.

As the hours ticked by, Paolo became frantic with worry. Had Teresa been caught? Had she revealed the hideout under torture? No, or he would have found out about it before now. Then he heard a noise. He pulled out the knife he kept tucked in his boot, then jumped to his feet and slunk behind a pillar. There, he heard a shaky voice calling his name. "Paolo, where are you? Paolo, it's me, Teresa. Everything's gone horribly wrong," she cried.

While shaking from head to toe, Teresa relayed the bad tidings. She had met with her older, pregnant sister near the drop-off point. As planned, they pretended to be a couple out for an evening stroll. They saw two suspicious-looking men dressed in black standing near the designated stone. The two young women ducked for cover. Then they cautiously crept near the men to overhear their conversation.

"I wouldn't wish to be in Don Alberto's shoes," one said.

"I'd never again get a good night's sleep if I had refused to pay the ransom," the other chided.

"Well, I don't blame him. I don't think I could have made that decision, but he's doing the right thing. To pay the bastards would bring dishonor to his family's name."

"I've no doubt the Don will find the boy, Paolo. He will get what's coming to him."

"Yeah," the second man added. "A bloody bullet with his name on it is what the bastard deserves."

Teresa and Natalia fled the scene.

It was all over. There would be no payout.

The sisters hurriedly hugged each other and said their good-byes behind a thick-trunked tree. Then Teresa raced like a cheetah back to the monastery, where she confronted Paolo. "What are we going to do now?" she cried.

Paolo's face contorted with rage. But he didn't have time to express it. He had to stay calm. He needed time to think, to figure out what to do next, but Teresa's shrill babbling was distracting him.

"We are dead. Do you hear me, Paolo? We are as good as dead."

After a short time, Paolo forced his scheming mind into overdrive. He scratched his chin as he crafted a plan. He wasn't sure it would work, but it was worth a try. He whispered his new strategy into Teresa's ear. She was all for it.

CHAPTER FIFTEEN

On the Run from Sicily

"The Devil watches all opportunities."
—William Congreve

The Messina dock was teaming with German and Italian military. Paolo, his cap pulled low, gripped Maria's hand. Teresa held the other, smaller hand. Accompanied by "parents" and disguised as a boy, Maria was led onto the overnight ferry crossing. Paolo's disguise and lies had secured their passage to the Italian mainland. Straight-faced and without the twitch of an eyelash, he told the officials they were Mussolini supporters who were being persecuted for their loyalty, and that they couldn't stay on the island any longer because they feared for their lives. Paolo ensured them he had family in Calabria who would take them in. The German official stared at the zonked-out Maria, who was wearing brown corduroy pants and a heavy winter jacket a size too big. "He's a good looking boy," the man remarked. "How old is he?"

"He is twelve," was Paola's lie. After all, Maria didn't look like a ten-year-old.

Paola and Teresa forced themselves to form proud-parent smiles for the guard's benefit.

They boarded the ferry.

With her body crumpled against a plastic seat on the top deck, Maria was in another world. Having been forced to drink a large quantity of alcohol, she was oblivious to the German soldiers sporting their weapons, or to any other passengers. Her hair had been cropped short with Paolo's knife, and she was wearing the boy's outfit Teresa had obtained from her sister.

Maria, a slight snore escaping her lips, slept like a baby, unaware of any wrongdoing.

As night plunged into darkness, the ferry, escorted by a German assault boat, sailed through the Strait of Messina. On the deck a full moon illuminated a couple whispering their congratulations to each other for eluding the Mafia informers and the scrutiny of the German occupiers. Then an alarming thought entered Teresa's mind. "What if she wakes up and starts blabbing?"

The wily Paolo immediately settled her fear. "She's going to be out for hours, and when she does wake, I'll scare the shit out of her."

Teresa couldn't wait to get it over with and start her life with the man she loved. She snuggled into him. "*Ti amo,*" she whispered.

"I love you, too."

Teresa released a happy sigh. Paolo was her hero, but not for long.

She was in for the shock of her life.

CHAPTER SIXTEEN

Two Days Later, the Eternal City, Rome

"Abuse manipulates and twists a child's natural sense of trust and love."
—Laura Davis

Sandwiched between Paolo and Teresa on a bench set in a six-teenth century plaza, Maria was expressionless. She was cried out and impervious to the damp, cold Rome weather. But, even so, she was concerned about what was in store for her. She didn't know where she was or what was to become of her, or why she had been brought to an ancient city steeped in historical splendor. She looked around. The cobbled plaza was thronged with German soldiers marching in steel-toed boots, all looking very much out of place. Behind her the morning sun shone brightly on the orna-mented facades of a cathedral surrounded by colorful flora.

The last thing on the ten-year-old's mind was history. She was hungry. The smell of chicken soup wafted across the square and tantalized her growling stomach. Her last meal had been a thinly cut tomato sandwich that Paolo had purchased on the cheap train ride to Rome. A picture of the wonderful meals Raphaela had pre-pared for her back home brought sadness to the forefront once more. She wanted to run home to her mama and papa and ask

Raphaela to make her favorite, *Fichi d'India*. But her inner sense knew that that would be impossible. She tugged at Paolo's shirt sleeve. "Can you get me something to eat? I'm hungry."

"I'm hungry, too," Teresa added.

Paolo reached into his pants' pocket and pulled out the lira he had left, the money Teresa's sister had given them from her biscuit-tin savings. The bulk of the funds had gone to ferry and train fares. Paolo realized he didn't have enough to buy one meal, let alone three, and there certainly was not enough to buy cigarettes. He could forego food but not his smokes. That realization incited urgency.

"Watch her," Paolo ordered Teresa. "I'm going to find a telephone, find out if we can go now instead of this evening." Teresa's insecure look impelled Paolo to add, "Don't worry. I'll be back as soon as I can."

Although she had heard what had been said, Maria was clueless.

Teresa wasn't.

In Calabria the day before, Paolo had left Teresa minding Maria while he purposely sought out people on the "wrong" side of the law. His criminal contact had been helpful, but had strongly warned Paolo that the man he was referring him to was extremely dangerous and would not be messed with. "I'm a big boy," Paolo had replied.

"Not with this guy!" was the man's response. "He'll cut your throat in the blink of an eye."

A few minutes later, Paolo, his face thunderous, returned to the bench where the girls were waiting. "The bastard wouldn't go for an earlier meeting. Seven as arranged. Not a minute sooner."

Teresa scrunched her face. "It's only ten o'clock in the morning. What are we going to do until then? We can't go all day without food! I'll die from hunger!"

His reply rang of cold inhumanity. "If you want to eat Teresa, then you will have to make the money."

Teresa's eyes squinted. "What do you mean?"

Paolo dropped the bombshell.

As if she were trying to catch flies, Teresa's mouth fell open. Then she stamped her feet and threw an unholy fit. Looking heavenward, she cursed God for making this despicable man, the Devil himself. She continued ranting upward. "You can have him. I don't want him." Nose to nose with Paolo, she exclaimed angrily, "Never in a million years! How dare you ask me to do such a thing, Paolo?"

"Please yourself," he said grumpily. "I'm not the one who's hungry." He made eye contact with his partner in crime and added, "When this is over, I'll find a woman who will do as I say without question."

His face tightened and his eyes pierced callously through her eye sockets as he spoke his next words. "And get this straight. You aren't going to get one lira from the sale."

"We'll see about that," she threatened.

Paolo clenched his fists. He wanted to throttle her where she stood, but this was not the place to do so. Cunningly, he switched his strategy. He embraced her and said, "Darling, I love you. You know that. There isn't anything I wouldn't do for you. Haven't I proven it? Remember, it was your idea to kidnap Maria. I did what you asked without question. All I'm asking you to do is give some guy a good time so we don't starve." Syrupy sweet, he finished with, "Can you do this for me?"

Although food rationing was enforced throughout Italy, Teresa's sexual exchange provided them with a decent meal.

Maria was none the wiser.

Afterwards, with her belly full of spinach and cheese cappelletti, Maria was taken by Teresa, on Paolo's instructions, to a public bathroom. Obediently, Maria washed her face and hands. Following the ablution, the trio entered a nearby park. Paolo dozed off, leaving Teresa to babysit. Somewhere in Teresa's antisocial personality, a gentler character lurked. "Maria, how about you and I go and find an ice cream?"

With her woes momentarily forgotten, Maria hugged Teresa warmly and asked, "Do you have money?"

Teresa laughed. "Of course. I'm not that stupid. I didn't hand over every lira to Paolo. But that's our little secret. Okay?"

The "children" walked across the park holding hands in search of an ice cream parlor. But soon, the memory of the glorious moments she spent devouring a humungous ice cream would fade forever from Maria's mind, to be replaced by the bitter taste of evil.

That evening, flanked by her bodyguards, Maria was shepherded out of the square. Yet again, her destination was a mystery. By the way Teresa was gripping her wrist, she knew her guard had stopped being nice.

The trio walked up the narrow street of Via Rasella past buildings with broken windows and smashed brickwork. They could not have known that in one year, on May 23, 1944, a time bomb in a garbage collector's cart would explode and kill a column of German soldiers. That blast would have devastating consequences.

Maria sighed compassionately when she saw the carcass of a little dog left to decompose on the street. The sight saddened her. She had always wanted a pet, but her father had always told her, "When you are old enough to take full responsibility, I'll get you the best there is."

Paolo reached into his trousers' pocket, pulled out a piece of paper, and examined it. "Yes. This is it, 508 Pensione Rasella. We are at the right place."

"Well, what are we waiting for?" Teresa urged, prodding him by poking her finger into his side. "Let's get it over with and get the hell out of here. I don't like this place. It's too creepy."

Not knowing what her fate was to be, Maria nodded in agreement. The piles of rotting garbage outside the doorway were making her nauseated.

They entered the rundown building and made their way to the top landing. Paolo knocked three times, waited a few seconds, then twice more. The door creaked open exposing the occupant. A fat, middle-aged, balding man, naked from the chest up, never took his lecherous eyes off of Maria. He spoke in a tongue the girl didn't understand. He gestured for them to enter.

In stark contrast to the decay outside, his living room was magnificently decorated, stuffed with expensive furniture, rugs, ornaments, and oil paintings. Maria didn't know what to make of this. Why was she in this creepy man's home? She saw the man hand Paolo an envelope.

After counting the money, Paolo exploded. "This is not what we agreed to! I want the rest of my money."

"Take it or leave it!" Schmidt fired through his rotting teeth. "That's all you're getting."

"I'm not leaving until I get what's owed," Paolo growled back.

Schmidt glared at Paolo with steel-cold eyes. Then he bent down and reached for the pistol taped underneath the table. Aiming it at Paolo's head, he threatened, "Go now before I change my mind and put a bullet through your bloody head."

Teresa screamed in horror. "For God's sake, Paolo, take the money and let's go." She grabbed his arm and pulled him toward the door.

Paolo had no idea how close he had come to death. But a bullet with his name on it was in the cards. *Once you have sold your soul to the Devil, you can't buy it back with a pile of dirty money!*

Maria didn't know what to think, but she heard their running footsteps and Teresa's last words: "*Arrivederci*, Maria, daughter of a dog."

A shiver of fear like no other she had ever felt ran down Maria's young spine. "Come back!" she cried pitifully. "Don't leave me here! I'll be good! I promise!"

Schmidt burst out laughing. "You're going to bring double what I've paid for your scrawny ass."

Maria felt warm liquid escaping. She had not only peed on herself, she also had slightly defecated. Her pimp wrinkled his nose and shook his head in disgust.

Tragically and brutally, Maria's innocent childhood ended that day. She'd been sold into the savage, underground world that traded in human flesh.

The happy world she once knew was gone forever.

Reliving her horrible past was more unbearable for Maria than she thought. It caused a flood of sorrowful tears to roll down her cheeks. She hurriedly replaced her veil to mask her pain.

Brianna felt as helpless as she had been when her mother had recounted her heart-wrenching story on cassette tapes back in Canada. Brianna couldn't help but be deeply moved and visibly upset by Maria's tragic narration. Suddenly, a tornado of empathy circled Brianna's saddened heart. She wanted to grab her grandmother and hug her, tell her how sorry she was, but Brianna found that she couldn't move. It felt as if her backside were glued to the chair.

CHAPTER SEVENTEEN

The Nightmare Intensifies

"Gott in Himmel, Forgive Me."
—Hauptman Günter Hornhauft

That same night a silent Maria was thrown in the trunk of Schmidt's car. The darkness was suffocating, but the numb child didn't cry. After what seemed like ages, the vehicle finally stopped in an alleyway behind an impressive building lined with cherub figurines. A black 1935 Duesenberg coupe pulled up alongside. After money was exchanged, Maria was handed over to a Waffen-SS officer with a thin grey moustache. "Hello, *Schatzi*," Rudolf said, stroking her face. "*Ve* are going to have a good time, *ya*?" His nose wrinkled. "First you can take a hot bath."

Clueless as to what he'd said, a terrified Maria shrunk away from his touch. She wanted to roll down the window of the coupe and leap out, but fear immobilized her.

Tightly gripping Maria's frightfully cold hand, the high-ranking, white-haired, blue-eyed officer led her into his private military quarter. The room was spacious and lined with books from ceiling to floor. A framed picture of Hitler hung above a bed. Rudolf began undressing, neatly folding each item and placing it on a chair.

When he was down to his underwear, Maria stared in puzzlement. She had never seen her mother or father this naked. A small voice inside her told her to bolt. She ran to the door. It was locked.

"Come, come, child," he said in a whisper as he gestured to the bathroom. "We are going to have a bath together. How do you like that?"

Maria stood rigid.

Rudolf's wrinkle-lined face twisted in annoyance. "Well, the bath will have to wait. I can't wait to taste your delights." He grabbed his victim and flung her on his bed and started removing what was left of his clothing.

Maria screamed in shock, "What are you doing?" Frantically, she tried pushing his hands away.

His raucous laughter hurt her ears as he ripped off her pants, exposing her feces-caked genitals. His amusement was replaced by a look of outrage. He stomped to the telephone and dialed out.

"Yes," the voice on the other side said.

"I want my money back," he screamed at Schmidt. "You tricked me. You sold me a *girl!* And not only that, she's covered in shit!"

"How the hell was I to know she was a *girl?*" Schmidt responded. "I got swindled, too."

"You better get out of Rome, and quickly," were Rudolf's final words to the trafficker.

The German officer's sadistic sexual desire had been foiled by the wrong gender. He stormed out of the room leaving Maria huddled at the back of the bed, grasping her torn clothing and holding it over her exposed private parts. A few moments later, her attacker returned with a young uniformed man at his side.

"She is all yours, a gift from me," Rudolf said, grinning like a Cheshire Cat. "Enjoy yourself, but wash her first. She stinks to high heaven."

The twenty-eight-year-old wasn't smiling. But Hauptman Günter Hornhauf's eyebrows were raised almost to the rim of his cap. "Sir, I thank you for the offer, but I have a girlfriend. I was with her last night. I don't need satisfying."

"You're refusing my gift," Rudolf retorted angrily.

"In a way, sir, I am. Like I said ..."

"Listen, young man," Rudolf interrupted, "when I give an order, I give a direct order. Do I make myself clear?"

Günter looked at his superior. Ever since being assigned as Rudolf's valet, he had feared his boss. Having strong moral beliefs, he saw this man as a descendant of evil and his sexual exploitation of little boys as a grave sin. However, Günter wasn't going to risk everything to disobey this sick creature of the Nazi regime. Rudolf had left him little choice. He quickly stepped toward the helpless Maria as his fingers flipped open his belt buckle. Rudolf left the room. His heinous laughter reverberated through the walls of the quarters.

Günter forced the terrified Maria's legs apart. Her rapist did not wrinkle his nostrils at the overpowering, repulsive odor of human waste. Instead, a detached face mask materialized, replacing any inkling of human revulsion. But it was the screaming he could not handle. He placed his hand over the girl's mouth, and then spoke in a contrite, almost confessional manner. "I want you to know that I don't want to do this to you, but if I don't, I will be shipped out to the front lines. I can't let that happen because I'm working on getting my nursing degree."

In a grip of pain and terror, his words were lost on Maria. She could not hear him through her piercing screams.

Günter shut his eyes tight. *Gott in Himmel, forgive me. She is but a child!*

Maria's tragic story had so far kept Brianna on the edge of her seat. Maria's pain had shaken her. Brianna's rage at Maria's treatment was melted by the tears in her grandmother's eyes. At that moment Brianna felt helpless, and she realized that history had repeated itself. Her grandmother and her mother had many things in common: both had been victims of violent sexual exploits as children. Brianna was sure no one had cracked down on these sick, sadistic, and destructive crimes during the war years. She would have given her eyeteeth to have been a judge at the Nuremberg Trials. She would have hanged the lot of them. Lorena Bobbitt came to mind.

Maria's face appeared wan, but she hadn't finished trudging down a road that had led her to the gates of hell. Her horrific life story continued.

Shortly after her deflowering, Rudolf ordered Günter to take her to a brothel on the outskirts of Rome. Wrapped in a bloody bed sheet, the silent, distressed child was handed over to a German brothel-keeper who looked like she belonged in Dracula's castle. Her long, pointed incisors clamped her bottom lip. She yakked in German to Günter for a minute; then he bent and kissed Maria on the head as if he were saying farewell to a relative. Maria didn't flinch. As young as she was, she was beyond hurt.

Following the rapist's departure, Helga led Maria to a concrete shower stall. The icy-cold water from the hosepipe didn't bother Maria. She felt disconnected from her ravaged body. The water couldn't wash everything away; blood was pooling at her feet. Günter had torn her to bits. Helga felt like crying. She hadn't been much older than Maria when she had been violated by a family member. She remembered it clearly and was still living with the psychological aftermath. But life had to go on. She had a job, while others back in Germany were starving and getting killed. Helga wrapped a towel around the numb girl and said compassionately, "Your body will heal, child, but your spirit is another thing."

Helga's German sentiment was lost on Maria, so the woman just shook her head. She had a job to do or her neck could be on the line, and she had three children back in Germany to feed. "I'll get you some clothes, and you can join the others."

When the lights in the dormitory were turned on, Maria was surprised at how many other girls her age were crammed onto bunk beds in one small room.

She wasn't alone in this debauched world.

The next morning Maria was befriended by a sixteen-year-old Jewish Italian girl named Bianca, who had been imprisoned in the brothel for over a year. She would be sharing her bed with Maria.

As time went on, these heartbroken girls spent the few hours they had away from their assigned work beds comforting each other in a separate part of the brothel. They spoke about their previous lives and collected colored stones from the yard to count the days of their captivity. Mostly, they talked about getting out ...escaping. Deep down, the older Bianca knew it was impossible. The girls were watched day and night by guards who wielded lethal, bone-crushing weapons. In the days that followed, the innocent little girl who had been Maria no longer existed. She had become, by force, a prostitute. However, her time in the brothel came to a sudden end in May 1943, nearly four months after she had been abducted from Sicily.

At the crack of dawn the brothel inmates were ordered to dress. They were then herded into canvas, camouflaged military vehicles. A baffled and sleepy Maria asked her friend, "Bianca, where do you think they are taking us?"

"I don't know," Bianca replied. She did not tell Maria what she had overheard from a female, Italian guard: "They won't be coming back. It's the end of the road for them." The heartless woman had cackled when she said it. "There will be another hundred fewer Jews contaminating our soil."

CHAPTER EIGHTEEN

May 30, 1943, Auschwitz-Birkenau, Polish Extermination Camp

"For the dead and the living we must bear witness."
—Elie Wiesel

In the middle of the night, thirty-seven miles from Krakow, the incessant sound of a locomotive's whistle was ear splitting. For the frightened and bewildered cargo—140 women and children rounded up in Italy and then tightly packed in grim freight wagons—that was the least of their discomforts. They had traveled without food or water, breathing only stale air, for thirty-three hours. In the sealed conditions of this death train, the occupants had little choice but to perform their natural functions in their cramped spots.

Groans and pleading hovered in the air, coming from all corners of the cars.

"I'm hungry," cried one six-year-old.

"I'm thirsty," sobbed another.

"Where are we going?"

It was 3 o'clock in the morning when the train rumbled through an arched, turreted, warehouse-style building toward the railhead.

Waiting on the platform were SS men and women and the camp's ferocious German shepherds, restrained by their handlers. The children stepped into formation. On the ramp to the side of them stood a slender man wearing an impeccable, dark-green uniform adorned with medals. He was omnipresent at all selections, and the wave of his gloved hand—*links* or *rechts* (left or right)—determined who lived and died.

With polished boots shining reflectively in the beams emanating from bright spotlights, SS Haupsturmführer, Josef Mengele, was an imposing figure capable of displaying deadly charm. However, his physical appearance did not meet Hitler's ideology of the pure Aryan race: tall, long-legged, blue-eyed, and blond-haired. Conversely, the thirty-two-year-old had many gypsy features: dark and tawny, brown-eyed, brown hair, with a bent nose. To some, Herr Doctor Josef Mengele appeared handsome with almost movie-star appeal. But to the miserable souls who had the misfortune of meeting the cold-blooded killer nicknamed "The Angel of Death," he was the ugliest, most evil monster. With his SS cap rakishly tilted to one side and his thumb resting on his pistol belt, the Camp "C" doctor was excited. Were there *zwillinger* (twins) in this shipment? Having a deep-seated ambition to achieve greatness, he had chosen to dedicate himself to genetics, to concentrate on unlocking the secrets and discovering the sources of human imperfections. Under the academic guidance of Professor Otmar Freiherr von Verschuer, Mengele, who was affectionately named "Beppo," postulated that *twins* held heredity secrets that would enable him to produce the perfect Germanic super-race for Hitler.

A shiver of excitement streamed through Mengele's veins.

What delights would he discover today?

The train's screeching brakes finally ground to a halt inside the compound, which was lit up like a football stadium. The guards leapt forward onto the ramp with dogs, whips, and machine guns at the ready. The doors were thrown open, accompanied by fiendish screams: "*Raus! Schnell, schnell!* (Get out! Quick, quick.) A new SS recruit clasped his hand over his nose, gagging from the stink of the decomposition of ten dead souls, and from the feces and urine of the living. The stench of the scene overpowered him, and he broke rank and retched.

A Nazi with a heart? Yeah, right!

Blows began raining down on the women and children. Some, too weak to stand, collapsed on the ramp. Others cried for their mothers. Still others held hands as if in a trance, staring up at the smoky gray clouds that rained human ashes down upon them. Some of the kids wrinkled their noses at the unfamiliar stench spewing from smokestacks. Others frowned at the sight of a pajama-clad man dodging flying bullets. They watched in bewilderment as he flung himself onto the high-tension current of the compound fencing. The youngsters were speechless. Suddenly the majority of their heads turned toward the sound of music being performed by a prisoner orchestra only yards away from the crematoria. *Der Ring des Nibelungen* by Richard Wagner (Hitler's favorite composer) was lost on most of these children, but it did spark an assuring comment from Bianca. "Listen, Maria. Nothing bad can happen if they are playing music."

Deluged by the cudgel blows and snapping dogs surrounding the new group, Maria, her thin body trembling with fear, whispered to her friend Bianca. "I'm afraid."

Bianca touched Maria's dirt-streaked cheek. "Don't be scared. We have survived the *freudenhaus* (brothel), haven't we? What could be worse? No matter what happens to us, we are together forever. Always remember ..." A violent head blow to the head ended Bianca's heartfelt sentiment.

"*Schweigen!*" The SS female overseer screamed for silence. Bianca came to, stood up, and glared at the skinny woman wearing a striped brown cap and striped pajamas who looked near death herself. Noting that they were surrounded by high, electrically charged barbed wire fences guarded by men with machine guns, Bianca asked the thin woman, "Where are we ...?" The butt of a male guard's weapon dropped Bianca's body to the ground. It was lights out for her. Maria screamed in horror. "You're a bad man! Why did you hit her? She didn't say anything wrong!" Maria didn't see it coming, but she sure felt it.

Now the friends shared something new in common.

Knocked unconscious by a similar blow to her head, Maria didn't see Bianca being dragged by the hair from the lineup. Nor did she hear the gunshot.

Bianca had gone to a better place.

A short while later, having regained consciousness, a wobbly Maria, bleeding profusely from the gash on her head, was shoved back into the lineup. The last thing she remembered was whispering a prayer for Bianca while she was being head-whipped. Had her only friend been taken to a hospital? Would she see her later?

Subdued and silent, with her head lowered, a sullen Maria advanced in the lineup. Mengele looked over his prey with dead, gimlet eyes. With a flick of his crop, children who didn't pass his inspection were waved to the left and to certain death. Their spine-chilling screams were muffled by the roaring flames coming from the petroleum-laced inferno. They had been thrown into open blazing pits, burned alive.

The camp doctor's eyes lit with excitement when he noticed two six-year-old sisters next in line. "*Zwillinger!*" he exclaimed. "This night is not wasted!" As a smug grin creased his lips, the doctor patted the girls on their heads. "'Uncle' Mengele is going to take good care of you. Would you like some candy?"

The girls looked at each other. His German tongue was lost on the identical twins.

Mengele dug into his jacket pocket and pulled out a couple of candies. Before he could offer them, the twins' little hands snatched the delights. "Grazie, grazie, Signor," they thanked him in unison. Mengele's smile was not one of "You are most welcome." He waved his gloved hand and ordered a female *kapo* (a camp prisoner given privileges in return for supervising other inmates) to take the twins to the children's barracks nicknamed "The Zoo."

The cudgel-wielding kapo, sporting a green triangle with the number 29559 sewn on her armband, marched the twins away with envy in her heart. How favored they were. They were able to keep their hair and clothing, as well as receive extra food rations and preferential treatment.

How absolutely wrong she was. Mengele's children were not allowed to keep the outfits on their backs. Instead, they were given apparel taken from the infamous "showers." Their heads were shaved. They were tattooed and starved like the rest of the deportees in the death camp. And in the name of science, Mengele's favored "patients" were subjected to diabolical traumas. They were put into pressure chambers, tested with toxic drugs, and subject to painful surgeries without anesthetics. To top that barbarity, toxic chemicals were injected into some of their eyes in an attempt to change their color. Was it possible to change an eye color into one that would complement the fanaticism of Hitler's idea of an Aryan race? Mengele thought so.

On this overcast night, Mengele waited on the selection platform. His diabolical heart raced in gleeful anticipation. What treasures would come his way this evening? Beyond the possibility of encountering twins, he was looking for anything else unusual that pleased his experimenter's eye. His delight magnified when he spotted the dark-skinned Maria, thinking she was a gypsy.

"A good-looking *Zigeuner*," he said, "this is my lucky day." In his warped, cruel mind, Maria was like the Jews, a subspecies, an unworthy part of the human race. He made his way to her, and lifted her drooped head with the handle of his cane. "What's your name, child?" he asked, making eye contact with the shivering Maria.

She stared blankly.

Mengele made a guttural sound that sounded like a strangled chicken, then lifted Maria's drooping chin. He repeated the question in Italian. "What's your name?"

Maria spoke only Sicilian, but she had heard her father once say, "The anti-Italian feeling on the island is such that Italians who do not speak the *lingua franca* cannot venture to leave their lodgings at night without running the risk of being stabbed in the back.

No true Sicilian admits to being Italian."

"I don't speak *ficken* Gypsy," Mengele hissed, "so if you want to live, you had better learn my language fast."

When Maria failed to open her mouth, an irate Mengele addressed the SS officer at his side. The man grabbed Maria roughly by the shoulder and led her away into a foul-smelling building behind the railhead. In there, Maria's head was shaved by an oberkapo (chief kapo).

Subsequently, Maria suffered the camp's painful registration process: being tattooed. On the inner side of her left upper forearm the letter Z (The identification for gypsies) was stamped followed by the number 19800. "From now on you do not answer by your name," the oberkapo informed Maria. "Your name is your number."

Her words, like Mengele's, fell on deaf ears. So the kapo tried hand gestures. Then, frustrated by no response, she lunged forward and began ripping off Maria's shabby brothel clothing, a scarlet red chiffon dress and silk underwear a size too big. It was too much for the already broken girl. She fought for her life, sinking her nails into the woman's face and using the foul language she had heard her father utter. Choice words spewed out in torrents.

Crunch! Blood trickled out of Maria's nose.

With tears rolling down her cheeks and horror on her face, a naked, shivering Maria was led to a tin-constructed shower cubicle. The cold water left her body numb but refreshed. It relieved her injured nose and the bloody razor nicks covering her head. The chill of the water also eased the pain of the needle punctures on her arm. She tilted her head and drank the murky water until her stomach was about to burst. The shower turned out to be enjoyable for Maria. But had she known about Zyklon B (a cyanide-based pesticide manufactured in Germany to eradicate vermin, and now used by Nazis to murder thousands of human beings) she would not have been so eager to jump into the shower.

After the degrading stripping, shaving, and cleansing, Maria was taken to another room and instructed to select something to wear from a heaped pile of discarded clothing. When she didn't make a move, the woman grabbed one of the garments and handed it to Maria. Under different circumstances the scene would have been hilarious. Maria was forced to wear a green strapless evening dress with a huge bow at the waistline. Not only was it two sizes too big, the hemline trailed on the floor.

Sometime in the predawn hours, when the stars were twinkling in the heavens, a barefoot Maria, wearing no underwear under her fancy ball gown, was frog-marched by a uniformed SS female to the children's barracks where the twins had been taken. There, the guard flicked on the light switch and exposed several rows of brick-walled compartments. Hundreds of dirty, ragged, sleepy children, six to eight in a slatted bunk, stared at the new arrival. Some laughed aloud. Others snickered. They were silenced when the officer's cudgel found their bare flesh.

Squished up against five other bodies on a bloodstained mattress riddled with lice, Maria wept. She cried for her mother, as she'd done every night since she had been abducted. They had been as close as a daughter and mother could be, always hugging and kissing. Now Maria was unloved, not even considered human any more. A burning feeling began in her gut and traveled to her throat. Why was God silent? How could He let humans perform such terrible deeds to other humans? Hadn't she faithfully attended Mass every Sunday? Hadn't she always kept His commandments?

Suffer the little children …

From that night on Maria never again turned her head heaven-ward. She was done with praying. Intellectually mature for her age, she knew she had to do what she had to do to survive, to return home, and to see once more her beloved mother. She missed her doting father. She would have thought otherwise had she known the truth. But most of all, Maria missed riding her beloved pony, Alfonso. Would she ever see him again?

A hand reached out for her. "Don't cry," the voice said. "Uncle Mengele will give you candies if you are a good girl."

Maria squinted in the dark at the shadow of a person huddled beside her. The girl, about her own age, had a black patch over her eye and was a mere bag of bones, without muscle or fat.

"I don't understand you," Maria whispered.

"Are you *Italiana?*" the voice asked.

Maria recognized the word, but was affronted. "No, no, no. I'm not Italian. I'm from *Sicilia.*"

Beata, a Polish twin aged six, yelled, "Does anyone here speak Sicilian?"

"Shut up, Beata," someone moaned. "I'm trying to sleep."

Out of nowhere a tall girl approached the bunk. She climbed up to face Maria. She introduced herself in Sicilian. "My name is Luciana. I'm from Catania. I was arrested by the Germans for stealing food from a container at the shipyard. I was first sent to an Italian prison camp and then here. What about you? What's your name? Where do you come from in Sicily? How and when where you caught?"

Bombarded with questions, Maria sat upright. Her outstretched arms sought out the girl. Hugging her tight, Maria whispered in Luciana's ear, "I'm so happy someone understands my language. *Mia chiama* (my name is) Maria Teresa Picasso Genovese," she said, pronouncing her full name with pride.

Luciana untangled herself from Maria's tight embrace and said, "Come down so we can talk privately."

The girls sat side by side on the wooden floor, and Maria filled in most of the answers to Luciana's questions. Then Maria asked, "What is this place?"

Sorrow lined Luciana's young face as she replied, "It's an awful place. But listen to me carefully, Maria. We have to survive … go home to our families when this war is over. And the word around the yard is that it won't be long until soldiers from another country rescue us. So do as you are told, and we'll make it to the end. That's if …"

"If what, Luciana?" Maria interrupted.

Luciana blew out a long, deep sigh. "Children are generally killed upon arrival, but we are the *lucky* ones." She sneered at the word. "We are guinea pigs, Maria."

Maria's eyebrows stretched high. "What's a guinea pig? I don't understand this."

"It means …" The older girl scratched her forehead with a dirt-encrusted fingernail. "How can I explain this? Ah. We are nothing more than animals used for medical experiments. Nearly every day the doctor sends someone to take one of us to the hospital.

Nobody has ever come back, except the girl with the eye patch. Mengele is finished trying to change her eye color."

"That's awful!"

The door burst open. The girls shot to their individual beds.

Two German guards brandishing sticks stomped in with their muddy boots. "*Achtung, der abschaum Jude!* (Attention, scumbag Jews!) *Raus, raus!*"

Beaten awake, the children fled the barracks into the frigid 4:30 A.M. temperature. Shivering from head to toe, Maria stood in line for her first roll call. It would not be her last.

She soon discovered that roll calls were dragged out, sometimes for hours, as a way to torture prisoners, especially on days of poor weather. Over the course of her incarceration, Maria lost count of how many hours a day she spent standing, arms at her sides, teeth chattering, in all kinds of severe weather.

During her first roll call, the frosty air chilled Maria's thin body to the bone, especially her feet. The girl standing closest to her began urinating, soaking not only her feet, but also Maria's. The warm body fluid felt glorious in the bitter cold. Someone behind Maria nudged her. She turned and looked at the girl, who was making strange faces and weird gestures with her eyes. Maria frowned. The girl pointed to the ground.

There between Maria's parted legs was a pair of well-worn shoes. She was so happy, even if they were both left-foot slip-ons. She thought, *Two left shoes will make you either weak or strong.* She chose to become the latter.

After an excruciatingly long roll call, the exhausted children filed back into their quarters. Sleep was almost impossible due to overcrowding and bed lice. Maria nudged Luciana, who also shared the bunk. "I'm so hungry, Maria said. When do we eat?"

"When Bronislaw makes it."

"Who's Bron ... ees ... laugh?" Maria pronounced badly.

"Oh, she's a political prisoner, considered a danger to the state. She's the daughter of a high-ranking Polish Jew. Why she's still alive, not sent to the gas chamber ..." Luciana took a deep breath before finishing. "She's *useful* to the Germans. She was a seamstress before she was imprisoned, and now she repairs their uniforms and makes new ones. It was Dr. Mengele who ordered her to make food for us."

Goosebumps appeared on Maria's skin at the sound of Mengele's name, but she had to ask, "What's a gas chamber?"

Someone moaned, "I'm tired. I want to sleep."

"Sorrreee," Luciana said while wondering, *Was Maria too young to comprehend this nightmare*? Somehow, she would have to make the naïve girl understand the diabolical work being carried out in the camp. Luciana did her best to quietly explain.

Maria couldn't believe her ears. There was a death factory right under her nose. Yes, she had firsthand experience with the twisted, wanton, and depraved brutality of the barbarian Nazis, but the idea of crematoriums right under her nose was unfathomable.

Maria lay awake, unable to absorb all Luciana had told her. Thoughts of the heinous possibilities besieged her: Would she be burnt alive? Would her beautiful eyes be plucked out? Would her stomach be cut open? Would she starve to death? Would her bones look like matchsticks? Would she get a terrible disease, like some of the girls in the brothel, and be left to rot?

Luciana took Maria's hand and led her to an area near the entrance of the barracks. There she introduced the frightened girl to the others. Maria noted that the other girls were as emaciated as she was. She touched her chest and felt her ribs protruding under her silly dress.

An hour later a short, blond woman who didn't look undernourished entered the barracks. She was wearing a brown, numbered armband and entered carrying a large metal pot.

"That's Bronislaw. We call her *Mamusia*," Luciana remarked as she pointed. "She's the only mother we'll ever have in this awful place."

In her early forties, Bronislaw, a political prisoner, smiled warmly at the hungry children holding their metal bowls at the ready. The least she could do was give them a tender smile. She put the heavy pot on the floor, dipped a wooden ladle inside it, and began dishing out the contents. She tried to ensure that each child received a scrap of potato peel from the bottom of the cook pot.

Maria, sitting on the cold floor next to Luciana, was handed her meager share of weak potato soup, her first nourishment in days. She was also handed a thin slice of moldy, rock-hard bread. As a newcomer she had to wait through the rotation for her first slice, but Maria wasn't bothered by the pecking order. When it was her turn, she crammed the tiny piece of bread into her thin-lipped mouth and, within seconds, began choking. A spew of vomit followed. No one spoke, snickered, or stared. They had all been there, rounded up and deported from homelands as far away as Holland. Most had suffered the long train journey without a morsel of food.

Bronislaw slipped out quietly. She couldn't bear to look into the girls' sad faces another minute longer.

"It's all right, Maria," Luciana consoled, wiping Maria's mouth with the bottom of her hospital gown. "I did the very same thing when I arrived here."

Maria, her bottom lip trembling and eyes filling with tears, turned to Luciana. "I need to go to the bathroom urgently. Where is it?"

"Bathroom!" someone sneered. While some of the girls laughed or snickered, others stared at the newcomer. One child pointed to the big barrel at the far end of the barracks. Maria sprinted towards it. As she got closer, the fetid odor assaulted her nostrils. The tub was full to the brim with feces. She felt like throwing up again. Unbeknown to her, dysentery was rife within the camp, threatening to infect her and the other inmates. But what choice did she have? She couldn't leave the barracks. She'd be shot. But doing what comes naturally in front of everyone else was dehumanizing for the crushed ten-year-old. But she accepted the situation understanding that she had no choice but to change in order to survive.

The remaining months of 1943 flew by.

The start of the New Year was just another day on the calendar for Maria. The now eleven-year-old had grown to love many of the camp faces who later had vanished from her life, including Luciana's. The girls were taken daily by hospital staff, just as Luciana had described, and they never returned. But their beds were soon filled with new faces from the nightly train arrivals. The loss of her best friends, Luciana and Bianca, was heartbreaking for Maria. She was lonely without them. The place felt empty, but it wasn't. Luciana and Bianca were connected to Maria's heart and soul. She would miss them, but life had to go on no matter what. Maria's once happy, privileged childhood was gone for good, destroyed beyond repair. Yet she considered herself lucky because she was tough. And she had promised Luciana she would survive. Luciana's last words to her were, "Live, Maria. Do what you have to do to survive. Tell the world what has happened here. I'll carry your love in my heart wherever I'm going."

Maria remembered how they had tearfully clung to each other until they were forcibly wrenched apart. The night Luciana didn't return from Mengele's hospital. Maria cried, "Dear friend, say hello to Bianca for me. I'll see you both in heaven."

Love is immortal ...

Shortly after losing Luciana, Maria was escorted by a kapo, but not to Mengele's hospital, as she had expected. Instead, she was frogmarched to the German officer in charge of the work force. As she entered his space, the stink of stale cigar smoke filled the air. Rudolf Hoess, the work force commandant, carried the same stench. The buttons of his immaculately pressed uniform protested his obesity. He looked at Maria as if she were nothing more than muck collected under his boot. "How old are you, Gypsy?"

"I'm eleven, I think," Maria replied in her best German. She asked, "What day and month is it?"

He shot her a filthy look, but then, for some unknown reason, obliged her. "It's January twenty."

Maria boldly fired back, "I am eleven. And I'm not a gypsy!"

His belly laughter cut through the room. "Really?" he said. "You don't look just eleven; you look at least sixteen." But in the blink of an eye, his amusement transformed into rage. Blood vessels mapped his ugly face and one of his neck veins pulsated visibly. He growled at Maria. "If Herr Doctor Mengele says you are a gypsy, then you are just that!"

His lecherous gaze, an undressing look, made Maia cringe. She had seen that look many times before. She stared down at her feet.

"Take the bitch away before I shoot her," the officer shouted to her escort.

Maria was more than glad to leave, but she wouldn't be too happy about the work Hoess assigned to her.

That night Maria slept soundly until the blinding light of a powerful flashlight woke her.

At 4:30 A.M., at the sound of the roll call gong, Maria was marched off to a drab, foul-smelling building at the other end of her barracks. What she saw there was horrifying: mountains of human hair, a large container of bloodied extracted gold teeth, child and adult clothing, and enormous stacks of shoes and suitcases. She was handed a striped, bloodstained prison uniform that looked as if it would fit her. She was thrilled to finally take off the threadbare evening dress, which she had been securing at her waist with a piece of string. She pulled the rough prison clothing tightly around her. It reeked of its previous owner's sweat, but the strong odor didn't faze her. Anything was better than the threadbare outfit—the sack—that she'd been forced to wear since she arrived at the camp. But she wasn't thrilled about her new job: stuffing human hair (for making socks) into bags.

As she began her task, she tried not to think about whose hair she was handling. But it was the brownish-black fleas—their constant, piercing, sucking bites on her ankles—that stressed her the most. When she couldn't take it anymore, she cried out, "I can't do this! Bugs are biting me ..."

Crunch! The truncheon hit Maria's scalp hard.

"Get on with your work!" the overseer ordered icily. "You should be thankful it's only fleas! If you don't want to taste shower gas, you better work harder. You're behind your quota for the day, and that's not good."

Another kapo piped up. "Yeah. You should be grateful the Commandant didn't assign you 'light' duties." Thankfully, Maria didn't understand. For if she had known that "light duty" was prostitution, she would have lost it.

No child or woman was safe from sexual violation in this abominable camp.

They were raped daily.

Maria reluctantly returned to her dreadful duties thinking, *If I get thumped on the head once more, I'm going to develop brain damage.* Her thought was not far from accurate. This would not be the last violent blow to Maria's cranium. She would suffer further head injuries, but not brain damage.

She couldn't have known that her speculation would one day become a surreal truth.

It was well past midnight when the exhausted child laborer, now covered in painful welts, was returned to the barracks. Maria fell into a dead sleep next to a stranger brought in during her absence.

The next morning, at the usual ungodly hour, Maria's hellish work schedule started all over again. This time she was given more tasks. She had to empty suitcases, examine clothing, look for hidden money or other valuables stitched inside garments. And she had another hardship to deal with. Against the odds, Maria was experiencing her first menstruation.

She was given old rags to stuff in her underwear. But she wasn't given anything for her thumping headache and intense cramping.

By December 1943, Maria had piled half a million suits and dresses and tens of thousands of eyeglasses. She had stuffed tons of hair into bags. The hard labor had aged her beyond her years. She was all grown up, and she felt old: cried out, shocked out, immune, and numb to the horror and sorrow of the gruesome goings-on taking place around her daily. They had become her everyday existence. Until ... one day it all changed.

A year later, as Maria was being escorted back to the barracks, the sky lit up with explosions, and titanic blasts shook the earth under her feet. Afraid, she hit the dirt.

"They are coming! They are coming!" her escort cried.

Bewildered by her attendant's energized, repetitive words, Maria asked, "Who's coming?"

"The Allies are coming, you stupid girl! Look over there," the woman said as she turned Maria's head. "See the flames. Those are from bombs. Soon, very soon, we'll be liberated."

What the woman told Maria didn't sink into her mind at first, and then ... *boom* ... it hit home.

Maria stood up, grabbed the kapo in a tango hold, and danced a happy dance with her in the snow.

It was over for Nazi Germany in December 1944. The German High Command ordered the staff to evacuate Auschwitz and leave no witnesses behind. Some prisoners were shipped by rail to Camp Dora. Sixty-thousand wretched souls were death marched out of the gates. Inmates too weak to stand were simply left behind. Maria was one of them. Mengele spotted Maria on her way back to her barracks. His smile was fiendish. Did he have time to perform one more experiment before he fled from the approaching Allies?

A naked Maria lay helpless on a gurney in Block 10 of the hospital's experimental unit. Her human parts were feeble, but not her mind. She knew she had joined the ranks of Mengele's "special" children.

Would she die like the rest? Would she be the exception? Would she live through whatever the doctor had in store for her? Would she survive to tell? Not if the man looming over her had his way. "Hello, Zigeuner," he smiled. "How is my Romany today?"

Maria didn't answer. Her heart was beating so fast, it drowned out all reason. Even though her jittery mind told her his voice was not mortal, she didn't take her eyes off the syringe he had in his hand. She had heard stories about lethal, phenol injections being plunged into hearts.

Panicked, she flew off the bed and tried to run out the door. With lightning speed Mengele snatched his seventy-pound victim in a vice hold. "Ah, we have a fighter," the vile demon scoffed. "We'll soon change that."

Strapped by the cot's leather restraints, Maria squeezed her eyes shut. Cringing inside, she awaited the doctor's next move. Seconds later, her screams shattered the stillness of the icy operating room. The chemical concoction injected into the iris of her right eye was excruciating. The second injection was just as bad, only this time he plunged a different syringe containing an unknown fluid into a neck artery. Finally, when Maria's brain could absorb no more pain, it shut down. She could hear her violent screams echoing in the recesses of her mind, but she felt nothing. And she wasn't aware of another presence entering the operating room. The tall, dashing male nurse and valet approached his mentor, Mengele. Without looking down at the patient, Günter Hornhauf, the man who had stolen Maria's virginity, touched Josef's arm and urged, "Herr Doctor, hurry. It's time to go. I have your suitcase."

A spasmodic twitch of Maria's arm toward Günter's waist made him look at the girl on the gurney. He bent and examined her closer. Did he know her? If so, where had he seen her before? Günter snapped his mind to attention. He didn't have the time to ponder these thoughts.

"Herr Doctor, we must leave now," Günter pleaded.

Mengele nodded in agreement, grabbed his scribbled notes, and shoved them into his briefcase. In the far corner of the operating room, he quickly undressed. His captain's uniform and doctor's coat lay rumpled on the floor. Disguised as a member of the regular German infantry, he slipped out the Auschwitz gate, his faithful servant at his side. Before getting into the waiting car, Mengele gave his last direct order to his medical assistant. It took one second.

Gott in Himmel (God in heaven), forgive me, were Günter's final words.

Maria, violently convulsing, was tossed out of the hospital unit by Günter into the freezing temperature. It was Christmas Day. Chilled to the bone, miniature icicles clung to Maria's bare flesh. Her life's blood seeped from a bullet wound in her head, turning the silent snowflakes into a myriad of pinkish shapes. Maria curled up in a fetal position. Miraculously, she was alive. The bullet had missed her brain entirely, exiting through the back of her skull.

An hour later Maria forced her frozen eyelashes open. Where was she? Who was she? What century was it? She remembered nothing. Was her amnesia a blessing?

Yes and no.

The unfortunate child became an android. In the days left in this horrible year, Maria walked aimlessly around the camp and slept in whatever bunk she could find. One frigid evening twelve-year old Maria Teresa Picasso Genovese, who had been wandering as if frozen in time, couldn't comprehend the excited chatter around her.

"They are gone!" one prisoner cried.

"The bastard Germans have fled!" yelled another.

"The war is over!"

Another inmate cried for revenge. "Every breathing German—man, woman, and child—should be shot."

"They are not all bad," someone said.

"Are you bloody nuts!" a Russian woman returned.

Unbelievably, there had been acts of courage and kindness, but on this day no one was willing to agree with the person who had defended the German race.

On January 27, 1945, the Auschwitz gate opened under a blanket of heavy snow. The liberating Russian army was shocked beyond belief when they looked into the emaciated faces and bodies of the silent, remaining survivors.

"These people are nothing but walking, breathing, living skeletons." a senior-ranking liberator said to a comrade.

"*Viva Ruski!*" a Russian prisoner shouted.

Some women dropped to their knees and kissed the soldiers' boots. The joyful scene appeared as a mirage to Maria. She hadn't a clue what was happening. But without hesitation she snatched the bar of chocolate handed to her. The Russians had located the stockpiled Red Cross parcels of food, clothing, and pharmaceutical supplies intended for the internees.

A stoic-looking Soviet first aid worker examined the delirious Maria. She was given powerful medication for the infectious malarial disease Mengele had injected into her bloodstream, antibiotics for the eye infection caused by the chemical dye injected into her eye to change its color, and medication for a sexually transmitted bacterial disease that was now full blown gonorrhea.

Two weeks later, when her body was able to tolerate some rich, fatty food—mostly items fried in pork fat furnished by the Allies—Maria regained a little of her lost body weight. That day she was told by her first aid worker that she was free to leave the camp. During all of her incarceration, Maria had never heard the word "camp," but it caused a question to cross her lips. "Where shall I go?" she asked.

"Go home. You have one hour to leave here," the medic replied.

"But this is my home," Maria returned.

He exhaled loudly. "Was," the official said. He had his work cut out for him in these foul surroundings. Some of the "left behind" survivors had typhus, dysentery, and had been infected by vermin and flea bites. All of the camp residents were lice infested.

"Next in line," he shouted.

CHAPTER NINETEEN

January 27, 1945, Liberation

"Thou shalt not be a victim, thou shalt not be a perpetrator, but, above all,
thou shalt not be a bystander."
—Yehuda Bauer

Maria, feeling physically stronger and wearing a thick soldier's coat, walked out of the gates following other lost souls. She had no idea where the others were headed, but she decided to tag along.

The frozen winter weather had been Maria's savior after she had been shot, and it would serve her well again on the walk to God-knows-where. But she had survived. She had beaten the odds. She would live, and, eventually, she would tell the world what had happened. She would keep her promise to Luciana from Catania. But there was no special key to unlocking her lost memory. She had endured so much evil, never knowing if love or hope would resurface or ever existed at all. The haunting legacy of child abuse bestowed upon her by human hands would remain with her until the day she died. The scars ran too deep.

Maria, twisted inside, would forever see the vivid faces of the evil monsters who had robbed her of her innocent childhood, many of whom would escape justice. Mengele was certainly one of them. His barbaric doctoring in Poland was at an end; it was believed he had caught typhus and died. Wrong!

Many years later it would be learned that Mengele used a fake identity to hide as a worker on a farm near his native Gunzburg. While he was there, he received word from his family that the Allies were not going to give up their search for the notorious war criminal. "You must leave the country, Josef," his father, Karl Mengele, had urged in a letter to his son. "Never come back. Your mother and I will miss you. We love you and are proud of you. With our dying breaths, we will never betray you."

With the net tightening around him, Mengele agreed to plan his escape from Germany. Financed by his father, he got a fake passport in the name of Helga Konig. He boarded a train to Austria disguised as a female. He crossed the Italian border on foot, and in Genoa in 1948 he boarded the *North Star*, an ocean liner bound for Argentina. Mengele would spend the next thirty years on the run.

Mengele escaped earthly judgment. Death, the act he had had so much control over, finally caught up with him. Supposedly, he drowned in 1979.

For Maria and the rest of the wicked doctor's victims, death wasn't good enough for the demon of Auschwitz. Forever after she would see Mengele's face along with other cruel faces from the past. She could never forget them, especially that of Günter Hornhauft. At the urging of his loved ones, he followed in Mengele's footsteps and skipped his country to God-knows-where. His whereabouts wouldn't remain a mystery for a long time.

And his demise would be far worse than that of his former boss.

Gott in Himmel!

CHAPTER TWENTY

Early February 1945, Bagnoli, Displaced Person Camp, Italy

"J'ai ecu — I survived.
—Abbé Emmanuel Sieyes

It was touch and go for the displaced refugees. Maria, like many others, was forced to travel a long, arduous distance on foot. Her feet became severely blistered, but in four weeks she made it to Bagnoli, a former Catholic orphanage now turned refugee camp on the western seaside district of Naples.

In the hospital at Bagnoli, which was run by the International Red Cross, she was given clean water, a small piece of cheese, and a spoonful of brown sugar—her first food in days. Then she was seen by the camp's doctor. On Maria's medical examination form he wrote:

EXAMINATION FORM

Unidentified gypsy female suffering from untreatable acute amnesia with severe malnutrition, vaginal disease, bullet wound infection, chronic eye infection (possible chemical burn).

Country of Origin: Unknown at this time. Unable to repatriate. Resettlement is unlikely.

Estimated Age: Fourteen.

Treatment: Penicillin.

Recommendation: Remain in camp until a further psychological evaluation can be performed.
—Dr. Charles Brown

Conditions were harsh in the refugee camp, leaving many legitimate uprooted souls sleeping on cold marble floors. Unbeknown to the Red Cross, hiding among the genuine needy were German and Italian soldiers who dreaded reprisal from the Allies. Everyone in the camp feared for their lives. Some were abused by other refugees. A number attempted suicide.

Maria wasn't exempt from the hardship and trepidation. She simply didn't know it existed. She spent most of her time lying still on her hospital cot staring up at the ceiling. Occasionally she walked around the ward.

One day as she was walking about, she heard moaning and went to see who it came from. A young man, writhing in pain, cried out for painkillers. Maria touched his bandaged head. "Why do you cry like a baby?"

Paolo's eyes widened in shock. He was stunned. There was no doubt in his mind. It was obvious that she had not recognized him or she would have said something. He risked it. "Maria, what are you doing here?"

"I don't know. Why do you call me Maria?"

"You mean you don't know who you are?"

"No. I can't remember."

A sigh of relief escaped Paolo's lips. The last time he had seen her was when he had handed her over to the child trafficker.

"What's wrong with you?" Maria asked plopping herself down on his cot.

"I was shot by a German."

"Oh, how awful," she said. "How many times did he shoot you?"

"Once ..." He sucked in a deep breath. "And the darn bullet is still in my skull."

"Then you'd be dead, silly," she said, with childish innocence. She had no idea that they had something in common; each of them miraculously escaped death by gunshot. But in her case the slug had not lodged. Instead, it went through and out. She did not know then that sometime in the future someone dear to her would also experience the trauma of being shot point blank and then live to tell the tale.

Paolo could only imagine what had happened to Maria after he had sold her to the trafficker, yet here she was sounding like the innocent little Maria he had known on the Genovese estate. But he cautioned himself. *What if she remembered? I'd be a dead man for sure.*

Paolo's thoughts were interrupted by a couple heading his way. Although moving his head hurt like hell, he shot upright. Could it be? No. It was too much of a coincidence. How could this happen? They had traveled three different paths for almost two and a half years! What were the odds of all of them ending up in the same camp? He was delusional from the pain, that's all. He gently placed his head back on his cot, but something made him sit back up. He looked again. His heart leapt out of his chest and his abdominal muscles tightened. "Mama, Papa," he cried.

Raphaela rushed to his side. She wore a glorious smile, one that could have captured the heart of Leonardo da Vinci. "It's my Paolo! Cesare, I've found him! He's injured!"

None the wiser, Maria quietly slipped away when the short woman appeared.

Raphaela smothered her son with kisses. "Oh, Paolo, thank God you are alive," she cried. She bent and hugged him. "You made it through the war. But what has happened to your head?" What her son had done to destroy her life in Sicily was the furthest thing from her mind. She said, "Look, Paolo. Papa is here too."

Cesare only half smiled. Deep in his heart he had hoped his son was dead. Had he not been the cause of him and his wife living their lives on the run? In a cool voice Cesare greeted his son. "Hello, Paolo."

Paolo felt his father's frigidness. He had to atone, and fast. "I'm sorry and ashamed for what I did. I would never have done such a thing if it wasn't for Teresa." He took a deep breath and asked, "Do you remember the *Normanne* girl who used to work at the mansion?"

His parents nodded in unison.

To save face, Paolo invented a tale straight from a scriptwriter's pen. It was her idea and hers alone. He didn't want to do it. He was bewitched. He was shot because of her. She was dead, thank God. His expression of internal pain for what he had taken part in continued. He had to convince his parents, wrap them around his little finger. "I'm still in danger. You see, Maria is here. But don't worry, she has a brain sickness. I'm pretty sure she doesn't remember me or anyone else."

Paolo didn't tell his mother the whole truth of what he had done to Maria, but what he did say was so convincing, his mother believed every word.

Raphaela's gloved hand clamped over her mouth and Cesare gasped loudly. "She's here?"

"Yes. Didn't you see her? She was by my bed when you came down here."

"No, no, no," Raphaela cried in disbelief. "Cesare, go and find her. See if she recognizes you."

Cesare walked away, shaking his head and muttering under his breath.

Raphaela's love for her child was unconditional. She forgave him. "Paolo, I love you with all my heart, but we have to move on from this tragedy or our lives will have been in vain."

"I agree, Mama. Tell me how you and Papa got off the island and what you've been doing until now?"

Raphaela closed her eyes for a moment. She didn't want to recall their flight from the island, or what had happened in the Nebrodi Mountains in Sicily. But she found herself explaining to her son their thirty months in exile: numerous train rides through Italy, finally ending up in a tiny town in the hills of Veneto in Northern Italy, the home of her distant cousin. She told her son how they had found work in the vineyards until a stranger came to town asking too many questions. Fearing it to be a Mafia informer, they hurriedly left Veneto, ending up in Bergamo. Feeling safer in the larger population of that Northern Italian city, Cesare found work as a butler and she as a cook in the home of an Italian General. But their positions crumbled to dust a few months later when the General became too inquisitive. Once more they fled. This time they were stopped at an Allied roadblock. Having no true identification, Cesare was quick to answer, "We are displaced Jews. The Germans took our identity documents at the labor camp."

The horrendous stories of death camps, death marches and

other dreadful goings-on, were on many Italian lips.

The American soldier, who was fluent in Italian, shook his head. They didn't look starved or frightened to him, but what the heck. They could be telling the truth. He passed Cesare a slip of paper with an address written on it. "Go there," he said. "The Red Cross will help you guys. Good luck."

After arriving at the Bagnoli Camp, Cesare had learned that it was an emigration processing camp and that leaving Italy for good was the best plan.

Paolo understood he had to come up with a viable strategy for his family.

Cesare combed the camp inch by inch until he spotted the girl his son proclaimed was Maria. With her head lowered to her chest, she was ambling aimlessly through a dormitory corridor. Cesare grabbed her arm and spun her around to face him. Even though she was older now and stick thin, there was no doubt she was Maria Genovese. But he had to be sure. "Hello, Maria from Solicchiata. Do you remember me?"

Dead eyes stared up at him with no recognition.

Convinced she hadn't a clue who he was, or even what he had said, Cesare returned to his wife and son and relayed to them the details of his meeting with Maria.

Paolo smiled in an "I-told-you-so" manner.

As the weeks flew by, Paolo became stronger, his pain lessening with a combination of medication and the constant support of his loving parents. But he couldn't get Maria out of his mind. What if she grows stronger and healthier? *What if she recognizes me on one of the daily walks required by the medical staff? What if ….?*

On a fine Sunday morning, after a restful sleep, Paolo was ready to divulge his cunning plan to his parents.

Paolo's parents, eyes wide, listened to his proposition. Blinded by her intense love for her son, Raphaela was easily persuaded. At first Cesare was hesitant, but in the end, he agreed it was the only solution for saving all their lives. So many other people had already been carted off by military officials to stand trial for one thing or another. Cesare was left with little choice.

At the camp's administration desk, Cesare glibly swore to the processing officer, "Yes, of course, I'm positive she's my daughter and he is my son."

CHAPTER TWENTY-ONE

Late February, Bon Voyage

"There are victories of the soul and spirit. Sometimes,
even if you lose, you win."
—Anonymous

The ocean liner *Rondane* was crammed with refugees as it sailed for South Africa in late February 1945. Among the passengers were the newly processed-for-immigration Girrdazzello family: Cesare, Raphaela, Paolo, and Maria. Oblivious to her new identity or her fake age—fourteen—she was happy to have a "family" who cared about her.

Paolo, recovering nicely from an emergency surgery that had removed the bullet from his head, was thrilled to be leaving his old life behind. He was no longer a wanted man with a target on his back. But there was no escaping his past. Maria was a constant reminder, and so was the memory of the depraved Father Rupolo who had molested him when he was a boy. He had learned through the grapevine that Father Rupolo had gotten his just reward, castration.

For the time being Maria was clueless of all that was happening and had happened. That suited Paolo just fine. But the image of a particular face still haunted him. Why had Teresa chosen that fancy restaurant the same night Maria had been sold? It was full of Germans guzzling Italian delicacies. One patron, a German captain, put down his fork and squinted at Teresa. He jumped up from the table and bellowed for all to hear, "That's the whore who stole my wallet."

The last things Paolo remembered were a loud bang and then the sight of Teresa's blood flowing across the floor. He couldn't recall the excruciating pain on the side of his head, or remember crawling under tables draped with long white tablecloths, or running down a dark alley, or the uncomfortable ride draped over a good Samaritan's bicycle handlebars. How he ended up in the displacement camp was another mystery. Maybe he and Maria did have something in common. Both had memory lapses. Some were convenient. Others were not.

Paolo leaned overboard and spewed his guts.

CHAPTER TWENTY-TWO

Late Fall 1998, the Genovese Estate

"Lift not the painted veil which those call Life."
—Shelley

"Mi desidero di non ricordare ... Mi desidero di no ricordare ..." Maria screamed.

Brianna jumped off her seat and placed her arms around her grandmother. "What did you say?

"Child, I don't want to remember, but I can't stop."

In graphic detail Maria told Brianna about her enforced life on the Hallworthy plantation (which included continual child sexual assaults), her escape, the birthing of the evil Lord's twins (one of which was Brianna's mother), and her encounter with Anele (the runaway slave who saved Brianna's mother from a shallow grave, then raised her in her village until Lord Hallworthy found the girl and claimed her as his own—in every way.)

Brianna had heard much of this before, from her mother's tape recordings. History had repeated itself within their bloodline. Maria and Shiya, mother and daughter, had both been victimized by the evil Lord Hallworthy.

Maria continued her story, picking up at the point where she had made up her mind to separate from Anele before the runaway servant discovered the truth, the real reason for the blood streaming down the inside of her thighs.

As soon as Anele, her only friend, left their hiding place to search for an African medicine woman, Maria swapped her own blood-stained dress for Anele's kitchen uniform. It was way too big for her, but where there is a will, there is a way. Maria lifted the skirt, rolled up some of the length, and tucked the excess material into the waistband. As she was fashioning a knot to one side of the improvised outfit, something fell to the cave floor. Maria's eyes lit up when she realized it was money. Would this be enough to pay for her passage home to Italy? She hoped so.

A few moments later a laughably-attired Maria exited the cave with no other thought in mind than finding a way back to her homeland.

Like a doe unaware of danger lurking in nearby grass, Maria sprinted down an animal-trodden pathway leading to nowhere she was familiar with. After walking for what felt like ages, her dry skin, lips, and mouth didn't even faze her. The thought of drinking replenishing water was the last thing on her mind. Unaware that the copious amounts of blood flowing from her post-birth canal caused her to suffer from dehydration, she obliviously weaved in and out of clumps of thorn trees. Out in the open with no tall grass or trees to shade her from the blistering sun, she picked up speed and ran as if she were competing in a marathon. Unaware that her blood pressure was dropping dangerously, she continued along a hard-crusted pathway.

Maria neither saw it nor heard it, until she ran headlong into it ... a bush truck that seemed to have appeared out of nowhere. The driver didn't bat an eyelid at the twig-like figure that had been tossed into the air like a windswept leaf, ultimately hitting hard on the metal hood of his truck and then thudding to the earth. The driver exited the vehicle. His euphoric laughter pounced on the dazed, sprawled Maria as her hands clutched her bloodied scalp, injured by the violent impact of flesh hammering into metal.

"Gotcha," Alan gloated in a sneering tone. He showed no spark of human concern as he straddled his 110-pound victory to check out her condition. Maria wanted to scream, *Oh, no. Not him!* She wanted to throw herself at Alan like a crazed cat, but she had little choice but to remain prone. No matter how hard she tried to get up, she couldn't move a muscle. It seemed that her wounded head and the rest of her scrawny body were frozen to the ground. As lethargic breaths escaped her lungs, blood slowly trickled from the gash in her head.

Alan bent down and poked Maria's pliable abdomen with his index finger. Instantly, a deep frown creased his tanned forehead. Her belly felt like the consistency of unset gelatin. Then it hit him. "Where's my fucking baby?" he screamed. "What have you done with it?"

Maria wasn't going to answer him.

Not giving Maria's injury or immobilization a second thought, Alan hog-tied her with a rope and secured her restraints to the vehicle's bumper. Spitting nails, a demonically possessed Alan began to retrace her dusty footsteps in the sandy soil, as methodically as a bloodhound. The footprints led him to the hideaway, the cave in which Anele and Maria had found refuge. A deep frown creased his tan forehead when he spotted a second set of footprints, larger and flat-footed. He had some knowledge of these types of prints. He had located many black runaways by the flatness of their feet. No doubt, these prints were African. What bothered him most, though, was that he had recently searched this very spot on horseback, not realizing Anele and Maria had been there all along.

Alan followed the large footprints of his former servant as far as he could … until they disappeared into thin air. She was long gone. But he set his determination that day. He would not give up searching for his runaway. The idea of scratching her name on a shotgun shell pleased his sick mind immensely.

The blood vessels on Alan's neck pulsated with uncontrolled rage as he made his way back to the now semiconscious Maria. From the back of his truck he removed a can of kerosene. After dousing the lifeless Maria with the flammable liquid, he lit a match.

Powers beyond human comprehension—Maria's guardian angel, perhaps—intervened and triggered Maria's survival instinct … a fight-or-flight response intended to keep her alive. Adrenalin released into her blood stream like a burst dam, prompting her to extinguish the flames by rolling in dirt. But her impulse for self-preservation wasn't enough to save her from further heartache.

With raw flaps of skin dripping down her face, Alan picked her up violently and threw her onto the back seat of his truck. The feeling she had had in Auschwitz that she might be thumped on the head once too often came true. Her mind emptied like a drainpipe, leaving nothing but a vacant void in her damaged skull. Maria's eyelids closed slowly. Her spirit floated into the domicile of dead souls.

Alan drove at breakneck speed toward the estate and to the cottage, where he flung the shallowly breathing girl onto the bed, locked the door, and drove to the manor house. Once there, he telephoned an unemployed East Indian doctor who was new to the area and living in a shantytown thirty miles from the estate's borders. Alan decided to take advantage of the fact that the young physician, having been being classified as colored, was having difficulty finding work. Alan offered to pick him up.

Within an hour, Dr. Singh, age thirty-two and fashionably dressed in ethnic Indian apparel, entered the cottage. What he saw not only unsettled his compassionate heart but also confounded his medical expertise. He wasn't prepared for such a serious medical emergency.

"Well, can you mend her?" Hallworthy asked in a lifeless tone.

"I'll have to examine her first."

Singh placed his doctor's bag on the floor and checked to see if the girl was breathing. He then covered Maria with a blanket to prevent her from going deeper into shock. The child had serious third-degree burns on one side of her face. Typically, healing from severe burns is a slow process because of the destruction of the skin's tissue. If untreated, these burns could cause extensive scarring. The doctor noted the deep gash on her head caused by blunt trauma (by Maria's head smashing into Alan's truck) and began covering Maria's burns the best he could with a moist sterile bandage. Then he checked her nose and ears for bleeding, a common symptom associated with head fractures. Was there bleeding in her brain? He could not know for sure. But he was sure of one thing: Alan's explanation that she had done this to herself—that she had tried to commit suicide—was impossible. What a lie!

Without even knowing it, Maria had gained an ally.

On further examination, the doctor was shocked to discover that this slip of a child had recently given birth. He didn't know where the baby was, but he suspected Alan was the father. If only he could do something, report this man to the police, do something to help Maria, but his hands were tied politically. Uncomfortable with the situation, he opted to say nothing, do his duty, and live up to the oath he had sworn.

Prior to this house call, Dr. Singh had heard horrendous stories about Hallworthy abusing his servants. At first he didn't believe them. *A descendant of royal English blood could never do such a thing*, he had thought. But Alan was one of the coldest people he had ever come across. And he had seen with his own eyes this man's capacity to injure. Only five days ago the doctor had stitched a lash cut on a field worker's arm. But this situation was different. He had seen her tattoo. She wasn't colored. She was white … and Jewish.

"Can you hear me?" Dr. Singh asked Maria.

The girl stirred. She suffered from a dry mouth, an intense thirst, and numb fingers. She stared at the white-coated man. "Was I in an accident? Was I in an accident?" she repeated.

Alarm bells sounded in Singh's head. What the long-term prognosis would be from this head injury he did not know. He urged Alan, "Sir, I've done all I can. She needs to go to the hospital or she will die."

Alan didn't care if she lived or died. But his inner voice reminded him that Maria could lead him to his missing newborn.

He threw his hands in the air and threatened the doctor. "Okay. But you better keep your mouth shut, if you know what's good for you! Or you'll meet Buddha sooner than you had planned!"

After the belittlement, Dr. Singh gave Alan a wan smile and then averted his eyes from the Lord's intimidating glare. He picked up the payment offered and placed it in his pocket. He grabbed his medical bag, exited the cottage, and headed toward his home, understanding that Alan would take the girl to the hospital. He wanted desperately to report the abuser and save this poor child, but who would listen to him? He was just an immigrant doctor trying to support his family in a country that judges skin color, not medical degrees. He wanted to vow never to return to this plantation, but he knew that someday his services might again be needed in this godforsaken place.

While Maria's broken body lay in purgatory on the cottage bed, her spirit temporarily absent of life, Dr. Singh returned to his home and documented what he had seen and done. His detailed journal notes, together with those of a psychiatrist, and, later, Dr. Mubani, who had also attended to Alan's victims, would be offered as evidence in a future sensational criminal trial. The Hallworthy name would become mud.

CHAPTER TWENTY-THREE

Boxing Day 1945, Saint Vincent de Paul Asylum, Durban, South Africa

"Something is dead in each of us, and what was dead was Hope."
—Oscar Wilde

Maria slipped in and out of unconsciousness as she was carried by Alan into a bleak, rundown, brick building. A black nun wearing a white doctor's coat over her habit rushed to meet him. "What happened?"

"All I know is her name is Maria. I believe she is sixteen, maybe seventeen," Alan said. "She's a migrant worker on my plantation. I found her lying in one of my fields all cut up. This is the nearest black hospital."

The nun sized up the East Indian looking girl dangling limply in Alan's arms. "We are not a medical facility, sir. We treat only the mentally afflicted. But she looks in bad shape. Follow me. Dr. Pataki, our resident doctor and psychiatrist, might be able to help."

The Devil Hallworthy wears many disguises; this time he came posing as a good Samaritan.

"Let me introduce myself. I'm Lord Alan Hallworthy of the Hallworthy Plantation. I have more than sufficient field workers to run my place, but months ago I took Maria and her destitute family in because I felt sorry for them, especially her," he said as he looked at the girl with an actor's compassion. "I was told that she was brain damaged at birth. So you can imagine my surprise when her colored family suddenly left my farm without her. That's probably why she tried to commit suicide. Whatever it takes, I'll pay for this poor girl to get the medical and mental help she needs."

"God bless you, Lord Hallworthy," the admittance nun responded respectfully. "We'll do our best to give this child all the help we can." She wanted to add, *I wish there were more kind white people like you*, but was interrupted.

Alan said, "I have to dash. Where can I put her?"

Sister Tulane pointed to a gurney. "There, please."

Alan dug into his jacket pocket, pulled out his checkbook, wrote an amount, and handed it to the nun. "This should help pay for her care."

With eyes as big as saucers, the sister stared at the amount: £1,000. What a godsend. The asylum for colored folk depended on charitable donations. The astonished nun gushed, "God bless you and thank you for your most generous donation."

When the nun tried to kiss his hand, the prejudiced Alan pulled it away in disgust.

"My telephone number is in the book," he said straight-faced. "I want to know her progress, and she's not to be released without my knowledge."

The nun didn't think twice about his bizarre request for information about someone he hardly knew. In her estimation, he was a saint. "Of course, Lord Hallworthy," she replied. "She will be well looked after mentally and physically, confined here until further notice."

Her words were hollow in his ears.

The charity-run hospital lacked the necessary X-ray or other scanning equipment necessary for neuropsychological testing, so when the elderly resident psychiatrist, Dr. Pataki, examined Maria, his hands were tied. However, he was thankful for the emergency room training he had completed in Pakistan before he decided to specialize in mental health. That instruction proved to be a blessing in disguise. First, he would treat her physical wounds. Because Maria's head wound was deep, the doctor couldn't investigate it internally. He hoped stitching and bandaging would suffice.

His patient's burned cheek flesh caused the doctor to question the validity of Alan's suicide story. The explanation didn't seem to contain a morsel of truth. With many years of practice behind him, Dr. Pataki was convinced that Maria's youthful mind, no matter how sick, could not have conjured up a bizarre dousing method designed to end her life. He noted the difference in Maria's eye color and the retinal burn, but he didn't pay much attention to her tattoo because the atrocities of the Holocaust hadn't yet been fully exposed by the South Africa media. Living under enforced segregation was more than enough for the mild-mannered doctor to digest. He also noted what looked like a bullet wound scar to her head. He couldn't imagine such a young girl having been shot in the past.

The hospital staff had no training in intensive care techniques, but under Dr. Pataki's supervision, they monitored Maria the best they could. The nurses were unaware of her medical history, the numerous blunt force traumas she had received in her short life. Maria remained comatose. She was hooked up to an IV to replace lost fluids and was numbed with a cocktail of sedatives. She lay at death's door, and her prognosis was poor.

Time slipped by with little progress in Maria's condition. The asylum's 1946 New Year's festivities remained uncelebrated by the brain-numbed girl, who turned thirteen on January 3. When Maria finally regained consciousness in the middle of the month, she was disoriented and confused. She had no idea where she was or who she was, yet again! Through blurred vision she looked around but became no wiser.

Later, when her physical injuries were much improved, Maria was released into the general hospital population and fell into despair. Lunatics touched her exposed welts. After having been treated for infection, the scarring was prominently raised. Some of the elderly souls afflicted with Alzheimer's, Parkinson's, or other unknown and untreatable ailments, simply stared at her. The nursing staff ignored her. The nuns were far too busy praying for the lost girl's soul to interact with her. Maria's days were spent taking medicine and staring blankly out of barred windows. She took no heed of a demented woman who repeatedly sang *"God bless Africa. Raise her spirit … Hear our prayers … Bless us."*

One dark day toward the end of January, with her fingers interlaced and placed neatly on her lap, Maria sat in her usual spot by the window gazing onto the concrete courtyard. Her memory was repressed, and she wasn't bothered by the heavy rains lashing at the windows. She didn't notice that the rainstorm was coloring the hospital lawns a deep, dark green. Nor did she flinch when lightning cracked through the gloomy skies. She simply sat alone in a corner rocking from side to side.

Her lonely presence was not unnoticed.

A German immigrant newly employed as casual labor came on duty. He stood behind a glass partition and began placing medications into paper cups. The day nurse gathered the patients and ordered them to line up to receive their doses. A look of fright paled Günter's face when it was Maria's turn at the dispensary. He stared at the tall, skinny, maimed girl with different eye colors. *Gott in Himmel! No. It can't be! It's impossible! Could it be?*

As she reached for her cup through the gap in the partition, Günter grabbed her arm, rolled up her sleeve, and saw "Z19800." He gasped so loud the pharmaceutical nurse rushed to his side.

"What's the matter, Günter? You look like you've seen a ghost." She stared at him and then at Maria, who was writhing under Günter's tight grip. "Do you know her?" the nurse asked the astonished man.

In shock and not thinking clearly, he quickly answered, "I don't think so." As his head cleared, he added, "But she does bear the identification mark of the same concentration camp where I was imprisoned."

"It must have been horrible for you, Günter," the nurse commiserated. "It's a blessing you got out alive and were able to make a new life here in South Africa."

The proverbial penny dropped. The nurse was hit with a wake-up call. She rushed out of the dispensary, latched on to Maria's arm, pulled up her sleeve, and stared at her tattoo. She gasped. "She's Jewish, not colored! I better go and see Mother Superior so she can notify the Jewish authorities."

Günter reacted quickly. "She's not a Jew. Her marking is that of a gypsy. In Germany that means she is colored."

"So she does belong here," the nurse agreed. "But the poor girl doesn't know what class she is. She has no memory. She's brain damaged."

Günter let out a sigh of relief. His fake identity as a Jewish refugee was not blown, and his previous occupation would not be revealed. It had taken him over a year to find this menial position. This country was swamped with refugees, and jobs were few and far between. In the meanwhile, his savings had dwindled. Thankfully, the head nun had swallowed his concocted story of his persecution in Germany, his lack of money, and his need for food and lodging. But she pointed out a potential problem. Under a South African political ruling, no black hospital, clinic, or sanatorium could employ whites. But her faith wouldn't let her abandon a soul in need. So she was prepared to break the rules for Günter. He looked so desperate. And if the hospital got wind of an outside inspection, she would simply hide him in her room.

Günter watched Maria return to her favorite spot. Her memory was damaged, thank God, but there was nothing wrong with his. He had taken her virginity in the military quarters in Rome. He was witness to the surgery performed on her to change her eye color, and, under orders, he had fired what he thought would be a murderous shot into her head. Never in his wildest dreams could he have imagined that the girl had survived.

"*Gott in Himmel*, forgive me, but I need your help," he mumbled as he made his way to the nurse's station.

When no one was around, he opened the filing cabinet, removed Maria's file, and hid it under his white coat. Back in his modest apartment on the hospital grounds, he read the file:

```
"MIGRANT FEMALE: Known as Maria
SURNAME: Unknown
   RACE: Colored
   AGE: (16?)
   COUNTRY OF ORIGIN: Unknown"
```

Her medical history listed her recent accident injuries. It continued with visible previous injuries, vaginal birth scarring, ongoing treatments, prescribed medications, and her psychological condition.

```
"NOTE: High risk—suicidal."
```

Even though Maria's amnesiac condition gave him breathing room, Günter Hornhauf wasn't sure what her condition would be in the future. What if she regained her memory? What if she recognized him? What if she blew the whistle? The Nazi net was being spread relentlessly throughout the world. A part of Günter wished he had never been brainwashed into believing Hitler's ideology, or joined the *Nationalsozialistische Deutsche Arbeiterpartei (Nazi party)* at his parents' insistence. He had dropped out of nursing school to join the army and had been decorated for bravery after the Polish invasion of 1939. After being slightly injured, he was sent to Rome. He wasn't happy about that job, valet to a high-ranking official. It was a huge letdown after soaking up the glory of his bravery. But he had learned never to ask questions. He was allowed, however, to continue his nursing studies, and that is how he became Mengele's assistant at the Auschwitz death camp.

After the war the net began to tighten around Günter and the other Nazi war criminals. Scared for his life, his parents gave him money to flee to South Africa. Using a fake passport, he entered the country as a Jewish refugee. He had had gotten away with his deceit, until now. He had drastically changed his appearance by shaving off his blond hair and moustache. He disguised his blue eyes with green contact lens, and he lost a lot of weight. But he knew he could be identified as a Nazi officer by the swastika tattoo under his armpit.

Things had taken a turn for the worse because of Maria. He couldn't risk losing his perfect cover and hiding place. The girl had to disappear. But how could he make that happen? Günter's mind raced. He could "doctor" her medication. Put a pillow over her head and smother her. Hang her in the bathroom. After all, she was listed as suicidal.

Stressed to the point of nervous exhaustion, Günter decided to sleep on it and make a decision in the morning. But sleep didn't come easily to the escaped Nazi war criminal. Nightmare after nightmare tormented him. Fingers of the dead pointed at him, grabbed him, and threw him into the same ovens they had been burned alive in.

While Günter was experiencing a nightmarish hell, Maria was wide awake, with a soft blue light from the beyond hovering over her. What she faced was not a dream, but reality. The hospital psychiatrist had miscalculated Maria's powers of recovery. *God works in mysterious ways.* Miraculously, she knew who the medicine dispenser was. Without warning, a blinding headache crushed her skull. She gripped the sides of her head and squeezed mightily to force out the pressure. As if the past became the present, Maria began to remember everything from her early childhood up to the present. But the images her brain released were more than she could handle. She screamed and screamed. Suddenly a flashlight blinded her. "Shut up!" the orderly ordered. "You'll wake everyone else."

Even though she had been programmed to be submissively locked up, Maria's body and mind had suffered enough cruelty. She went into survival mode, a superhuman spiritual endurance that she had mustered and utilized for years, starting with the day she was abducted from her home. Being headstrong with an unending will to live, she had survived a child-trafficker, the loss of her virginity, life as a child prostitute, a notorious death camp, a displacement camp full of fragile survivors, sexual violation by Alan Hallworthy, and childbirth at a tender age. Having gone through so much in thirteen years, she couldn't sit back and let what was left of her life fall to pieces. No. She would be strong and scheme her way out of this enforced confinement. At that moment, Maria felt ancient. Then a clear, sharp picture developed in her mind. *Will it work? It has to, or I will be lost forever.*

The next morning Maria waited her turn in line. As she faced the glass partition, a smiling Günter handed her a paper cup. His cheerful face soon vanished. Maria latched on to his wrist and in perfect German murmured, "I know who you are. How could I ever forget the man who raped me and shot me? If you want to save yourself, then you will help me get out of here."

His shocked expression boosted Maria's courage. She continued. "Don't try anything stupid," she threatened. "That would be unwise because I've written down everything you did to me. If anything happens to me now, my detailed notes will hang your pathetic arse."

For a moment, Günter was speechless. Then he drew close and whispered in her ear, "I'll meet you in the garden near the fountain when I'm done here."

Maria nodded in agreement. She felt nothing but utter disgust for this despicable animal. He had robbed her of her innocence, taken her virginity. And he was her failed executioner.

I hope he rots in hell! There will be no God in heaven for the likes of him.

On Sunday morning when everyone else was attending services at St. Mary's chapel, Maria, wearing a nun's habit, slipped out of the unlocked gates. Down the road an old Ford sedan idled, spewing gas fumes. The driver was impatient.

"*Schnell* ... Hurry up," Günter shouted out the window.

Maria scrambled into the vehicle and slouched in the rear seat. The driver extended his arm and passed an envelope to her. "It's the best I could do on short notice," Günter said. "Now go."

Maria opened the flap and stared at the wad of crisp English pound notes. She was at a loss. She didn't know what their value was or if the total was enough to get her out of the country. A shiver of fear prickled her spine. "You are going to have to hide me at your place until I can sort my head out."

"Impossible," he exclaimed. "I live on the grounds, Maria. It would be an obvious place for them to check."

Angry, Maria threw back her head and said with heat, "Then you'll have to find a way. Take me somewhere away from here."

At his wits' end, Günter scratched his chin. One possible plan was to kill her and throw her body onto the road, but his conscience stopped him from executing it. He became overwhelmed with guilt at what he had done to the girl. Instead, he longed for her forgiveness. He'd do anything to get it, even if it meant risking his own life.

A Nazi with a heart?

Günter's white knuckles gripped the steering wheel tightly as he drove the car into the city of Durban with Maria hidden in the trunk. An hour later, under the cloak of darkness, the odd couple entered a high-rise building in an affluent area. They rode the elevator to the sixteenth floor. Günter knocked three times on the door marked "1601." After a brief moment, the door opened a fraction. A buxom woman with a fleshy abdomen glared at Günter. "I told you never to come back here!"

She slammed the door shut.

Günter pressed the buzzer. This time the woman, displaying a red, emotional face and protruding blood vessels, noticed Maria and looked her over. The woman wanted to laugh at the girl's ridiculous, ill-fitting outfit. The black-and-white nun's habit hung in folds over her bare feet, and was being held together by a braided cord belt and a dangling crucifix. The starched white bib was askew, and the *wimple* (stiff head covering) reminded Bronislaw of a sixteenth century French peasant headdress. "Why is this kid wearing this outlandish outfit?" she asked Günter. "She's no more a nun than I am!"

Maria stared at the woman's sagging jowls. They were bouncing like a turkey as she traded heated words with Günter. He argued, "It was the only way she could get out of the asylum. She's not mad. She's a camp survivor. She needs help, Bronislaw. I didn't know where else to take her but here."

When a door opened down the corridor and a nosey neighbor popped her head out, Bronislaw quickly said, "Come in."

Ushered into a nice apartment filled with creature comforts, Maria immediately felt at home. She headed to a white sofa, sunk down onto the soft leather, pulled off the black-and-white headdress, and flung it to the side. She ran her fingers over her head. Her sweaty, braided hair felt like straw. Oh, how she longed for the smell of the lavender shampoo her mother, Sofia, had used on her. The thought of her dear mother brought tears to Maria's eyes. Would she ever see her again? Would she hear her beautiful singing voice? Her thoughts then drifted to her father. Could she forgive him? Could she hug him without wanting to kill him? Paolo had said, "He doesn't give a shit about you, Maria, because if he did, he would have paid any amount of money to get you back."

Not knowing what the future held, Maria blocked out these family reflections and waited for the heated German voices to die down.

She was in for a surprise.

Maria's eyes darted around the room. She saw several framed photographs on a sideboard. But one picture in particular caught her attention. She got up to examine it. Her eyes went wide. She gasped. Could it be? Was it really her, or was her own weakened state of mind playing tricks on her? No.

Maria rushed up and flung her arms around the big woman. There were tears rolling down her cheeks when she said, "*Mamusia*. Mother of the camp, I remember you. I'm Maria, one of Mengele's girls. You used to bring us food."

Bronislaw's unplucked, unruly eyebrows locked in a deep frown. She held Maria at arm's length, looking over every inch of the girl. "Yes, yes. You're the gypsy girl who told me such wonderful tales about the island of Sicily."

"Oh, Bronislaw," Maria sighed. "I'm not a gypsy."

While immersed in their dreadful, intertwined past, Bronislaw and Maria didn't notice Günter slipping out of the apartment. With his head lowered, he proceeded to his car and drove away, racing down back streets as if his life depended upon his speed.

Back in the relative calm of Bronislaw's apartment, Maria clasped Bronislaw's hand tightly and led her to the couch. Sitting close, Maria told the kindly ex-prisoner how she ended up in South Africa. And Bronislaw reciprocated with an astounding story of her own.

Shortly before the war ended, Bronislaw had fallen in love with a German officer. They met when she was making a new uniform for him. Under a cloak of secrecy they met and made love. When he received orders to flee the camp, Bronislaw's soldier-lover tearfully informed her that it would be the last time they'd be together. She couldn't bear the thought of losing him and begged him to smuggle her out with him. It couldn't be done, he had said. But before he left, he had handed her a metal tin. To her amazement it was filled with uncut diamonds.

At the end of the war Bronislaw, the daughter of a high-ranking Polish official, was branded a German whore by witnesses who wanted more than a pound of flesh. They wanted her tried with the other war criminals. Shamed and in fear of her life, she decided not to return home to Skwierzyna in the far province of Lubuskie. Instead, she sold some of her diamonds to a Russian general and sewed the five thousand zlotys he paid for them into her bodice. She hid the rest of the diamonds in her padded bra. Bronislaw then swapped her life in war-torn Europe for a life in South Africa. She married a South African, got divorced, and began to hit the bottle.

Maria couldn't have been happier in the days that followed, safe and comfortable in her guardian's home. She had a roommate, a mother figure, a best friend, and someone who understood her and what she had been through. And she had left the ugliness of the sanitarium behind—though she did not abandon her secrets.

Back at the asylum, Maria's disappearance was the talk of the staff. Somehow, Alan got wind of it. Dr. Pataki had to face Maria's enraged "guardian." Alan went berserk. "How could this have happened?" he snarled. "How could she simply disappear from this so-called secure facility?"

The psychiatrist responded honestly. "I'm just as baffled as you are, Lord Hallworthy. This has never happened before, not since I've been in charge. The police have been notified. I'm sure they'll find her." In the back of his mind, though, the doctor wanted to put this man in restraints, perform a lobotomy on him, and rid the world of his evil.

"You're not getting another penny from me until you find her and bring her back here where she belongs."

Dr. Pataki didn't know how to respond. Alan's healthy donations had helped to renovate the aged 1827 building, which had once served as a holding pen for slaves. Even though medical ethics nudged at his conscience, the conflicted doctor couldn't let the money source dry up, so he broke a cardinal rule. Betraying his patient to gain riches, he bit the inside of his cheek and said, "Maria is probably trying to return to the place where she buried the twins."

The look on Alan's face could have sunk a battleship.

"Twins!" he shouted. "What fucking twins?"

Alan's shocked reaction was the doctor's cue. After all, it was his job to read between the lines. He knew Hallworthy was the father of Maria's twins. During a therapy session Maria had mentioned a woman with an African name. "A Zulu woman, her name is Anele Dingane and ..." The doctor nearly jumped out of his skin when Alan slammed his fist on the desk with force.

"I know that bitch!" screamed Alan. With that he stormed out of the office, hurling foul language into the air. Taking off like an enraged bull elephant, he nearly knocked over a janitor mopping the steps. "Get out of my way, *kaffir!*" Alan roared.

"Sorry, *baas,*" Kumdi apologized in a strong Zulu accent. Little did the servant know this would not be the last time he would see this irate white man. Or that he'd be fired from his job and forced to return home to Zululand. Eventually, Kumdi would become a scorned wannabe chieftain in Tswanas Kraal, Anele's home village.

After Anele ran away from Alan Hallworthy, she returned to Tswanas with Shiya, the newborn baby Maria had left for dead. Five years later, Kumdi would betray both Anele and Shiya by playing a part in the abduction of the loved and contented girl by her evil biological father, Alan Hallworthy.

CHAPTER TWENTY-FOUR

Wanted by the Police

"I have not yet begun to fight."
—John Paul Jones

Police "Wanted" posters of Maria's scarred face were planted everywhere. Her crimes were listed as felony theft, illegal immigration, and, the most damning, murder of an unborn child. Living as a virtual prisoner now, the trapped girl soon became bored. She begged the well-educated Bronislaw to teach her and help her study so she could one day achieve her dream of becoming a doctor. Her guardian was happy to oblige. She purchased every high school textbook she could lay her hands on, along with anatomy and physiology books checked out from the local library.

Maria was every teacher's dream, an adept, determined student who had the potential to choose any career she wished. But even with her remarkable acceleration to an eighth grade level, Maria realized her learning was pointless. She could never receive a legitimate graduation certificate, and she couldn't enter an honorable profession without one. Bronislaw was heartbroken at Maria's change of heart. But it didn't stop her from filling Maria's head with other forms of education. She introduced her to Shakespeare,

Greek mythology, Roman history, and anything else she felt would keep her pupil's bright mind sharp.

Over time the two displaced refugees spoke of many new things, no longer dwelling on their ugly pasts. Forgive and forget became their motto. Maria was willing to block out everything that had happened to her except one event—the birth of her babies … and her abandonment of them when she buried them alive in a shallow grave, hoping desperately to spare them the painful reality of her life. The hole in her maturing heart ran deep.

One morning, in the early hours, Maria's nightmarish screams brought Bronislaw rushing to her bedside. Maria's protector soothed, "Hush, *dziecko*, (child)," as she cradled the shaking girl to her large bosom. Bronislaw didn't have to ask. It was obvious. Nightmares from the death camp disturbed her own sleep, too, regularly. But the woman wasn't prepared for what her ward was about to reveal.

"I didn't know what to do. I buried the twin girls," Maria confessed. "I don't know if they were both dead. I'm sure the first one was." She fiercely scrunched the top sheet on her bed. "They hate me. They hate me. I can feel it. I didn't mean it …" her voice trailed. "I didn't mean it." Maria looked up at the ceiling and added, "If it takes the rest of my life, I'll make everyone who destroyed my innocence and my life pay. I'll get my pound of flesh."

Bronislaw hid her shock with a soft voice. "*Szlachetne dzieko* (precious child), your babies don't hate you. They are joined to you with their invisible umbilical cords and are being cared for by mothering angels in heaven." She continued comfortingly, "It's not your fault. Maybe it was for the best. You have your whole life ahead of you to have more babies and know a mother's bond."

A tearful Maria shook her head. Nothing Bronislaw said or did could ever erase what she had done. She could not know that one of her babies, Shiya, had survived and was being happily raised by Anele in Tswanas Kraal, Zululand. But that would all change in 1950. Shiya would become a victim of evil circumstances, as had Maria, her biological mother.

The Genovese legacy—curse—had found a surrogate host, Lord Alan Hallworthy. Already blighted by the manor's bad omens, he would stop at nothing to find what belonged to him.

History, in fact, repeats itself.

CHAPTER TWENTY-FIVE

Six Years Later, 1951

"There are no coincidences in life."
—Shannon Alder

On a rainy morning, Maria's mentor and only trusted friend, Bronislaw, left the apartment to go grocery shopping, as she normally did on weekends. She always brought back new clothing or some other delight for her now twenty-two-year-old roommate. Even with Maria's visible facial scars and different eye colors—one blue, one green—she was attractive. She was over six feet tall and slim, in spite of Bronislaw's fattening Polish meals. Her black, flowing, waist-length hair glistened like a raven's feathers. And her dark, olive skin had turned marble white due to a lack of sunlight. Racially, Maria now looked more British than Mediterranean.

Despite Maria's attractive qualities, no Mona Lisa smiles would be accompanying her new, maturing look. Her unrelenting inner pain, her torment from the past, ensured that her smiles would only appear when they were needed to appease others.

Being cooped up for so many years had not been easy for Maria. She longed to walk in the sunshine along the beach that she viewed daily from the window. She hungered for a swim in

the aquamarine waters of the Indian Ocean. She yearned for a female companion of the same age (boys were the furthest from her
mind). But mostly, she ached for her parents, her home in Sicily,
and the smell of harvested olives.

Maria couldn't admit she had any outer beauty. She felt she
looked like a scary freak. She was an illegal immigrant on the run
from the wicked Alan Hallworthy, and, according to him, she
was a child murderer. Maria realized he would never give up his
hunt for her. She had little choice but to accept her lot, just like his
other victims had. So she waited patiently for Bronislaw to return
with some tasty food and another surprise. But what Bronislaw
returned home with this time was more than Maria could have
expected.

When Maria heard the key turn, she rushed to the door to
help her friend with the groceries. She looked down at Bronislaw's
empty hands and frowned. "Where's the shopping bags," she asked.

Bronislaw didn't reply straight away, but she smiled broadly.
She shut the front door behind her and walked over to the kitchen
table. She removed a package from her handbag and announced,
"This is for you, *szlachetne dzieko*." She handed the mysterious
brown envelope to Maria.

With a baffled look, Maria hurriedly opened it. The contents
bearing her name brought a squeal of delight. "Is this real?"

"Yes. That's your new passport. I'm sending you home. That is
where you belong, young lady. But I must say that I have dreaded
this day for years because your youthful spirit, laughter, and love
have made my life more bearable. But I told myself that I was being selfish keeping you here for my sake. No, darling, you have

your whole life ahead of you, and it should be on your own soil."

"I'm going home! I'm going home!" Maria repeated. "At long last!"

Holding her new passport high above her head, she danced around the room and then flung her arms around her benefactor. She squeezed tightly and said, "I can't wait to see Mama and Papa and tell them how much I love them and have missed them. But I won't tell them the truth, only that I was sick, unable to come home until now. Please come with me, dear Bronislaw. My parents will love you like I do."

"Darling, I can't leave here," Bronislaw said softly. "I've made what little of a life I have right here. To start all over in another country is too much for an old woman. But thank you for asking me."

Maria examined the Polish passport. It had a photo of her that Bronislaw had taken. Maria smiled.

"My contact in the underground is darn good, don't you think?" asked Bronislaw.

Maria nodded happily. To her this was better than receiving a bar of gold. But how was she to get out of a godforsaken country governed by the Republic of South Africa's Grand Apartheid policy? Africans couldn't travel from the country that easily.

Many years later, Steve Biko, an anti-apartheid activist and the founder of the Black Consciousness movement would proclaim, "The most potent weapon in the hands of the aggressor is the mind of the oppressed."

How true for most of those left behind in South Africa, but not for Maria. She would be spared the indignity of being classified "colored" under the Mixed-Race classification system and of having no rights. With Bronislaw's help, she was leaving as a documented Polish white female.

Bronislaw read her mind. "You will not be judged by the color of your skin again. A trustworthy contact of mine is going to help ... to see you home safely."

"I hope it's not Günter!" Maria blurted.

"You don't ever have to concern yourself about him. He won't be hurting anyone ever again."

Maria frowned. "Why?"

"He shot himself two days after he brought you here. I was going to tell you, but at the time, I thought it was best to let it rest. But I must say, his suicide surprised me because he didn't strike me as a person who could take his own life."

Maria didn't know how to respond. He deserved a bullet, yet she felt some pity for him. And although their recent contact had been brief, she, too, did not think of him as a person who could kill himself.

"As I was saying," Bronislaw continued, "you'll be driven to Kenya. There you'll board a plane to Palermo."

Maria gasped as fear tingled up and down her spine. "Bronislaw, I've never flown in an airplane. I wouldn't know what to do."

"Don't worry your pretty head," she replied. "My dear friend has offered to accompany you. She's Italian. I believe she's from Naples. Her name is Battistina. She is five years older than you ..."

"Can you trust her?" Maria interrupted.

"With my life," was Bronislaw's quick response. "You see, I met her in Auschwitz. She was a political detainee, and in those dark days she kept me sane by making me laugh, telling me dirty jokes. She only escaped the gas chambers because she was strong, built like a giant man. After the war she moved to Israel."

"She's Jewish?"

"No. And she never married. She works on a chicken farm outside Tel Aviv. We have kept in contact, and when I wrote asking for her help, she didn't hesitate. You will love her like I do, Maria. She's not pleasing to the eye, but you could never wish for a better protector or true friend. Battistina has the heart of an angel." That night, Maria tossed and turned. A good night's rest before her long trip was the furthest from her mind. All she could think of was Bronislaw. She would miss her dear friend and benefactor, but she missed her mother more. "Precious Mama, I'm coming home," she whispered into her pillow.

CHAPTER TWENTY-SIX

Maria Returns to the Genovese Estate

"All that we see or seem is but a dream within a dream."
—Edgar Alan Poe

A heavily veiled Maria stared at the tangled Mass of overgrown weeds hugging every inch of the entry gates to the estate. Compared with her childhood memories, they had never looked so neglected. She watched in admiration as Battistina, with pit-shovel hands, ripped the weeds from the wrought iron gate. Maria's companion had promised Bronislaw to see her safely home, and to not leave her side until she was safe and sound in her parents' arms. Thinking about her parents, Maria couldn't wait a moment longer. She removed her cumbersome ankle boots and left Battistina and her luggage behind as she sprinted up the overgrown pathway toward the mansion. What she found there overwhelmed her. Gone was the splendor of the eighteenth century home. The house was trashed—vandalized. Window glass littered the courtyard. The magnificent front door was missing.

Maria walked through layers of windswept leaves lining the hallway. Gone were the marble slabs and the furniture that had once adorned the area. She ran through the rooms of the abandoned house, now stripped of its grandeur.

"Mama, Papa, where are you?" she called on the verge of panic. She rushed to a room she remembered well. She stood like a statue in the bare kitchen, paralyzed with fluster. Questions flooded her panicked mind. Where were her parents? How had their home become nothing more than a shell? She couldn't imagine her proud father ever letting this happen. With tears in her eyes, Maria flew out of the house and caught Battistina as she was about to enter the courtyard. Tugging the big woman's arm, Maria pleaded, "You have to drive me into the village. Something terrible has happened. I just know it. Someone in the village has to know where my parents are and what has happened here!"

Both women's heads turned toward a voice that was yelling at them from atop a horse heading their way. "Who are you? What are you doing here?" a church-frocked man shouted. He had been out riding when he spotted the sleek black car heading up the hill. No one had approached this house in many years. There was nothing left to steal. Looking both women up and down, he introduced himself. "I'm Father Bettino from the village. And you are?"

"I'm Maria Teresa Picasso Genovese," the younger woman answered haughtily. "I'm the daughter of Don Alberto and Sofia. I live here."

The aging priest couldn't believe his ears. Because Maria was wearing her mask, he couldn't see her face or the spellbinding green eyes he remembered so well. But she sounded just like the overconfident child he'd known. He had prayed for her well-being every night after her abduction, consoled her parents, and even prayed for Paolo to do the right thing and return the child. It didn't happen. Now she was no longer a child. He was eager to ask the obvious question: Where have you been?

Maria beat him to it. "I've been away. Do you know what's happened here and where my parents are?"

"Oh, Maria," he said softly. "They are long dead." He dreaded telling her of Sofia's suicide, and, subsequently, of her father's murder.

"No. They are not!" she screamed in disbelief.

"I'm afraid it's true."

Maria felt her knees buckle. Battistina was at her side before you could say "Jack Robinson." She carried Maria in her arms and sat her down on a stone bench that had been untouched by vandals. "I will find water for you to drink," the mammoth woman said. She rushed off to find a water source.

In the meantime, Father Bettino placed his hand on her shoulder. "It pains me to tell you this, but I feel you should know the truth now." He began, "Your kidnapping ..."

After the father had filled Maria in, she broke down and sobbed. It was final. She would never see her beloved mother or father again, or Alfonso, her beloved horse. She wondered if he had died of old age or had been stolen in the rampage on her home. Thinking of her adored pony triggered thoughts of his caretaker, Paolo. Maria felt a wild rage racing through her. The intensity of it was like nothing she had ever felt before.

Under her veil, no smile, enforced or not, would ever be revealed again.

Maria's lips curled into a revengeful snarl. "Priest, you are not going to like what I have to say. If it takes me a lifetime, I'll get every *bastardo* who has darkened this soil with evil."

Father Bettino felt her pain, but as a servant of a Higher Power, he couldn't and wouldn't comment. What he could do was pray for her. "Our Father who art in Heaven ..."

Maria gave him a look that stretched straight from Hell. "You can stop that right now! There is no God, and if there were, my family and I would not have suffered as we have."

Father Bettino sighed. He wasn't going to give up on the wounded, abused girl. There was one more thing he could do. "If you and your friend intend to stay here in Solicchiata, you can room with me at the church until you have sorted things out. And I have the name and telephone number of your father's Palermo lawyer. I believe he was appointed executor of Don Alberto's estate. It's rightly and legally yours now. It would be wonderful if your father's magnificent vineyards came alive again. Unfortunately, like this home, they have been woefully neglected."

Maria vowed, "In no time I'll have the Genovese estate back to its former glory."

And that's exactly what she did.

Shortly after a visit with her father's attorney, Maria reclaimed her land. Together with her inheritance—the exquisite jewelry her parents kept in a Palermo bank box—and Bronislaw's diamonds, Maria brought the Genovese mansion back to its former splendor. She never asked what had happened to the rest of her father's wealth. She assumed it had lined the lawyer's pockets—something she would deal with later. Nor did she seek assistance from her mother's Spanish family.

With no one around to poke their noses into her business, Maria became a force of her own. There wasn't anything she could not handle head on. Nevertheless, she cared deeply about her new role. She orchestrated drastic changes in the running of the property, new rules that would prevent anything like the earlier vandalism from happening again. She would make sure no men, young or old, were allowed to work at her home or in the fields. The women in the village were delighted; they became bread winners now.

On rare occasions, with Battistina by her side, Maria would visit the vineyards at the bottom of her estate to talk with her new workers—to see how they were doing and if they needed anything. But mostly she took long strolls through the magnificent land-scaped gardens that surrounded her large home.

At this time in her life, Maria seldom ventured outside her gated fortress. She left outside matters to her most trusted servants, Battistina and Francesca. Over the years, Battistina witnessed a capable young woman grow into the most powerful woman in all of Sicily. Donna Maria, a fearless Roman Empress, was reborn.

CHAPTER TWENTY-SEVEN

Present Day, on the Genovese Estate

"Nobody grows old keeping their soul unblemished."
—Anonymous

Throughout Maria's harrowing narration, Brianna sat upright, not moving a muscle. Her grandmother's tale of woe had kept her so riveted that she only now realized her bladder was ready to burst. She quickly excused herself and headed toward the bathroom. In the quiet of the space, Brianna collected her thoughts. During her years at law school, she had developed a keen sense of observation, especially of criminality. Without a doubt, Maria had not told her everything. She was hiding something.

Brianna's revelation was right on. Her grandmother had not revealed the darkest revelations hidden in the bowels of the mansion, or what was in the yeti's little black bag.

Day turned to dusk.

"It's getting late, Brianna," Maria said. "Perhaps you should freshen up before dinner."

Brianna readily agreed. She was hungry, as always.

Apart from the customary chitchat at the dining table about how tasty the evening meal was and how nippy the nights were getting, Maria didn't mention another word of her life story. Brianna was relieved because her mind was already bursting to the brim with her grandmother's earlier revelations. Not to mention that her mother's alarming past was still lying heavily on her.

Brianna brought up a new topic. "Nona, why are there no TVs in the house?"

"I did think about having television installed," Maria replied, "but decided I preferred reading books to watching crap on a square box."

Brianna smiled.

"But if you want to watch TV, I can get it installed," Maria said. "However, you'd better learn our language fast!"

"Thanks, but no thanks," Brianna responded. "Reading books would suit me fine, too, if they are in English. And I could do with a baby book, as well."

"I'll look into that tomorrow."

"Thanks. Anyway, I'm going to have a bath and retire early tonight. I feel pooped."

"*Buonanotte, nipote,*" Maria said in her strong Sicilian dialect.

"Goodnight to you, too, Grandmother.

After a long soak, Brianna pulled her bed linen back and started to climb into the comfort of her bed when she heard it—a loud, continuous thumping sound. Was it merely the groaning of antiquated plumbing? Was the bath water rebelling within the pipes as it drained? She rushed into the en suite of the bathroom. No, the bath water hadn't backed up. Was it the toilet? No. That seemed okay, as well.

She returned to her bed, but now the sound was coming

through as clear as day. She felt she had to investigate it or she'd never get any sleep, so she walked out of her room in search of an answer.

"Nonna, there is an awful noise coming from under my bedroom." She pricked her ears. "Can't you hear that?"

Maria's crow's feet wrinkled. "I don't hear anything," she replied glibly.

"Then you need hearing aids," Brianna countered rudely. "Can't you feel the reverberation? It's shaking the damn walls."

With her best poker face Maria propped herself up on a sofa cushion and bellowed, "*Battistina!*"

The yeti rushed into the living room. Maria spoke in dialect to her faithful watchdog. Battistina was not wearing a happy face when Maria finished speaking to her. It seemed to Brianna as if the two women had butted horns.

Maria turned to Brianna. "I believe the time has come to let you in on another secret," she said in a flat emotionless voice. "Go with Battistina. She will show you the source of the noise! Then we can all get some sleep."

With an inquiring look, Brianna followed the huffy Battistina, who was making her way briskly toward the kitchen. Her skirt bellowed, exposing her unshaven legs. Brianna wanted to laugh, but her mirth froze in her throat. She watched in amazement as the elderly servant wrestled an enormous wood dresser away from a wall without spilling any of its contents.

Brianna saw a newly exposed steel trapdoor, securely padlocked. Surely, Battistina wasn't taking her under the bowels of the home just to look at plumbing pipes. The idea was too absurd to entertain. There had to be another explanation.

Battistina unlocked the trapdoor with a cathedral-type key, flicked on a light switch, and beckoned a puzzled Brianna to follow her. Brianna tucked the ends of her robe into her pajama pants and climbed down the stone stairway behind the servant. On the way down, Brianna was confronted with a musty, dank, mildew odor. It smelled sickening, and she felt as if she could throw up. But for everyone's sake, she held the nausea in and kept it under control. She walked through a cold, stone-walled tunnel until a cellar door came into view. Unbeknown to Brianna, this underground cellar was used during the war to hide wine, food, and other valuable items from the marauding, looting Germans.

The yeti unlocked the door with another gothic-type key. Wedging the door open with her foot, she beckoned to Brianna. "*Immettere,*" she said sternly. "Enter."

Brianna's sixth sense told her to turn and flee, but her curiosity prevailed. She tiptoed through the doorway and into the room, where the dark secret was shockingly revealed. Brianna was witnessing a gruesome, ghoulish scene straight out of hell. It was more than Brianna's rational brain could handle. What she saw took her breath away and made the hairs on her neck bristle.

In the dingy room, shackled to a cot bed, was an excrement filthy, naked old man with hunched shoulders. His skin hung from his body like old rags. Chunks of gray hair were missing from his head, and his beard flowed down his torso. Squinting in the bright light, his dead eyes searched Brianna's frozen face. It was only when Battistina spoke to her that Brianna moved. "You wanted answers, Signórina," the servant said in broken English. "There they are. Meet Paolo Girrdazzello, the *bastardo* who abducted Maria when she was ten."

With her legs glued to the cement floor and her eyes unblinking, a stunned Brianna stared at the poor creature foaming at the mouth like a rabid animal. His eyes were dull, but not his guttural cries. "Mama, Mama, Raphaela …"

Battistina slapped him into silence.

He sunk down onto the urine soiled mattress.

It took a split second for the truth to sink in. Brianna gasped. "The cook is his mother?"

Battistina nodded. "She's Maria's prisoner. So was her husband." She pointed to a corner. "He lies there, quietly."

The numb girl's legs moved in slow motion towards where Battistina's had indicated. There, heaped in a corner, was what was left of Cesare—skeletal remains with handcuffs dangling from bony wrists and ankles. Brianna's insides screamed in disbelief: *This isn't real! It's a friggin' nightmare.* Overcome with incredulity, her Latin blood boiled. Maria's heinous vengeance aroused fury in her like she had never felt before. Chasms of rage spewed through her veins. Like a seasoned prosecutor, Brianna declared, "I'm going to nail her psychopathic arse."

The yeti was none the wiser.

Until today Brianna had felt safe, even vital and alive, in Maria's secluded abode. Now Brianna felt as if she had been violated by a woman who had no conscience. The law student's thoughts raged like a forest fire. She had been duped.

Finally, Brianna's legs found momentum. She stormed from the ghastly, horrible sight. She was livid and made no bones about it. Yelling at the top of her lungs, she screamed, "You evil, friggin' witch! I'm going to call the poli- …" Brianna never made it up the stairs. Battistina's balled fist saw to that.

Eventually, Brianna opened her eyes. She was in her bed. Was it a nightmare? Was it real? Was the caffeine overload she'd enjoyed earlier the cause of her thumping head and the ghastly images? She sniffed. Then she smelled it—the musty cellar odor clinging to her pajamas. Every nerve in her body stood at attention. It was crystal clear to her that you can never justify murder!

Her thoughts caused her to shudder in fear. They drove her need to get away quickly. However, she had to ask herself, *Will I get out of this place alive?* After seeing Paolo and what remained of his father, Cesare, her paranoia was understandable. She had not grown up in this shadowy world. Her inner voice told her, *If you had a scintilla of a brain, you would have got the hell out of here long before this!* But she had seen him!

Brianna would soon learn what she could and could not do.

She shrunk under the bed cover when she heard the doorknob turn. Maria, accompanied by the yeti, entered. Maria spoke, "Battistina wants me to tell you that she didn't mean to hit you that hard, but you scared her."

Brianna didn't respond. Her anger, hatred, and disgust flowed through her, but she kept her mouth shut. She wanted nothing more than to knock both women out with a baseball bat.

The tension in the room hovered like thick smog.

With a look that expressed *I'm not made of stone*, Maria sighed. "Don't be mad at me, Brianna. I did what I had to do, and, besides, you swore *Omerta.*"

Brianna shot up from under the cover. She shouted the cold-blooded murderer down. "That's a crock of horseshit! I don't know what demon drives you, but you can't take the law into your own hands by torturing and destroying human life. Period! I can't turn a blind eye. I'm going to be a prosecutor. How on earth can you expect me to remain silent about this? You have taken criminality to its lowest level. You are a murderer! And keeping a man alive just to hurt him is beyond murder. You'd better start looking for a good criminal defense lawyer."

Maria, her face thunderous, gave a sharp rebuke. "That's bloody enough!"

By her grandmother's body language and foul words, Brianna felt she had given the crazy woman something to think about. But the law student couldn't have been more wrong. Instead, she had detonated a ticking time bomb.

Undaunted, Maria's face contorted into a vicious, sardonic mask. "I am the law!" she snorted. "Welcome to your new world, Brianna. You will learn that 'sleeping with the fishes' is the only world I know now. So don't say I didn't warn you."

Brianna glared at her grandmother, thinking the woman had more dirt on her than a litter box. Her immediate thought was, *You and my mother had nothing in common.* Even though Lynette had had her faults, she was gentle hearted, while Maria was nothing more than a thug with no feeling or conscience, hiding behind a veil. Even though her mother had been no saint, she had deeply regretted using a young prostitute, Naomi, as bait to trap Lord Alan Hallworthy in a statutory rape situation involving lurid behavior with a minor. Yet, in her own way, Lynette had atoned for her bittersweet revenge. The girl's extended family now wanted for nothing.

Brianna growled brazenly, "You don't scare me. I'm not going to keep silent about this. I'm packing my bags and leaving this house of horrors ..." Stopped by a clicking sound, Brianna watched Battistina open a black bag, the very same case she had seen carried into her mother's room before she died. Before Brianna knew what was happening, the yeti was on top of her. Brianna's assailant plunged a syringe into the girl's thigh and then patted her on the head like a newly found stray animal. Brianna felt as if she had been hit by a bus. Her voice dropped to an inaudible whisper. "My baby, my baby," she repeated.

In a heroin-induced opiate daze, Brianna's tear-filled eyelids closed. The last thing she heard was the rustling of Maria's starched nightgown. Brianna wanted to fly on a magic carpet into sweet dreamlands, but the demons of a hallucinatory hell took her on a ride to the last place she ever wanted to be—the room below the house. Cesare's headless corpse floated toward her. Brianna screamed and screamed.

The next day Brianna awoke sometime after two in the afternoon. At first her memory was blank. But after what seemed to be an endless moment in time, her mind awakened ... fearfully. She swallowed hard. Had the knockout drug harmed her child? She didn't have the peace of mind of knowing her baby was okay, but at least the injection hadn't killed her—if that was a blessing at this point. Her mental torment was relentless, like a long-playing record. Brianna clutched her head in her hands. What was to become of her now? Was she free to leave this house? Or would she be held as a prisoner, like Paolo? Or die like Cesare? Or become a slave, like Raphaela? A question lingered in her mind: *How the heck did Paolo end up in Maria's cellar?*

It was impossible for Brianna to have known at that time that Maria had hunted Paolo and his parents down. Eventually, the stunned granddaughter would come to learn firsthand about her grandmother's tyrannical deeds. With the snap of slender, witch-like fingers, terrible things happened to Maria's enemies.

Brianna didn't know that after fleeing South Africa in early 1945, Paolo, Cesare, and Raphaela had sailed to Italy. Once there, Cesare learned through the grapevine that Don Alberto and Mistress Sofia were dead. However, Cesare was painfully aware that even though they had died, their revenge did not. He had lived long enough with this powerful family to understand their ways. No matter how long it took, he would always have to look over his shoulder. Don Alberto's "cursed" blood would be relentless.

The first thing Maria did after getting the mansion in order was send out well-paid spies to track down any surviving Girrdaz-zello family members. After some string-pulling, it wasn't long before their hideout in Naples was discovered. The little family was smuggled back into Sicily, where Maria had Battistina shoot Cesare. She kept the mother and son alive.

That wasn't all.

Maria had unfinished business.

After pulling more strings, she phoned a contact who knew a friend who knew a fixer. Maria purchased the monastery ruins where she had been held prisoner and ordered it demolished. At her expense an orphanage was built in its place. She named it

Sofia's Home for Little Children. Then she had Teresa's body exhumed from the graveyard in the village and her remains thrown into the monastery sewer. Also, in the dead of a winter's night, she had the well water in Giuseppe's home poisoned, but he, Teresa's father, survived the rat contamination.

Bent on revenge, Maria recovered most of the stolen mansion items and most of her mother's Picasso paintings, including a family portrait of Dad, Mom, and baby Maria. The canvas was badly damaged. It had been gouged with a sharp object. Maria paid a small fortune to have it professionally repaired by the best restorer in Rome.

Later, after Maria had purchased a "retired" cargo ship and made it sea worthy, she entered the drug world by bringing shipments of heroin and cocaine from North Africa. Eventually, the cargo hit the shores of America.

One aspect of Maria's transition required no extra thought. She vowed she would never marry, thinking no one could replace the most precious man she had ever known, her father, even though he had betrayed her. But the naked truth was that she had been violated too many times for her gaping wounds to heal permanently. To her, sexual intercourse was an abomination.

Que sera, sera ... what will be will be ...

After the drug worked itself out of her system, a more focused Brianna propped herself up on her pillows. Through the window she saw trees forming smiles out of raindrops. The lovely sight momentarily sidetracked her intention to have it out with Maria and finish off what had been interrupted by brutality. She would give her grandmother an ear bashing and demand Paolo's release. However, if that didn't work, she'd give her the silent treatment until she could do something about it herself. Obviously, Brianna didn't know Maria well enough to understand that she was immune to human emotions. Even so, Brianna did not doubt for a minute that whatever she chose to do would have consequences. How long would she have to fudge the truth about how she felt about her own flesh and blood?

Unable to stop her ponderings, a more pressing urgency overcame her. Her growling stomach nagged: *Feed me ... feed me!* Brianna had missed breakfast and was ravenous. She knew that if she didn't eat something soon, morning sickness would torment her more than the aftereffects of the unknown drug that had been injected.

Brianna sat on the toilet for the longest time staring at her toes. She was hesitant to leave the confines of her room. What was the best thing to do? Should she try to sneak into the kitchen without bumping into the ever-present Raphaela? Not possible. Brianna couldn't look at the old woman now without feeling wretched, helpless, and a tad guilty for not understanding her earlier plea for help. For her son to be held captive by a madwoman for his crime was incomprehensible. Brianna sighed. Should she go down the stairs and attempt to be her cheerful self? Pretend nothing had happened? Perhaps she should just toady up to her grandmother until she devised a way out? It was a long shot, but she had to try.

Once downstairs, Brianna breathed a sigh of relief. Maria was nowhere in sight. But Raphaela was. Unaware of what had happened the previous night, she smiled at Brianna and said, "I have kept your lunch warm, Signórina. Would you like me to serve it now?"

Brianna rubbed her hand over her swollen abdomen. The baby was kicking the crap out of her. It obviously wanted food. Brianna nodded.

Raphaela couldn't help the sorrow that had seeped into her heart. But she understood the joy Brianna must have felt when she'd learned she was pregnant. Raphaela's second baby lay cold and alone in a stony grave on the mountain she and Cesare had been fleeing on. And her first baby, Paolo, was at death's door. Somehow, she would try to tell the foreign girl of her woes, but first she must feed the mother-to-be. A few minutes later the cook approached the dining table. "I made special food for you and your baby," Cook said, setting down a plate heaped with sausage, eggs, and stewed tomatoes.

An appreciative Brianna felt an overwhelming desire to hug the woman, to assure her that somehow she would get word to the authorities to free her and her son.

But Brianna couldn't tell the cook anything. There was a huge obstacle—the language barrier. So she swapped her good intentions for another thought. Could she bear to see her grandmother, her only living relative, handcuffed and taken off to jail? Hadn't the woman suffered enough incarceration? Hadn't she endured unspeakable anguish? If it was any consolation, Paolo and Raphaela were alive. However, Maria was, in Brianna's opinion, already dead.

Although the food smelled delicious, Brianna only picked at

the fare. As her appetite wilted, her courage renewed itself. She went in search of the woman who held her life in her hands. Brianna was more than ready for a showdown. She found the veil-enfolded Maria in the terraced garden. Brianna's grandmother was sitting on a stone bench in front of a massive, empty pool. She was sipping espresso from a tiny china cup. Staring down at the layers of dead leaves and debris that had accumulated at the bottom of the mosaic-tiled, piano-shaped pool, Maria didn't have to look up to identify who was approaching. Brianna's perfume was overpowering.

"I was thinking of having this rebuilt," Maria said casually.

Only then did Maria look over her shoulder and ask, "Do you like swimming?"

Expecting the cold shoulder, Brianna was taken aback. "Um … I love swimming," she sputtered. The thought of plunging into soothing water brought a spark of life into her troubled heart, and for a moment she didn't think about the close shave she'd had with her grandmother the night before. Yes, she pitied her grandmother, but, at the same time, loathed her.

As if nothing had happened between them, Maria said, "Then that's it. I'll have it repaired. Swimming is good for pregnancies, I'm told."

Brianna, her mouth open, stared confusedly at Maria. Last night she had become a demon from hell trying to harm her and her child, and now she was acting as sweet as apple pie. A caring granny! Yeah, right!

The law student delivered her final verdict: It would take a lifetime to understand Maria. The woman needed a psychiatric evaluation. Brianna believed her grandmother was mentally afflicted with a borderline split personality. What Maria came out with next could have bowled the mother-to-be over with a feather.

"How would you like to fly to Palermo and spend a few days there?" Maria proposed. "We could shop for baby things: clothes, a crib, books, toys, and anything else you want. I can arrange a private hospital visit for an ultrasound scan if you'd like to know the gender of your child."

Brianna shivered. Fighting the anger clinging to her like cactus spines, her mind snapped to attention. Get away from this hostile, deadly place? Maria had given her food for thought. Could an ultrasound detect any possible harm done to her unborn child by the drug injection? She decided to seize the moment before it was too late. All she had to do now was make her eagerness believable. An inner voice screamed a warning: *Don't screw this up! Bluff it out.* This was a do-or-die situation.

With her heart pounding, Brianna crossed her fingers behind her back, stood on an imaginary podium, and performed her first acting role. "Absolutely!" she squealed. "Nonna, you've made my day! When can we go?"

Maria's eyes locked on Brianna. She looked down. Had her grandmother seen through her charade? Brianna heaved a sigh of relief when Maria returned with, "We can leave first thing tomorrow morning, if you like."

Despite Maria's evil deeds, Brianna, being young and inexperienced, couldn't help but marvel at this woman who had beaten the odds. Brianna gave a mock curtsy. "I'm at your command, m' Lady," she said playfully.

As if a magic spell were cast that reversed past inclinations, a natural, broad smile crisscrossed Maria's mouth. She wagged her finger and said, "I'll 'm' Lady' you!"

Cue. Act One/Scene Two. Brianna grabbed Maria's shoulders and twirled her around in a tango embrace. "Then let's go."

Maria laughed so hard her chest hurt. It looked as if she was going to get along just fine with her granddaughter. She would spoil Brianna as if she were her own child. She would relive all of those missed years.

Brianna, on the other hand, didn't give a fig about her grandmother's sentiments. Her inner voice said it all: *What goes around comes around!*

Having been fully awake for most of the night, Brianna felt like it took an eternity for the sun to rise the next day. Remaining on tenterhooks, she continued to modify her scheme until she was sure her plan would work. She was prepared to leave almost everything she owned behind, but not her most treasured possessions: her mother's photos, jewelry, and heartfelt notes, all stored in a wooden memory box. She could hide those items in her backpack, together with her passport and credit cards. It was still a mystery at what point she could get away from Maria. She thought of Lusia at Villa Favola, the place she had stayed in earlier. That kind woman would certainly help her. Brianna could stay there until she could arrange a flight out of Sicily. Feeling confident, she said aloud, "Where there's a will, there's a way."

Maria, too, was having a tough time sleeping; nightmare after nightmare plagued her subconscious. Her excursion with Brianna would be the first time she had left her fortress gates in a long while. That thought troubled her because she had angered most of the drug lords she had dealt with. She was overly bossy and way too controlling for the likes of them. And she was a woman! Yes, she was more intelligent. Yes, she could outsmart the lot of them. And no, she would never become romantically involved with any of the eligible men. She was living her life her way. But would Maria become a target when she traveled outside the safety of her confines? Why was she taking such a risk just to take her granddaughter shopping?

The next morning Brianna gawked at the sight in front of her. As its single-engine warmed up, the red-and-white Skyhawk Cessna looked brand new. "Who does this belong to?" asked Brianna.

"I bought it a few years back," Maria replied. "However, I seldom go in it."

Brianna didn't ask her why not. She was anxious to get going, to get away from this dreadful place and its "disturbed" occupants.

It seemed strange, though, that Maria would buy this luxury item but not a road vehicle. Her explanation had been, "Why do I need a car when I have horses that can outrun them?"

The plane took off in the half-light of dawn. The droning of the aircraft was music to Brianna's ears. She looked admiringly at the pilot, who was wearing a fake leather pilot's jacket. Not only was Francesca Zanatta a fearsome gatekeeper and skilled horsewoman, she was also a certified pilot, her flying instructions paid for by Maria. Brianna was impressed as Francesca guided the four-seater aircraft over the towering Monti Nebrodi Mountains toward the ancient city. Brianna's stomach churned with pregnancy acids as she clung to her seat belt.

Although she was scared of heights, Brianna stole glances at the scenery below. She saw endless mountain tops and many fields dotted with buildings. Beside her, Maria was fidgeting in her seat. Maria was no stranger to fear, but she was terrified of flying. Under the fine lace of her veil, her face was pasty white. She couldn't wait to get her feet on solid ground.

A while later Francesca skillfully landed the aircraft and taxied to its designated spot. There were no arrival or departure gangways, no passport control desk, and no luggage searches for this privileged traveler. Francesca had telephoned ahead to the Mafia-controlled airport.

A black Range Rover was idling next to the private hanger. A suited driver, his green chauffeur's uniform limp with perspiration, stood alongside the vehicle. All three women disembarked from the plane and walked toward the car. As they neared it, Brianna's sunglass-shielded eyes grew as wide as the Nile. There was no iota of doubt.

Giuseppe rushed toward the veiled Maria, kissed her hand, and gushed, "It is an honor to drive you to the hotel, Donna Maria."

Maria did not respond. His presence was not a coincidence.

On her boss's instructions, Francesca had telephoned Giuseppe and requested his service. Teresa's father had not yet been crossed off Maria's to-do list. Somehow, after Maria had returned home, he had survived the toxic chemicals that had been added to the well water that had supplied his home. His wife, Lena, his daughter, Natalia, and her children had not survived. But the last of Teresa's family wasn't going to escape Maria's new plot, planned the Mafia boss. After the hotel drop-off, Giuseppe was a goner.

The unsuspecting Giuseppe gently took hold of Maria's arm and helped her into the back seat without a backward glance at Brianna. Still stunned at seeing him, Brianna made her way to the other side of the vehicle and slid onto the plush seat next to Maria. Comfortably ensconced in the bulletproof, gilded chariot, Brianna wondered where the rust-bucket Floria was. Had she gone to a metal graveyard? And why was Giuseppe wearing such silly Al Capone attire? Had he adopted a new role? Had he been acting when he told Brianna he was afraid to meet up with the infamous Donna Maria? Did he know about Paolo and his mother? Had Maria blackmailed him? Or was it simply a taxi fare?

Brianna felt her skin crawl. Had Maria hired him to keep an eye on her?

Giuseppe's face was as red as the Chinese flag as he sat down behind the wheel. Brianna was dying to say something to him, but she held her tongue. *I'll never understand the makings of mysterious, secretive Sicilians!* She couldn't wait to get off the island, but she could no longer think of involving Giuseppe in her plans, as she had intended. She wanted to knock his head off, the wily old fox. He, like Floria, was history to her. But she would inscribe this episode into her diary when she got the chance.

Each of the two women was preoccupied with personal thoughts as they stared out the tinted windows.

Twenty minutes later Giuseppe pulled up in front of the luxury, five-star, palatial Grand Hotel Villa Igiea overlooking the sea. With his head modestly lowered, he let them out of the car, said something to Maria, and drove away.

Brianna's analysis of Giuseppe's strange behavior was interrupted by the breathtakingly rich hues surrounding her. Abundant multicolored beauty stopped Brianna in her tracks. A tapestry of scents from exotic plants wafted her way. Equally pleasing was the elegantly furnished penthouse suite she was sharing with her grandmother.

Francesca wasn't given the same luxurious accommodation. So Brianna instinctively asked, "Why not?" Maria's snobby reply was, "She's a servant, Brianna. She knows her place." Sofia's aristocratic, belittling ways lived on in Maria's blood. Brianna filed that thought in her memory bank. She hoped her ability to remember wouldn't abandon her. She had hundreds of entries for her journal.

Francesca unpacked Maria's overnight luggage while her boss rested on the bed. The servant didn't offer this service to Brianna, who was fine with that because she didn't want her secret luggage contents to be discovered. Brianna walked across the room and stared hypnotically out the window. She spotted the hotel's enormous swimming pool; it was perched above the seashore, waves cresting below. But as much as she would have loved to swim and sunbathe, she wasn't here for pleasure. She felt frightened, and she needed someone to help her control the fear rattling her senses.

Brianna had no one to talk to. She knew that no power on Earth or in heaven was going to help erase the horrors she'd seen and heard at the mansion. She had never before felt so alone.

Suddenly, Brianna heard a strange gurgling sound coming from the en suite of the bathroom. She dashed to the door and knocked. "Are you okay, Maria?"

Silence.

"*Nonna*," she shouted in a cold sweat.

All she heard was her own exhalation.

"This is not happening! This absolutely is not happening," Brianna uttered on the verge of tears. At that moment she wished she were Tinkerbell—*poof*—up and away from here. But she had to face this new reality.

Brianna tried the bathroom doorknob. It was locked. A sinking, foreboding feeling overcame her. "Maria, open the door!" she shrieked.

The eerie silence pressed Brianna's heart to beat faster.

It was déjà vu.

Brianna rushed to the in-house phone. In a panicked voice, she said, "Send someone up immediately. My grandmother is locked in the bathroom."

She was afraid of what she would encounter as she watched the maintenance man unlock the door, but she was not prepared for what was inside. She struggled to breathe and felt like she was about to die. There on the marble floor lay Maria, sprawled, with her underwear down by her ankles. As Brianna choked for air, her hands clutched her chest.

"Call an ambulance!" Brianna screamed at the workman. "I think she's having a heart attack."

The man shot out of the bathroom.

Brianna immediately began to resuscitate her grandmother, and, at the same time, soothed her. "You're going to be okay, Nonna. The hotel is calling an ambulance, and I'm not leaving your side until it arrives." Silently, she pleaded inwardly to Maria's god: *No matter how bad she is, please let her live*. Brianna's earlier hopes for this day evaporated. Her current reality was that she wanted

Maria to survive. The aging woman was severely disturbed and had committed horrible acts; nevertheless Brianna had a tremendous amount of respect for the woman, for all she had suffered and how she had survived. Brianna could no longer see this hardliner as her enemy. She remembered it was not so long ago that she had wanted to protect her grandmother.

Maria looked up at her granddaughter. As she lay on the floor, the color was drained from her cheeks and her breathing was labored. "Promise to look after my home and my people," Maria garbled. "If I die, I can't let what happened to my parents' home ever happen again. Ten generations have occupied the Genovese estate. You and your offspring will be the eleventh. You belong there."

Brianna nodded and exhibited an inherited trait: trying to appease an awful situation with humor. "You'll probably outlive me, Nonna!"

Maria put her ring finger into her mouth and, using her teeth, slipped the silver band off. "I want you to make sure that Paolo gets this," she said. "My father gave it to him, and only God knows why I've worn it all these years."

Brianna was speechless. Why on earth would Maria keep Paolo's ring on her finger after what he had done to her? When he kidnapped her, she never had a chance to say goodbye to her loved ones, so why was she saying goodbye in this way to the boy who had abducted her? That ring was the only piece of jewelry Brianna had ever seen Maria wear, even though she could afford Cartier finery. The whole scene was confusing. In the quiet moment that followed, Maria, her vision light years away, sighed. That was her last breath.

Brianna was not mentally prepared for Maria's death. However, she felt a certain relief. She didn't have to get even with her grandmother anymore. Donna Maria would not be darkening anyone's doorway again. Maria had escaped the punishment allotted to mortals who break the law, but she would not escape the all-seeing eyes of the netherworld. No angels from heaven would come to take Maria. This unscrupulous woman would be more than welcome in hell.

Brianna shuddered when she felt something warm on her arm. Then she heard it, clear as day. "Shame on you, Brianna!" the female voice admonished. "I did not raise you to be like this."

Subconsciously Brianna said, *I'm sorry, Mom.*

Then she wept.

After the necessary formalities and paperwork were dealt with, Francesca flew Brianna back to the mansion. There, in a spiritual torpor, Brianna flung herself onto the bed Maria had occupied, just as she had flung herself onto Lynette's bed when she had died, and curled up like a potato worm. Nothing could have prepared her for the loss of two family members in such a short period of time, even though she wasn't so keen on one of them. Her eyes burned with unshed tears as she clasped her palms together and prayed silently. "*Dear God, if there is a God, and you are listening to me, please, help me. I don't know what to do. You've taken my mother and my grandmother from me. What about me and my child? Don't we count?*" She caught herself. What was she thinking? She could no longer believe in higher powers after what her mother had revealed on those tapes ... torture and suffering beyond imagination.

How could He have let this happen? So much agonizing misery could have been prevented with one stroke of His powerful hand. But then, where was this almighty spiritual being when millions of His children died at the hands of a hateful German maniac? Brianna shook her head and sighed. The answer was obvious. He didn't exist except in the minds of those who choose to have faith in an invisible being. With her mind still set in an unbelieving stance regarding religious contradictions, a disturbing image suddenly popped up: the dirty Catholic priest who had exposed himself to her mother and others. Pairing that picture with the recent media coverage of priests around the world abusing children in their charge made Brianna spit fumes. A sardonic thought crossed her incensed mindset: Did God personally pick these "bad seeds" to serve Him?

The frenzied sounds of barking dogs brought Brianna back to Earth.

Francesca knocked. "Do you want me to see who it is?"

"Of course," Brianna replied, keeping her tone as light as possible. "And, Francesca, the gates are to remain open from now on, until I tell you otherwise."

Brianna didn't see Francesca's dark scowl. Her manner was as barren as a lime tree in autumn.

Left alone with her thoughts, Brianna wondered, *Could it be Dr. Caldrese?* The hospital pathologist had told her that he would be in contact with Maria's family doctor. Who else could it be? A shiver went down Brianna's spine. Could it be that Maria's partners-in-crime got wind of her passing and had come calling? She hoped not.

Earlier, in the Palermo hotel, Francesca had fallen to pieces in disbelief. "Oh, no!" she had cried, proclaiming, "She was a saint, my guardian angel! If it weren't for Donna Maria, I would have starved to death. She gave me work! Made sure my family didn't go hungry, and made me who I am today." Brianna wasn't buying the goody-two-shoes story about her grandmother. Maria may have had a soft moment or two, but she was still the Devil incarnate. Maria wondered if her grandmother had already ousted the Devil from his throne. But, despite her bitter feelings, Brianna felt grateful to Maria. She had eliminated the orphan feeling that had overwhelmed Brianna after her mother died. And now, there was no turning back.

Brianna had promised Maria. She now had to calm her fear of the unknown. Could she fill the shoes of one of the most powerful women in Sicily? No, and she wasn't even going to try. But she did want to change things. She was anti-Mafia, anti-drugs, and anti-everything else that is standard in crime organizations.

True to her word, Brianna squashed the idea of departing from the island.

How long she would stay was anyone's guess.

Brianna couldn't take her eyes off the visitor Francesca had escorted in. She thought her guest, with golden hair flowing from under his tweed cap, was divine, drop-dead gorgeous. And his Brad Pitt blue eyes were hypnotic. He wore an angelic smile as he extended his hand. He introduced himself in English. "I'm Father John Risso, Father Bettino's replacement. I've come to offer my condolences on the death of your grandmother."

As Brianna's female hormones raced out of control, she clasped the frocked priest's hand a little too long for his liking. "Thank you, Father," Brianna said. Blushing to the roots of his blond hair, Father Risso withdrew his hand and looked into her eyes. A shiver in her spine prompted her to think he was looking straight into her soul. She guessed he was around her age, maybe younger. They were about the same height. His lean, muscular body rippled through his cassock. A deep longing to be passionately loved by a man suddenly possessed her. She would have slept with this eye-candy in a nanosecond.

Brianna was seized by a flirtatious urge. Fluttering her long eyelashes, she said seductively, "It's really nice to meet you." She was then struck with a jab to her conscience. The internal wake-up call hit her hard. *For bloody sake, stop undressing him with your eyes. He's a priest!* At that moment she couldn't help but recall one of her favorite miniseries: *The Thorn Birds*. In it the Cleary girl was hopelessly in love with a handsome priest. The reflection nudged at Brianna's conscience. *Men who pray to statues and have no wives are a waste of space.* Or are they?

Father Risso was also sizing up Brianna, who was wearing an alluring, low-cut top that snugly fit her extended midriff. He had learned from Francesca, who attended Sunday Mass regularly, about Brianna's pregnancy, Shiya's death, and most of the other goings-on at the farmhouse, except its most sinister secrets. Although he was thrilled to meet the new owner of the estate, he wanted to set out the reason for his visit. "I've come to ask if you would like me to conduct the funeral Mass for Maria."

"There won't be a funeral. I'm having her cremated, and I haven't yet decided what I'm going to do with her ashes." She waited for his response, and when one did not come, she added, "Or should I refer to them as her pulverized dried bone fragments?"

Father John sighed. Her cruel anti-religious words came as no surprise. She was young. She was a foreigner. And she was now alone in the world.

His heart went out to her, but it was his duty to enlighten her that the Catholic Church discouraged this practice in favor of sending Maria's soul into God's pure light. "I assume you are not a Catholic," he replied.

Brianna immediately acknowledged she was not. "No. I don't believe in God. There is no God! I'm my own God!"

Visibly shocked by her answer, Father John proceeded to help her understand that it wasn't up to her. "Even though your grandmother was a lapsed Catholic, she was baptized in the Roman Catholic Church," he told her. "I'm sure she would not wish this forbidden practice performed on her remains. You see, Brianna, denial of a proper burial interferes with God's ability to resurrect the body of His daughter, Maria. Her body was an instrument through which the sacraments were received, a holy object. It's imperative that she be buried, given absolution, and her departed soul prayed for."

With a contemptuous face Brianna said, "Oh, I'm positive He won't want to resurrect Maria. Her body and soul are beyond redemption."

The Father let out a sigh of frustration before he responded. "No soul on Earth is ever past redemption. But something tells me that something is hurting you deeply for you to make such a statement."

Brianna was struggling to keep up her tough-cookie façade. She felt tears stinging her eyes. As if she were lifting an anvil off her brain, she broke down. Clinging to Father John's hand she started from the beginning. She retold her mother's and Maria's tragic life stories, and her own. Then she divulged Maria's darkest secret. Father John's body flew off his seat as if he had been propelled by a Scud missile. "He is alive! Dear God in Heaven. Take me to him."

Too weak to stand, Paolo was piggybacked by Father John to Dr. Caldrese, who was outside waiting in an ambulance.

CHAPTER TWENTY-EIGHT

The Elaborate Funeral of a Mob Boss

"Death is so terribly final ..."
—George R. Martin

A low-lying, dense morning mist shrouded the various Geno-vese tombstones. Many of them were weathered by the cen-turies and spotted with patches of moss. They stood as testament to this family's grim and morbid tenure upon Earth.

Brianna—somberly dressed in black pants, top, and flat shoes—stood silently beside Father John at the rectangular pit that was waiting to consume Maria's body. At that moment the new mistress of the estate felt like a distant observer of a surreal scene frozen in time. It hadn't been that long since her mother had been laid to rest, and now she had to go through it all again. But this time was different. She didn't feel this loss as she did the loss of her beloved mother. Brianna deliberately avoided looking at the spot where Lynette had been buried.

A cool, sharp breeze ruffled Brianna's long hair, and an icy chill stroked her exposed face. She wasn't happy about the pomp and ceremony bestowed on her wicked grandmother. Unlike Lynette's quiet, private burial, Maria's funeral would leave her with memories of an internment equal to one of a passing president.

Brianna heard a rumble. She turned and stared in disbelief as an elaborate horse-drawn hearse—carrying coachmen dressed in traditional livery—made its way to the gravesite. She was dumbfounded. She had no idea so much antiquated, Victorian pomp had been arranged. The whole scene was bizarre. Father John had told her to leave Maria's funeral arrangements to him. Had he lost his mind? Hadn't he only a few days earlier been stunned and horrified by her revelations of her grandmother's evil ways? Hadn't he witnessed Paolo's release and the discovery of Cesare's skeletal remains? Why was he giving this immoral woman a burial fit for a queen?

Brianna scowled at Father John. His brows furrowed and his shoulders heaved in a questioning posture. Before she could confront him, four black Shire horses—sixteen hands high and plumed with ostrich feathers—entered the cemetery pulling a hearse with front and rear bowed-glass doors. Black-suited men of all ages walked beside the hearse. Behind them followed Francesca and Battistina, both sporting dark veils, funerary garments, and bowed heads.

Maria's exquisite coffin was removed from the purple-and-silver draped interior. Six strapping field workers carried the casket to the gaping hole next to Sofia's mausoleum.

Brianna noted the photograph of a smiling child pasted onto the coffin's lid. Maria was no longer her father's little princess. But one thing was certain, neither a Catholic nor a Jewish send-off could redeem Maria's soul from the fires of hell. As Giuseppe had mentioned to her on her first trip to the estate, Maria had probably already ousted the Devil from his throne.

With his missal opened to the correct page, Father John signaled with his hand that he was ready to start the litany. The Latin service was lost on Brianna, as it had been when her mother was buried. But it gave her the opportunity to observe the hundreds of mourners. The mob bosses in designer suits stood out like sore thumbs. They were the only attendees wearing sunglasses and fedoras. She wondered if they were glad to be rid of Maria and move forward with men's rule. Brianna had learned that although Maria wore the pants in this part of Sicily, she could never equal these proud men of long-standing tradition. They had only tolerated her because of her Genovese bloodline.

In a way, Brianna was thankful she was of mixed blood, not belonging to the true-blooded Genovese clan. Being so, she felt she was not a threat to the hard-core bosses. Or so she thought. While she stood at the burial site, though, the thrill of having that much power did cross her mind briefly.

When the funeral rites were concluded, two men, each gripping a strap in each hand, gently lowered the casket to its final resting place. One by one the mourners, some teary-eyed and others stoic, stepped forward and threw a white rose onto the coffin lid. Brianna couldn't bring herself to follow their example. The thornless rose she had been tightly clutching stayed trapped in her hand.

Brianna, who not so long ago was a skeptic, turned her head heavenward—just in case Father's John's powerful Being was listening at last—and prayed silently. *If there is justice in Your realm, then grant me the strength to put right the wrong that has been done. And give Maria the courage to face the demons that threaten to engulf her…* Brianna's heartfelt message was interrupted by the mourners approaching her, kissing her on both cheeks, and offering condolences in broken English. One elderly, portly man, who looked strikingly like Marlon Brando, whispered in her ear, "If there is anything I can do for you, don't hesitate to contact me."

Another said, "Maria was an excellent businesswoman, and I'm sure you have her blood. I look forward to working with you one day."

Dr. Caldrese said for all to hear, "You have the face of an angel, just like your mother. If it is your intention to stay in Sicily, you and your offspring will be welcomed and respected by all of us."

It was the first time since the burial day began that Brianna let go of some of the tension trapped inside her. She began to weep. Were her tears genuine tears of sorrow? Or was she simply overwhelmed by the mourners' outpouring of sympathy? Neither. She was thinking about what her mother would have said about all this: "What a waste of money! The Sicilian worms will get fed while the poor hungry souls in Africa eat their nails."

As if Brianna had made a tape recording of her mother's words in her mind, they played over and over again. Brianna lowered her head and mumbled, "Mom, I need you. What is going to happen now that you and Maria are gone? What should I do? Return to Canada … or what?"

The mourners dispersed, leaving Brianna deep in thought. The Mob men returned to their sleek black cars, chauffeured by uniformed drivers. The hearse and its magnificent horses departed, leaving Brianna alone with Father John. Noting Brianna's faraway look, the priest asked, "Are you okay?"

Brianna clenched her jaw and retracted his hand from hers. "I'm fine. I'm going back to the house. I have a lot to think about."

"Do you want some company?"

"No, thanks," she responded in a grouchy tone.

"I'll pop in and see you tomorrow then," he said.

"Whatever," Brianna replied in a detached voice.

Francesca and Battistina, now unveiled and displaying long, wilted faces, accompanied Brianna down the path that led through the back of the vineyards toward the estate house. On the way down the hill, spreading her arms out like a cross, Brianna cried, "Why me, God?"

As Brianna neared the house, she was surprised to see Raphaela waiting for her on the doorstep. The old lady grabbed Brianna's hands and kissed them repeatedly. Then, with tears in her eyes, she declared, "You are an angel sent by the Virgin Mary. Thanks to you, my son is recovering. Thanks to you, my poor husband's and baby's remains have had decent Christian burials. They are together in the arms of our Lord. Thanks to you, I have my cottage back, the home I shared with my husband and Paolo. To repay your kindness, I will work until my last breath for you, Signórina Brianna. And when my son is better, he can work for you, too."

Francesca translated.

Brianna closed her eyes. She felt humbled. "Francesca, please tell her that although she is the best cook in the world and I will miss her culinary art, she needs to enjoy what is left of her life. She should take it easy now.

"I've set up a bank account for her and Paolo. I want them to spend whatever is left of their lives together without monetary concerns. And if they need anything, please tell her to contact me."

Raphaela wrapped her arms around Brianna and kissed her on both cheeks. "I love you like the daughter I never had," she said sincerely. Hearing the translation of Raphaela's warm sentiment brought tears to Brianna's eyes.

CHAPTER TWENTY-NINE
Brianna's Inheritance

"She drowned in the thick sweetness of shameless opulence."
—Anonymous

As October came to a close, Brianna, having inherited her grandmother's fortune, brought about many changes to the mansion she had unofficially renamed "She" after a fictional character in a book by H. Rider Haggard. "She-who-must-be-obeyed" was an immortal queen, a goddess, who ruled the caves of Kôr. Brianna, as the new "cave" owner, now ruled the hills of Solicchiata. Brianna was in seventh heaven. It looked as if there was a Garden of Eden.

Brianna's first priority was to seal with concrete the trapdoor that led to the old cellar. Despite her age, the yeti had no problem lifting heavy bags of concrete, and she proved to be a skilled plasterer. The job was done in no time, and the quality of the work was so good that no one could ever tell a door to hell ever existed there.

"You like?" Battistina fished.

"Yes. You did a great job."

Brianna had mulled over the decision of whether to fire Battistina, but in the end, she couldn't do it. The uneducated woman's behavior had been motivated solely by loyalty and dedication to Maria. The servant had merely been carrying out orders. But despite that, Brianna actually liked the woman. Her charm eventually overcame her physical appearance. Battistina was thrilled when Brianna decided to keep her on as her bodyguard and general maintenance manager. The servant beamed, "*Ees* my honor to protect you."

"Is," Brianna corrected.

"*Ees,*" came the reply.

Brianna smiled. She made a mental note to help Battistina speak English, a language she intended to use in the house. That would be a lot easier than her trying to speak the local language. However, Brianna made one thing clear to her bodyguard: she was to get rid of the black bag and any drugs that might be in it. There would be no more intakes of illegal substances. Period!

Brianna brought about other changes, as well. She ordered the fortress gates to be dismantled, much to Francesca's dismay. Francesca argued that she was the keeper of the gate. What would she do now? Brianna assured her that she would always have a job, just a different one. The highly intelligent, delighted, and relieved Francesca was assigned to be Brianna's girl Friday, secretary, bookkeeper, pilot, general gofer.

Lynette's and Maria's bedrooms were nailed shut, their shrines sealed behind their doors.

Brianna ordered a distasteful painting—the depiction of a wild creature holding a heart—removed from the house and burned. Battistina and Francesca were not happy to see the artwork Maria had commissioned destroyed. Both women felt as if Brianna were trying to remove every trace of their former boss. And, in a way, they were right. Everything in the house was a sore reminder, but there was only so much that could be erased. The rest of Maria's possessions would be cared for, but not the ship. It was donated to the International Red Cross. Brianna later learned that Maria's "cronies" were livid and would have bought the vessel from her. Had Brianna made enemies already?

Power equals violence; they go together.

Life was running smoothly for Brianna and her staff. Raphaela's position was filled by a young widow from the village. Three male gardeners were hired to keep up the magnificent gardens. Francesca took care of the horses and had other duties, as well. The yeti brought the dogs in at night. The female dogs were spayed and let loose to roam, play, and explore during daylight hours. Brianna kept a puppy she named Brutus in the house, as well as three stray abandoned kittens she had rescued from the stable. The four-legged as well as the two-legged were now free of abject misery.

Even more happy changes were on Brianna's agenda. In the servant's wing, which until now had consisted of nothing more than bare essentials, Brianna ordered an up-to-date makeover: fresh paint, new furniture, drapes, bedding, efficient wood burning stoves, and new kitchen appliances.

The Olympic-size swimming pool was restored for children of the village to enjoy after Sunday Mass.

Brianna had feeders and baths strategically placed around the courtyard for resident birds. Shortly thereafter she was delighted to spot highly colored parrot look-a-likes in the bird sanctuary. Francesca pointed out that she had never seen this species before and that it was an omen of good things to come.

The rundown stables were updated, housing not only Francesca's favorite stallion and a mare, but also two retired donkeys and a miniature horse Brianna named Alfonso.

Happy husbands, wives, and children worked the orchards and vineyards for decent wages.

All the village homes once owned by Maria were rent free and repaired at Brianna's expense, as well as the village church and the chapel on the estate.

Brianna employed a retired man from the village as a cemetery keeper.

Was the Genovese curse finally to be lifted?

CHAPTER THIRTY

November's Cool Breath

"Be the unafraid mistress of your own fate."
—Anonymous

November's breath cooled the air. Brianna was looking forward to the birth of her baby and the end of a dramatic 1998. She was especially looking forward to her first Christmas on the island.

A week earlier Francesca flew her to the city, and the Cessna had returned crammed with expensive baby items, gifts, Christmas decorations, and luxury foods. Through Father John, her appointed spokesperson, she had invited nearly the whole village to a Christmas feast. It would be the first communal invitation ever to be held at the mansion. Sofia, and those before her, would never have invited "peasants" into their home.

Brianna didn't want to think about one of her pet turkeys gracing the table. She made up her mind not to partake of its flesh, even though, Father John assured her that the creature was sent from God to enhance her table, and that the dark meat was, indeed, heavenly.

The image of this gorgeous man popped into Brianna's head.

She sighed. She was struck by his good looks, intelligence, and charm. She wasn't a daydreamer, though. She was hopelessly in love. So much so that she had stopped biting her nails, wore make-up daily, and, in spite of her expanding figure, dressed provocatively. When Father John wasn't around, she felt lost. However, she knew the heart-tugging feelings she was experiencing were hers alone. Why was she attracted to a man who was married to his God? Could Father John keep both—his faith and Brianna? Was there any chance her fantasy of becoming his wife would come to fruition?

Brianna and Father John had become inseparable, even though they didn't connect on the level Brianna yearned for—the love of a man and woman. Father John seemed to spend every free moment with her. When he was engaged elsewhere, they met in cyberspace and e-mailed their thoughts. In one of his messages, he wrote, "God loves you because you are so giving."

What Brianna wanted to hear was "And I love you."

But that was a tall order.

Brianna and Father John had a lot in common. Both were avid wildlife lovers. They shared the same favorite creature—a black leopard. They both loved country music, enjoyed outdoor sports—tennis, swimming, and hiking—and were volleyball and football fans, except Brianna rooted for Canada and John for Italy.

What most excited Brianna was that Father John was studying Law. This was a colossal interest to have in common. Not only had he supplied her with Italian law books, he had also shopped for baby books. And he accompanied her to all her maternity visits at Dr. Giovanni's clinic. What delighted Brianna most, though, was that Father John no longer held her awkwardly in his arms. They were comfortable with one another. However, he did continue his attempts to convert her. "It wouldn't hurt just to come and listen to the church choir," he would say.

"Nice try," was Brianna's usual response.

Two weeks into November, near the time of her due date, Brianna received a letter from Mike Rodriquez, her mother's lawyer, enclosing Detective Marquand's Notice of Attendance for the trial that would address Anele's homicide and the attempted murder of Lynette Martinez (Shiya) in South Africa. Even though Anele had saved her mother's life when she was a newborn, Brianna had no intention of appearing at the trial even if she was capable of doing so. She gave her response in writing: "I'm not allowed to fly due to the advanced state of my pregnancy."

Her valid excuse not to attend was accepted without further question. The day after the trial ended, Mike called again and informed her about the proceedings.

He stated, first, that the courtroom had been packed to capacity and that he couldn't believe his eyes when he saw people of color segregated—divided by an aisle—despite the fact that the political scene had changed since Nelson Mandela's rise to power. It sounded to Brianna that white supremacy still ruled in the South African courthouses.

Mike went on to relay what had occurred during the trial, and as he talked, Brianna found herself in the courtroom, witnessing what had happened. The scene was surreal.

"Order please. All rise," the court attendant ordered.

The Crown's attorneys and the men and women in the public seats all stood. On the raised podium, a white, wigged judge lowered his large derrière into his seat. Behind the judge hung a portrait of Queen Elizabeth II.

The reprehensible people in the dock—Lady Corrie Hallworthy (Alan's wife), Bryan Durval (Shiya's South African lawyer), Captain Johannes de Klerk (the murdering helicopter pilot), and the segregated witch doctor, Sliman—were ordered to remain standing after the judge was seated.

Prior to the trail, and after many hours of grilling, Sliman had confessed. He was being detained behind bars. He appeared at the trial dressed in prison garb, looking thin, gaunt, and haggard.

Corrie, had been released on her own recognizance. She looked well dressed and well fed, appearing to be several pounds heavier than she had been.

Bryan Durval was also released on his own recognizance. Wearing a pinstripe suit, white shirt, and shiny black shoes, he looked as if he were in the courtroom ready to defend a client.

Missing from the mix was the real felon, Lord Alan Percival Hallworthy. He had slit his own throat and died an hour or so into the day of Anele's August funeral. He got an easier death than his victims did.

The trial lasted only four days. The twelve white jury members delivered their verdict in less than two hours. Of course, the accused white folk got a slap on the wrist. The murdering pilot, de Klerk, was acquitted due to lack of evidence. And Lynette's betrayer, Sliman, the man she had loved without rhyme or reason, received his own brand of justice. The once noble African witch doctor was hanged a month later.

Immediately after the trial, Bryan Durval left South Africa for parts unknown.

Pilot Captain de Klerk and his family immigrated to Australia.

Lady Corrie Hallworthy died of a massive heart attack two days after the verdict was delivered. Most shockingly, she left everything to Shiya, (Lynette Martinez).

Brianna was informed of Corrie Hallworthy's change of heart toward her mother by the estate's lawyer twenty-four hours after the woman died. As Shiya's legal next of kin, Brianna was now sole owner of the Hallworthy manor, the refinery, and the plantation. She sought the help of a reputable South African law firm and gave them instructions: the manor, cottage, and outbuildings that once housed slaves were to be demolished immediately. (To her dismay, Brianna was to learn many years later, that this instruction had not been carried out for reasons unknown). She retained the lucrative refinery and plantation, renamed KwaZulu Holdings, and employed blacks only, which she was informed was her right as a foreigner.

The business income from the refinery, after wages and expenses, was distributed to black hospitals, schools, and gravesites in Tswanas. In addition to tending to Anele's resting place and those of her relatives, Brianna added to the caretaking list all living family members of Naomi, the teenage prostitute who had been murdered by Brianna's grandfather, Alan Hallworthy. They were to receive a monthly allowance of 40,000 rand (about $3,600 Canadian dollars).

The thought of the Polaroid pictures taken at the moment of Naomi's death, which to Brianna's knowledge were still knocking around in some police file, made Brianna weep for that lost child of Africa. Naomi, like so many others, hadn't stood a chance against the most brutal killer, AIDS. Antiviral supplies were also on Brianna's list.

Another thing Brianna wanted desperately to do, but was hesitant to start, was investigate the many skeletal remains, especially those of Anele's sisters, she believed lay hidden on the Hallworthy estate. She eventually decided against the search, though, because it would unleash a hornet's nest and dredge up a past that could never heal. The tragedy inflicted upon the forgotten daughters of Africa would remain with them in their silent graves.

Not only had Brianna grown wise beyond her years in a short amount of time, but she had graduated from the University of Life.

CHAPTER THIRTY-ONE

Motherhood

"Frequent tears are running the colors from my Life."
—Browning

B rianna gave birth to twins by Caesarean section at midnight on November 20. She had cried out for her mother during the childbirth. Now that the babies were born, a warm, maternal glow of love swept through her as she tenderly gazed at her two tiny bundles swaddled in white linen, looking very much like Egyptian mummies. Brianna had never before felt anything like her connection to her children. Pride radiated from every pore, and her heart burst with happiness. But never in her wildest imagination could she have foreseen what Fate held in store for her son and daughter.

In the twilight of deep sleep, Brianna felt a worldly presence. A willowy female bathed in a radiant blue sphere of light approached her. Lynette's face was somber and her long arms outstretched. She floated toward the hospital bed as if she were an astronaut wrapped in the timelessness of space.

Brianna bolted upright, not sure if she was still dreaming. "Oh, Mom, is it really you?" she called out. "Come and see. You have two beautiful grandchildren. I've named my little girl Shiya, after you, and my son, Alberto, after your grandfather."

"Oh, precious child of mine, what have I done? I've passed on the cursed blood."

Shiya's visionary words triggered Brianna's quick response. "Oh, no you haven't. I've given birth to a daughter and a son!" Much to Brianna's annoyance, the spectre vanished in a blink. Typical of her mother, she thought. She always knew how to conveniently disappear!

The emotional high Brianna had been experiencing vanished, and now she felt deflated. She wanted to shout, "Mom, come back." But she knew it was fruitless. Besides, she felt like a fool talking to thin air.

A strange feeling came over Brianna as she looked adoringly at her children lying in their crib. She couldn't put her finger on its meaning, but it was a sense that her children were different. And they *were!*

Brianna looked again at her bundles of joy. The dark-skinned Alberto, Jr., stirred and lazily opened his eyes. They were jet black, as was his mop of thick hair. Shiya, on the other hand, was a fair-skinned blond with sparkling emerald eyes. There was no doubt who had delivered her daughter's gene profile.

"Phew!" Brianna muttered in relief. The indentation on the tip of Roberto's nose was positive identification, as clear as day. Thank God she had given birth to her ex-boyfriend's children, and not Mike's, her mother's lawyer. She could now get on with her life. She no longer had to feel pangs of reckless sexual guilt. Deep inside, though, she wondered if she should tell Roberto. *No, wrong move!* He has gone on with his life, according to Mike. And he had

replaced her before her side of the bed cooled. "Let sleeping dogs
…" she muttered.

A few moments later, a snore escaped from the exhausted
mother's nose. Finally, a time to snooze. Or so she thought!

Brianna was abruptly shaken from her slumber by a firm stroke
on her hand. "I'm sorry to wake you. You have visitors, Signórina.
Do you wish to see them?"

"Who is it?"

"The foreign man wouldn't give his name, Signórina, but he
says he knows you well."

"Okay, let him in."

Brianna blinked several times to focus on the face standing beside her bed. She couldn't believe her eyes. Her jaw dropped. In a
stunned voice she said, "Oh, my God!" He was the last person she
thought would dare show his face. She had only seen a photograph
of him, but there was no mistaking the aquamarine eyes, sun-
bleached hair, chiseled features, and over six-foot height. It was
the South African lawyer who she strongly believed had betrayed
her mother during the time of the shooting in Tswanas Kraal.

If the surgery pain hadn't prevented her, she would have stood
up and socked Bryan Durval hard, and socked the man who was
trying to hide his face behind the door. She never expected to see
Giuseppe again. Had he come to visit her? No, she didn't think so.
He must have been Bryan's transport to the hospital. That's all.

The last time Brianna had seen the taxi driver, whom she
had once regarded as a friend, was in Palermo on the day Maria
died. To this day Brianna couldn't shake off a suspicion that he
had something to do with her grandmother's sudden heart attack.

Brianna recalled that he had whispered something to her grand-mother before she died, and that Maria had clenched her fists in anger in response.

Giuseppe had, indeed, escaped death that day. The bomb that had been strapped to the undercarriage of the hired limo had been detected long before he left his Messina home to take his fare. And he had whispered the finding to Maria. Had he threatened her? It was anyone's guess! Brianna refocused her attention on her most uninvited visitor.

With a bouquet of flowers in one hand, a smiling Bryan Dur-val approached Brianna's bed. "This is for you," he said. "Congrat-ulations!"

Brianna's lips curled into a snarl. She remembered it was not long ago—back in South Africa in Detective Pieter's Marquand's office—that she had said, "Bryan Durval is nothing more than a deranged animal, and that is putting it lightly." Now he was here.

"You've got balls!" she spat. "What in the world do you want?"

"I have something for you."

Brianna watched as he dug into his khaki safari shorts and pulled out a small velvet box. He handed it to her.

"Open it and see for yourself."

With bold flashes of princess pink, two rare diamonds spar-kled under the neon lighting of the hospital room. Brianna gasped. "Are these for real?"

"Yes. They are rare pink diamonds."

"You mean blood diamonds!" Brianna retorted. "I don't want them. Why have you brought them to me?"

Without invitation, Bryan lowered himself onto a bedside

chair. Brianna gave him a look that could have brought down presidents. But she felt she had to hear him out before she called hospital security.

"Please, let me explain," he said. "They are not blood diamonds. No human blood was spilled. They were found in the same river your mother used to play in ..."

Brianna interrupted, "By whom?"

"Kelingo," came his soft response.

"Not the same guy who tried to kill her!"

Bryan looked down, away from her intense, probing stare. "Yes. Just before he was arrested, he learned that your mother had survived. He came to me and begged me to find out how she was doing in the Durban Hospital."

Brianna's features contorted. She couldn't take another word. "Well, that's bloody ironical! He shoots her and then, when his conscience pricks, he wants to know how she's doing? Go on. I'm listening."

"For the record, old Kelingo was not Anele's killer. He did not have a weapon. The pilot, Johannes de Klerk, was the shooter ..." Putting up his hand to silence Brianna's threatened interruption, he continued. "Hear me out. I am just as anxious to get this over with as you are. You see, Kelingo gave me the diamonds to give to your mother as atonement for the role he played. He believed that he would never be able to enter the Invisible Kingdom of Souls if he didn't try to make amends."

An acidic reprisal came to Brianna's mind: *The dog knows what happens to him when he steals food off the kitchen counter.* To Brianna, words had to be truthful.

Bryan continued. "Lynette has passed away, and I was saddened to hear that."

Sure you are, asshole! Brianna's insides screamed.

"I'm sure Kelingo would want you to have them. These diamonds could command prices up to $400,000 per carat, and what you have here is 3.14 carats."

Brianna clenched her lips, trying not to show astonishment. Of course, she didn't need this additional wealth, but being in possession of pink diamonds was an exciting idea. It was nice being filthy rich.

"Okay. On behalf of my precious, mother, I'll accept them. But there is one thing I have to know. Why didn't you keep them yourself? No one would have been the wiser."

"I know you are not going to accept my explanation, but I'll tell you why, anyway. When I met your mother, I was overcome with a feeling I can only describe as love at first sight."

Brianna's guttural raspberry resonated around the room.

"I was expecting that," Bryan said. "But I did love Lynette. She was the most fascinating and adorable woman I had ever met. My feelings only soured when she held me and my family at ransom. And as God is my witness, I had nothing to do with the assassination plot … I swear. It was Lady Corrie Hallworthy who arranged the hit. All I did was comply with your mother's blackmail demand, and I did that under duress. I falsified travel arrangements to make immigration and law enforcement officials believe Lynette was not in the country when Lady Hallworthy went for her throat. I don't know if you are aware of this, but your mother tried to murder her father, Alan Hallworthy, while he was incarcerated in a mental facility for the death of Naomi, a prostitute.

Even though Brianna already knew almost everything there was to know about her mother's past, her head was reeling. The shocking revelations her mother had left for her on cassette tapes in February of 1998 at her Canadian cottage had left nothing to the imagination.

Suddenly, Brianna wanted no more stories from Bryan. She just couldn't handle any more drama or dark remembrances. She didn't want to hear another word.

"My babies are due for their feeding, so I would like you to leave. And never darken my life again!"

With that said, Bryan slunk out of the room.

Brianna's next visitor would send her to the brink of insanity.

She didn't have to turn to see who entered the room next. His aftershave was an ugly reminder. She glared at Mike as he made his way toward her. Wordlessly, she looked him up and down with a confrontational face.

Her mother's attorney was dressed in an expensive Italian suit, crisp white shirt, and a black tie, shoes, and fedora. He was wearing sunglasses ... in a hospital! His pathetic Mafia attire was the least of her concerns. Her secret was out, but thank the gods she could happily inform him that he was not the father of her twins. She didn't take much notice of the gray-haired man standing outside the swinging doors engaged in conversation with Father John. She couldn't have known that the priest's eyes were as large as saucers, or why he couldn't keep his eyes from alternating between this man and Brianna.

"What brings you here, Mike? I thought we had dealt with all the issues last time I saw you." Glancing toward the glass door, she added, "Who's that out there with the priest?"

He didn't answer her right away. His eyes were now glued to the twins. Brianna was one step ahead of him. "No, they are not yours. Look at their noses. They are definitely Roberto's."

"Does he know?" Mike asked.

She pushed truth to the back burner and glibly replied, "Of course."

Mike removed his sunglasses and looked into Brianna's eyes. She turned from his intense stare. Mike knew she wasn't being honest. He had attended Roberto's wedding two weeks earlier, and Brianna's name wasn't mentioned.

Mike, too, had put the past behind him: built a great law practice and paid more attention to his long-suffering wife, who had turned a blind eye to his infatuation with Brianna. Mike couldn't help but feel a flutter in his heart as he looked at the beautiful Latina who had once stolen his heart. But now he had to deliver a blow. "Brianna, I brought someone here to see you."

She frowned. "Is it that guy out there?"

Mike didn't answer. He turned and beckoned with his hand to the man who was looking his way.

"What the hell is going on?"

She was even more perplexed when Father John rushed to her side and held her hand with a forceful grasp.

She never saw it coming.

"What the hell!" she screamed. "It can't be! You're dead! You fell off a roof! My mom scattered your ashes in El Salvador."

Lionel wrapped his arms around his shaking daughter, and in

Spanish he said, "My darling daughter, your mother wanted me dead."

Brianna's insides screamed. *It can't be real. This only happens in movies. No more ... no more ... no ... no ... no ... no ...*

EPILOGUE

"Truth is the cry of all, but the game of few."
—A.D. Posey

In the days to come, Brianna's heart would be filled with the worst kind of hatred toward the woman who bore her. Shiya's name was not to be mentioned; it was to be forgotten forever. She even considered renaming her baby daughter, but changing a name on a Sicilian birth certificate was a complicated, daunting legal procedure.

Brianna removed her mother Shiya's remains from the Genovese cemetery and reburied them in the outskirts of Solicchiata. There would be no tree bearing fruits of forgiveness beyond the grave … until her angry daughter could find a way to pardon her, and that wouldn't be anytime soon.

Will Brianna have a change of heart?

Yes, because she will need all the help she can get—from the Catholic Church, Father John, her biological father, her trustworthy servants, and the "all-seeing" eyes who offered spiritual guidance from beyond the grave.

How else could she cope with the never-ending Genovese

curse—the booby prize—that had now been bestowed on the newest members of the bloodline, babies Shiya and Alberto?

Can hope be worse than despair?

The End

Historical Facts

*O*n August 23, 1833, the Slavery Abolition Act outlawed slav-ery in the British Colonies. But that did not stop the colo-nists, or future heartless apartheid rules, from treating the ethnic races with nary a modicum of humanity.

> "Colonialism has led to racism, racial discrimination, xenophobia, and related intolerance, and … Africans and people of African descent, and people of Asian descent and indigenous peoples were victims of colonialism and continue to be victims of its consequences."
> —Durban Declaration of the World Confer-ence against Racism, Racial Discrimination, Xe-nophobia, and Related Intolerance, 2001

Ten million or so Africans who crossed the Atlantic as slaves were shipped in British vessels before 1850.

Sicily
The Motherland of the Mafia

The origins of the Mafia are highly disputed. Some historians believe the word "Mafia" originated in 1282 during the French invasion of Sicily. Another theory claims "Mafia" began as early as the ninth century when Sicily was ruled by Arab forces. In Arabic the word "mafina" means "refuge." In every invasion of Sicily—the French in the twelfth century, the Spanish in the thirteenth century, followed by the Germans, Austrians, and Greeks—native tribes sought refuge in the hills of the island. The refugees eventually developed a secret society based on their Sicilian heritage. "Mafia" as defined by the Sicilian translation means boldness and bravado. From these refugees, the Mafia was born.

The Mafia godfathers generally lived in country mansions and left their lands under the charge of local managers called Gabelloti. These men intimidated the poor people to work the estates for low wages. And some workers, fearing retribution for a petty crime against the ruling Mafia lord, worked for free.

With the abolition of Feudalism in 1789, the Mafia intimidated the peasants to pay taxes to the Barons with a cut going to the Mafia. Even so, the Mafia represented the will of the local farmers, tradesmen, and other common people. The locals often paid the

Mafia to settle scores or to receive justice, frequently by killing or maiming someone. From these actions, a conception arose of the Mafia acting as a Robin Hood or a knight. In addition to being known as the "friends of the friends," they were also known as men of honor. But these self-acclaimed descriptors are far from true.

The clannish nature of most Sicilians and their dislike of law enforcement ruled by an oppressive, hereditary, aristocratic government, created a favorable climate for the Mafia to develop. The nobility may not have actually created the Mafia, but it unwittingly permitted the development of social conditions that facilitated its macabre growth into criminality, which is how it exists today. The Mafia's hereditary code of silence, *Omerta*, is a thing of the past, shattered by modern-day informants.

If the code of Omerta were put into words, it would read something like this: *Whoever appeals to the law against his fellow man is either a fool or a coward. A wounded man shall say to his assailant, "If I live, I will kill you. If I die, you are forgiven."*

After fascism, the Mafia did not gain power in Italy again until the country's surrender in World War II and the U.S. occupation of Italy.

The U.S deliberately allowed the Mafia to recover its social and economic position as the anti-state in Sicily. The Mafia-U.S. alliance forged the invasion of 1943, and this became a turning point in the history of the Mafia. They exploited the chaos of post-fascist Sicily to re-conquer their social base, like they had done on previous occasions without a U.S.–Mafia alliance.

By the late 1990s the Sicilian Mafia was weakened and had to yield most of the illegal drug trade to American and Italian crime organizations. In 2006 the latter was estimated to control 80 percent of the cocaine imports to Europe. However, other criminal activities of the Mafia have remained the same and are as strong as before.

These days an annual Mafia turnover is estimated to be more than 120 billion U.S. dollars.

The Holocaust

The Holocaust was the systematic, bureaucratic, state-sponsored persecution of over six million Jews, and others, by the Nazi regime and its collaborators. The word "Holocaust" is of Greek origin and means "sacrifice by fire."

The Nazis, who came to power in Germany in January 1933, believed that Germans were "racially superior" and that Jews, deemed "inferior," were an alien threat to the so-called German racial community.

Between 1939 and 1945 the German government, under the rule of the despot Adolf Hitler, first methodically and then frantically, gassed, starved, shot, hung, burned, and tortured to death anyone born of Jewish parents. Between 1945 and 1953, more than 80,000 Holocaust survivors immigrated to the United States.

The question becomes: Could the danger of unchecked racial hatred reinvent itself? Most likely, yes!

Afterword

DIABOLICAL SLAVERY STILL THRIVES AFTER THE 150ᵀᴴ ANNIVERSARY OF THE EMANCIPATION PROCLAMATION

On September 22, 1862, in the United States of America, President Abraham Lincoln set the date of *freedom* for his country's three million slaves. The opening statement of the Declaration of Independence of 1776 reads:

"We believe these truths to be self-evident: that all men are created equal with the right to life, liberty, and the pursuit of happiness."

In 1865, almost 100 years after the Declaration of Independence, the Thirteenth Amendment extended this sentiment to "Negroes."

To this day, involuntary servitude is outlawed, and yet, *it still exists!* **Why?**

"In its many dark forms, slavery did not die when America

abolished it in the 1800s and Great Britain in 1834," says Lucia Mann, author of *Beside an Ocean of Sorrow, Rented Silence, Africa's Unfinished Symphony,* and *A Veil of Blood Hangs over Africa,* the final book in the series. Mann's books are historical, African-set novels that explore British Colonial slavery in South Africa and the victims who survived the institutional brutality before and after abolishment.

According to the United Nations, there are more than 37 million slaves worldwide, a number that represents more than twice the number of those who were enslaved over the 400 years that transatlantic slavers trafficked humans to work in the Americas. ***Why?***

"Today, many slaves are forced into prostitution while others are used as unpaid laborers to manufacture goods bought in the United States, Canada, and globally," Mann says. "It's almost impossible to buy clothes or goods anymore without inadvertently supporting the slave trade." ***Why?***

Fifty-five ghastly, sobering, little-known facts about modern day slavery/human trafficking

1. Approximately seventy-five to eighty percent of human trafficking is for sex.

2. Researchers note that sex trafficking plays a major role in the spread of HIV.

3. There are more human slaves in the world today than ever before in history.

4. There are an estimated 27 million adults and 13 million children around the world who are victims of human trafficking.

5. Human trafficking not only involves sex and labor, but also organ harvesting.

6. Human traffickers often use a Sudanese phrase "use a slave to catch slaves," meaning traffickers send "broken-in girls" to recruit younger girls into the sex trade. Sex traffickers often train girls themselves, raping them and teaching them sex acts.

7. Eighty percent of North Koreans who escape into China are women. Nine out of ten of those women become victims of human trafficking, often for sex. If the women complain, they are deported back to North Korea, where they are thrown into gulags or executed.

8. An estimated 30,000 victims of sex trafficking die each year from abuse, disease, torture, and neglect. Eighty percent of those sold into sexual slavery are under twenty-four years old, and some are as young as six.

9. Ludwig "Tarzan" Fainberg, a convicted trafficker, said, "You can buy a woman for $10,000 and make your money back in a week if she is pretty and young. Then everything else is profit."

10. A human trafficker can earn twenty times what he or she paid for a girl. Provided the girl was not physically brutalized to the point of ruining her beauty, the pimp can sell her again for a greater price because he has already trained her and broken her spirit. This saves the future buyers the hassle. A 2003 study in the Netherlands found that, on average, a single sex slave earned her pimp at least $250,000 a year.

11. Although human trafficking is often a hidden crime and accurate statistics are difficult to obtain, researchers estimate that more than 80 percent of trafficking victims are female. Over fifty percent of human trafficking victims are children.

12. The end of the Cold War has resulted in the growth of regional conflicts and the decline of borders. Many rebel groups turn to human trafficking to fund military actions and garner soldiers.

13. According to a 2009 Washington Times article, the Taliban buys children as young as seven years old to act as suicide bombers. The price for a child suicide bomber ranges between $7,000 to $14,000.

14. UNICEF estimates that 300,000 children younger than 18 are currently trafficked to serve in armed conflicts worldwide.

15. Human traffickers are increasingly trafficking pregnant women for their newborns. Babies are sold on the black market, where the profit is divided between the traffickers, doctors, solicitors, border officials, and others. The mother is usually paid less than what is promised her, citing the cost of travel and the creation of false documents. A mother might receive as little as a few hundred dollars for her baby.

16. More than 30 percent of all trafficking cases in 2007 to 2008 involved children sold into the sex industry.

17. Western presence in Kosovo, such as NATO troops and civilians, has fueled the rapid growth of sex trafficking and forced prostitution. Amnesty International has reported that NATO soldiers, UN police, and Western aid workers "operated with near impunity in exploiting the victims of the sex traffickers."

18. Lady Gaga's Bad Romance video is about human trafficking. In the video, Gaga is trafficked by a Russian bathhouse into sex slavery.

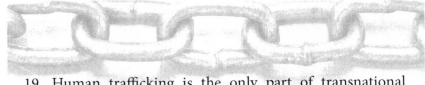

19. Human trafficking is the only part of transnational crime in which women are significantly represented—as victims, as perpetrators, and as activists fighting this crime.

20. Global warming and severe natural disasters have left millions homeless and impoverished, which has created desperate people who are easily exploited by human traffickers.

21. Over 71 percent of trafficked children show suicidal tendencies.

22. After sex, the most common form of human trafficking is forced labor. Researchers argue that as the economic crisis deepens, the number of people trafficked for forced labor will increase.

23. Most human trafficking in the United States occurs in New York, California, and Florida.

24. According to United Nations Children's Fund (UNICEF), over the past 30 years, over 30 million children have been sexually exploited through human trafficking.

25. Several countries rank high as source countries for human trafficking, including Belarus, the Republic of Moldova, the Russian Federation, Ukraine, Albania, Bulgaria, Lithuania, Romania, China, Thailand, and Nigeria.

26. Belgium, Germany, Greece, Israel, Italy, Japan, the Netherlands, Thailand, Turkey, and the U.S. are ranked very high as destination countries of trafficked victims.

27. Women are trafficked to the U.S. largely to work in the sex industry (including strip clubs, peep and touch shows, massage parlors that offer sexual services, and prostitution). They are also trafficked to work in sweatshops, domestic servitude, and agricultural work.

28. Sex traffickers use a variety of ways to "condition" their victims, including subjecting them to starvation, rape, gang rape, physical abuse, beating, confinement, threats of violence toward the victim and victim's family, forced drug use, and shame.

29. Family members will often sell children and other family members into slavery; the younger the victim, the more money the trafficker receives. For example, a ten-year-old named Gita was sold into a brothel by her aunt. The now twenty-two-year-old recalls that when she refused to work, the older girls held her down and stuck a piece of cloth in her mouth so no one would hear her scream as she was raped by a customer. She later contracted HIV.

30. Human trafficking is one of the fastest growing criminal enterprises because it holds relatively low risk and high profit potential. Criminal organizations are increasingly attracted to human trafficking because, unlike drugs, humans can be sold repeatedly.

31. Human trafficking is estimated to surpass the drug trade in less than five years. Journalist Victor Malarek reports that it is primarily men who are driving human trafficking, specifically trafficking for sex.

32. Victims of human trafficking suffer devastating physical and psychological harm. However, due to language barriers, lack of knowledge about available services, and the frequency with which traffickers move victims, human trafficking victims and their perpetrators are difficult to catch.

33. In approximately 54 percent of human trafficking cases, the recruiter is a stranger, and in 46 percent of the cases, the recruiters know the victim. Fifty-two percent of human trafficking recruiters are men, 42 percent are women, and 6 percent are both men and women.

34. Human trafficking around the globe is estimated to generate a profit of anywhere from $9 billion to $31.6 billion. Half of these profits are made in industrialized countries.

35. Some human traffickers recruit handicapped young girls, such as those suffering from Down syndrome, into the sex industry.

36. According to the FBI, a large human-trafficking organization in California in 2008 not only physically threatened and beat girls as young as twelve to work as prostitutes, they also regularly threatened them with witchcraft.

37. Human trafficking is a global phenomenon that is fueled by poverty and gender discrimination.

38. Human traffickers often work with corrupt government officials to obtain travel documents and seize passports.

39. Women and girls from racial minorities in the U.S. are disproportionately recruited by sex traffickers in the U.S.

40. The Sunday Telegraph in the U.K. reports that hundreds of children as young as six are brought to the U.K. as slaves each year.

41. Japan is considered the largest market for Asian women trafficked for sex.

42. Airports are often used by human traffickers to hold "slave auctions," where women and children are sold into prostitution.

43. Due to globalization, every continent in the world has been involved in human trafficking, including a country as small as Iceland.

44. Many times, if a sex slave is arrested, she is imprisoned while her trafficker is able to buy his way out of trouble.

45. Today, slaves are cheaper than they have ever been in history. The population explosion has created a great supply of workers, and globalization has created people who are vulnerable and easily enslaved.

46. Human trafficking and smuggling are similar but not interchangeable. Smuggling is transportation based. Trafficking is exploitation based.

47. Sex traffickers often recruit children because not only are children more unsuspecting and vulnerable than adults, but there is a high market demand for young victims. Traffickers target victims on the telephone, on the Internet, through friends, at the mall, and in after-school programs.

48. Human trafficking has been reported in all fifty states, Washington, D.C., and in some U.S. territories.

49. The FBI estimates that over 100,000 children and young women are trafficked in America today. They range in age from nine to nineteen, with the average age being eleven. Many victims are not just runaways or abandoned, but are from "good" families who are coerced by clever traffickers.

50. Brazil and Thailand are generally considered to have the worst child sex trafficking records.

51. The AIDS epidemic in Africa has left many children orphaned, making them especially vulnerable to human trafficking.

52. Nearly 7,000 Nepali girls as young as nine years old are sold every year into India's red-light district—or 200,000 in the last decade. Ten thousand children between the ages of six and fourteen are in Sri Lanka brothels.

53. Human trafficking victims face physical risks, such as drug and alcohol addiction, STDs, sterility, miscarriages, forced abortions, and vaginal and anal trauma, among others. Psychological effects include clinical depression, personality and dissociative disorders, suicidal tendencies, PTSD, and Complex PTSD.

54. The largest human trafficking case in recent U.S. history occurred in Hawaii in 2010. Global Horizons Manpower, Inc., a labor-recruiting company, bought 400 immigrants in 2004 from Thailand to work on farms in Hawaii. They were lured with false promises of high-paying farm work, but instead their passports were taken away and they were held in forced servitude until they were rescued in 2010.

55. According to the U.S. State Department, human trafficking is one of the greatest human rights challenges of this century, both in the United States and around the world.

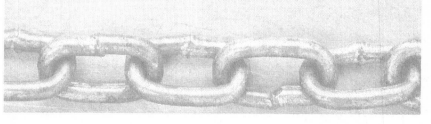

Millions of Modern Day Slaves
Need Our Advocacy

If we fail to address this plague of crimes against humanity, we'll never be able to bring an end to the unconscionable, heinous trade in human flesh.

WHAT CAN WE DO IF WE SUSPECT A
CASE OF HUMAN TRAFFICKING?

- **Catholic Sisters congregations:** (888) 373-7888.

- **Victims hotline and online tips reporting**: The *Modern Day Slavery Reporting Center*, created by Mann, is a Web site that makes it easy for third parties to report suspicious activity by clicking "File a Report." This section allows visitors to volunteer information. www.ReportModernDaySlavery.org

- **Federal Bureau of Investigation, report human trafficking:** (888) 428-7581. This number can be used 9 A.M. to 5 P.M. EST to report concerns to the FBI. They also offer plenty of information about human trafficking on their Web site.

- **Various easy-to-find anti-trafficking organizations:** Type in "human trafficking" on any online search engine, and several sites will appear promoting various methods of combating modern slavery. The important part, Mann says, is to follow through on an interest to help.

"Although I have a firsthand account of dealing with national prejudice and human slavery, many other people are compelled to help victims of human trafficking because freedom is a universal desire," Mann says. *"Any individual can make a difference in someone's life. That is the motive behind my books. I want victims to know that, like me, their tragedy can become their triumph."*

TOGETHER LET US TIRELESSLY PURSUE THE FIVE A'S:

- Awareness
- Acknowledgement
- Action
- Abolition
- Accountability

WE ARE MAKING A DIFFERENCE!

www.LuciaMann.com

Help Report Modern Day Slavery
www.ReportModernDaySlavery.org

About the Author

Lucia Mann, humanitarian and activist, was born in British colonial South Africa in the wake of World War II. She now resides in British Columbia, Canada. After retiring from freelance journalism in 1998, she wrote a four-book African series to give voice to those who have suffered and are suffering brutalities and captivity. The other books in the series are: *Rented Silence*, CBC Book Award; *Africa's Unfinished Symphony*, Indie Excellence Award; and *A Veil of Blood Hangs over Africa*.

Visit www.LuciaMann.com and
www.ReportModernDaySlavery.org
for more information on how you can help
alleviate the scourge of modern-day slavery.

57376255R00200

Made in the USA
Charleston, SC
10 June 2016